THE THERMALS
OF AUGUST

At fifteen thousand feet, the air is thin and painfully crisp. The sunlight feels like it's striking my eyes with sharp edges until I polarize my visor. Now that it's time to leave the thermal, I exit on the upwind side to minimize altitude loss in the cooler surrounding air.

Lark and I stalk each other like soaring birds. These Dragons are not the Indian fighting kites of childhood. There are no sudden moves—or rarely. Maneuvers tend to be graceful and conservative, to minimize loss of altitude.

We sweep by each other in a wide pass and I estimate I'm about one hundred feet higher than Lark. We circle each other like hungry, cautious predators.

Lark loops back in a figure eight and sails along still below, but parallel to me. I assume he is offering bait and try to guess how many moves ahead he's thinking. My craft and I are slightly heavier than he and his; my sink rate is higher and so I'm gradually descending to his altitude. I'm in a position to wing over and pounce, but that's the expectable thing. Lark doesn't expect me to do the expected; so I do it.

PARTICLE THEORY

Edward Bryant

A TIMESCAPE BOOK
PUBLISHED BY POCKET BOOKS NEW YORK

Another *Original* publication of TIMESCAPE BOOKS

A Timescape Book published by
POCKET BOOKS, a Simon & Schuster division of
GULF & WESTERN CORPORATION
1230 Avenue of the Americas, New York, N.Y. 10020

ISBN: 0-671-43107-2

First Timescape Books printing October, 1981

10 9 8 7 6 5 4 3 2 1

Printed in the U.S.A.

ACKNOWLEDGMENTS

"Particle Theory" Copyright © 1977 by the Condé Nast Publications, Inc. originally appeared in *Analog Science Fiction/Science Fact* in February 1977.

"The Thermals of August" Copyright © 1981 by Edward Bryant originally appeared in the *Magazine of Fantasy & Science Fiction* in May 1981.

"Hayes and the Heterogyne" Copyright © 1974 by Mankind Publishing Co. originally appeared in *Vertex* in June 1974.

"Teeth Marks" Copyright © 1979 by Mercury Press, Inc. originally appeared in the *Magazine of Fantasy & Science Fiction* in June 1979.

"Winslow Crater" Copyright © 1979 by Mercury Press, Inc. originally appeared in the *Magazine of Fantasy & Science Fiction* in March 1979.

"Shark" Copyright © 1973 by Edward Bryant originally appeared in ORBIT #12, published by G. P. Putnam's Sons in 1973.

"Precession" Copyright © 1980 by Edward Bryant originally appeared in *Interfaces*, published by Ace Books in 1980.

"Stone" Copyright © 1978 by the Mercury Press, Inc. originally appeared in the *Magazine of Fantasy & Science Fiction* in February 1978.

"Strata" Copyright © 1980 by the Mercury Press, Inc. originally appeared in the *Magazine of Fantasy & Science Fiction* in August 1980.

"The Hibakusha Gallery" Copyright © 1977 by Penthouse International Ltd. originally appeared in *Penthouse* in June 1977.

"giANTS" Copyright © 1979 by the Condé Nast Publications, Inc. originally appeared in *Analog Science Fiction/Science Fact* in August 1979.

"To See" Copyright © 1980 by Edward Bryant originally appeared in the *Berkley Showcase, Vol. II* published by Berkley Books in 1980.

This is for some special
women in my life:

Mrs. Louise Natwick
Nedalyn Dover Testolin
Ruby Preuit
    and
Florence Axford

Who sees with equal eye, as God of all,
A hero perish or a sparrow fall,
Atoms or systems into ruin hurl'd,
And now a bubble burst, and now a world.

—Alexander Pope,
An Essay on Man.
Epistle I, l. 87

What we shall have in the next cultural revolution is the reintegration of the Male (Technological Mode) with the Female (Aesthetic Mode), to create an androgynous culture surpassing the highs of either cultural stream, or even of the sum of their integrations. More than a marriage, rather an abolition of the cultural categories themselves, a mutual cancellation—a matter-antimatter explosion, ending with a poof! culture itself.

—Shulamith Firestone,
    from *The Dialectic of Sex*

The trouble with our times is that the future is not what it used to be.

—Paul Valery

Contents

PARTICLE
THEORY

Introduction:

The Legacy of
Hans Christian Sauropod

At intervals I indulge the fantasy that someday I will be discovered lying dead in a gutter with crumbs of Ko-Rec-Type on my fingers. What will the coroner's report say? "He wrote short stories. He didn't write enough novels." The conclusion will be that I perished of starvation.

There is the belief in some quarters that the novel is, finally, the only economically viable form of fiction; that short fictions, like poems, are a species of deprived literary stepchild that no right-thinking reader of commercial fiction would pick up, purchase, and read. Maybe so.

I write short stories almost exclusively. I do that because I love to. I value the feeling of having compressed a cast of people and their entire worlds into a universe of five or ten or twelve thousand words. I understand well that when I come anywhere close to accomplishing this, I am practicing a writing art form that is distinct from being merely a truncated novel (or, for that matter, a poem, a play, an epigram, or a limerick).

This does not constitute a declaration that I will never write novels. Believe me, I have fifteen or twenty in mind, even though I've never crashed the sixteen-thousand-word barrier. I've warily circled the project: *Cinnabar* is a "fix-up" book composed of preexisting short pieces. *Phoenix Without Ashes* is based on a teleplay by Harlan Ellison. I have in my files a sixty-thousand-word work called *At the Mouse Circus*. For good reasons, I have never submitted it to any publisher. Eventually I will cannibalize it for a future project. At this point, I have never done a prolonged work from scratch that I can point to proudly and say, "Oh, yes, that's my latest novel."

In the meantime, colleagues, concerned friends, readers, and booksellers all sadly repeat to me the litany: "Readers don't buy short stories. They want to read novels. Especially *thick* novels."

I wearily reply, "All right, I'll eventually write novels. Even a thick novel or two. All in time." A person could starve to death "all in time." And that's why I'll be found lying there in some future gutter. A manuscript of not more than sixty pages will be erected as my headstone.

But now, while I'm waiting for either novels or gutters, here is a collection of my more recent fiction. That seems at last a straightforward way of introducing *Particle Theory*. Here are eleven stories and a poem. I'm going to continue the introduction with comments about the individual pieces. You may wish to skip ahead directly to the stories and return to these notes later, if at all. I will not be particularly offended if you don't return to the introduction. The stories are the important thing. They are the reason that this collection exists at all. They can stand on their own.

So why a compilation of notes and comments? I'm one of those people who sit in an emptying theater until the bitter end, watching the credits scroll up the screen as the management brightens the lights. With books, I love to read the introductory and other extraneous matter. I must assume there are fellow readers of like mind. Most of all, I hope there are some readers whose curiosity goes on beyond the primary work to wonder how it was that a specific story came about: Why do I write about sharks when I could be staking out my own non-Benchleyan turf among the barracudas? Why does Vince Blake, newcomer to Cinnabar, have a distinctive quality of 1963 wimpishness about him? What does the protagonist of "Stone" have in common with Bette Midler? And so on. Not as historical or bibliographical notes, but more as lagniappe, I want the introduction to lend the book something extra; worth the trouble of reading, but not vital.

* * *

Here's a sample account—in abbreviated form—of the creation of just one story. "Particle Theory" appeared originally in *Analog,* the last great bastion of "traditional" science fiction: nuts-and-bolts-and-grommets SF, full of shiny hardware, concerned more with idea content than in generating flesh-and-blood people as characters. *Analog*'s editorial policy has never seemed to parallel most of what I liked to read—or to write. Over the years, though, placing a story there became a challenge. On a number of occasions, I tried to sell a story to John Campbell. I never succeeded during his editorial tenure.

In June 1975 I attended the Milford Writers' Conference, held that year in Michigan. At one of the nightly bull sessions, Milford founder Damon Knight peered at the rest of us from above his biblically patriarchal beard and wondered aloud why contemporary authors, grounded in the arts and humanities, didn't take some of the hoary, beloved old SF clichés and utilize them—turned inside out —in new stories. Everyone said "Hmm" and "Yeah. . . ." So Damon suggested informal assignments for a number of us. The luck of my draw was to "do the old Ray Cummings thing—worlds within worlds: What if the atoms of our universe are actually tiny solar systems, and our world, in turn, is the equivalent of an electron circling the nucleus of an atom in an inconceivably larger macrouniverse." Hokey stuff, but when I'd read those stories in junior high school, my mind had appropriately boggled. I thought about Damon's suggestion and wrote one word on a notepad. I combined the words "microcosm" and "cataclysm" and got the ugly neologism "microclysm."

Months later I read a feature account in the *Rocky Mountain News* about experiments in pion-beam therapy —shooting beams of charged nuclear particles into cancerous tumors. Some magic linkage occurred among my neurons. I got out the Milford notepad and considered "microclysm." I had a title.

The story accreted like coral—gradually. I talked to novelist and doctor Karl Hansen about prostate cancer. I spent an evening over coffee at my local Sambo's with Bob Vardeman, who had spent four years as a nuclear physicist before turning to full-time writing. He briefed me on the geography of Los Alamos and the salient characteristics of both Ross Airlines and the DeHavilland Twin Otter. I appropriated from my friend Jenni Caldwell the visual image of a character named Jackie Denton who would be a radio astronomer. So it went. No one should ever suspect that writing is either quick or easy for me. "Particle Theory" was no exception. The story was an organic construction, a slow, accumulative process of gathering details and images and information.

Finally a draft of the story was on paper, just in time to take to Eugene, Oregon, for the 1976 Milford Conference. Proudly I showed it to Damon, the story's godfather. He loathed it. A writer learns to recycle almost anything. I took some of Damon's acid comments, adapted them to the phraseology of my characters, and put them into the mouth of my protagonist's wife. The other conferees' reactions to "The Microclysm" were, to put it charitably, mixed. But I received considerable valuable criticism—and I wasn't so egotistical as to believe the story didn't need a rewrite or two.

I even reworked the title and "The Microclysm" became "Particle Theory." Finally I decided that there was little use in further nitpicking the story, and sent the manuscript off to Campbell's successor at *Analog*, Ben Bova.

One month later, four days before my birthday, I returned to my apartment to find a message from Ben on my answering machine. He said that he liked the story and wanted to use it in *Analog*, but felt there were just one or two small things he wanted changed. And would I call him back the following Tuesday?

It was a long weekend.

So I called him four days later. Ben repeated how much he liked the story; I thanked him and asked about the "one or two small things" that needed changing.

"Well," said Ben, "if you don't mind, I think we ought to take out the material from the final paragraph on the first page of the manuscript all the way to the top of page four."

I recall choking. "One or two small things?" I finally said.

"I figured if I told you I wanted you to cut three pages, you wouldn't have called back."

We negotiated. Ben told me to take a week and think about it. He felt that the material in question was too static and "people-oriented." *Analog* readers would hate it, lapse into boredom, suffer other unpleasant effects. On the other hand, I termed the disputed pages "characterization."

I pondered this situation for a week. I talked to *Analog*'s then associate editor, Victoria Schochet, who urged me to stick to my convictions—*if* I were positive I was right. Ben and I negotiated again. We finally agreed that I would delete only one paragraph—a chunk of bathos both Ben and I fully agreed was inappropriate. Otherwise the story was published as written.

Later on I was rather delighted that a few *Analog* readers had taken umbrage at the revolutionary science-fiction concept in the story that concerned my male protagonist having a female GP as his doctor. Then there was the gentleman who apparently was upset by my dealing with prostate cancer in SF; he canceled his subscription after writing the letter column to the effect that he couldn't stick with a magazine that published stories "more appropriate to the pages of *Penthouse,* or perhaps the walls of public restrooms."

And all I was trying to do in my story was to suggest that the most important victories tend to be quiet ones, personal ones; and that their importance is not diminished by external events (such as the sun blowing up—or the end of an individual life). I didn't *mean* to write scientific pornography. . . .

"Particle Theory" is one of my two particular favorites in this collection. "Shark" is the other.

It may at first seem odd, but "Shark" is about love.

Considering the backdrop and subject matter—sharks, assassination, an apocalyptic world war, the ruins of civilization being glued together by a rather nasty totalitarian regime—the reader might initially take exception. But then I never claimed to essay another *Love Story*.

Yet "Shark" *is* a love story, the uncomplicated moral of which is summed up in the character Valerie's quoting the Hindu proverb, "The woman you love, you must not possess." My plot may seem standard: a love affair initiated and ongoing, a separation, and then an ultimate reunion and consummation. At heart, apparently, I am a romantic.

"Shark" was not specifically designed to be a love story; like Topsy, it simply grew. I can trace two seeds which germinated in the spring of 1971, and then sprouted in the summer.

First, and more generally, there was the problem of the Great Dolphin Stereotype in science fiction. There are, if you haven't noticed, an inordinate number of affirmative porpoise stories floating around. I expect this has something to do with the dolphin's reputed high intelligence and the correlative theory that dolphins might be another intelligent species on this planet. Then there are the benign acts and services dolphins are alleged to have performed for humans—piloting ships through treacherous reefs, rescuing exhausted swimmers, all the rest. My suspicions were aroused. Could all this one-sided publicity be only a façade?

Epiphany came when I read documented reports observing that one of the less publicized attributes of dolphins is their propensity for rape. Dolphins will forcibly screw anything, be it one of their own kind, a sea turtle, or even a wounded shark. If their object is disabled and unable to resist, so much the better.

I have my other doubts about dolphins. It is true there is no documented case of a dolphin attacking and killing a human being. But could that be only because dolphins are sufficiently clever to cover the traces of their crimes? Perhaps they are more human than any of us suspects. I began considering the possible virtue of a nonrespectful dolphin story; and one natural enemy of the dolphin is the shark.

The second progenitor, more important because of its function as a catalyst, was the request of a very close friend to "write a story about sharks." My friend was fascinated by sharks; had, in fact, dreamed about sharks much like the character Valerie. She thought that perhaps my writing could turn her interest into something tangible. It did: this story.

I've never regretted researching sharks. There is an intrinsic fascination to a marine creature so perfectly adapted to its environment that it has survived and thrived for something like three hundred million years. There is also something brutally seductive in the shark's sheer power; in its defined role in the oceanic ecosphere—sharks do not sleep; their entire lives are spent awake solely to kill and devour. I suspect it's not mere coincidence that the sections of Peter Benchley's *Jaws* which flare to life are those which deal directly with the eponymous fish.

I'll stop. This is intended to be neither a sermon forbidding dolphins nor proshark propaganda, but rather an illustration of a story's beginnings.

"The Thermals of August" exists because of Telluride. Telluride is a tiny former mining town in southwestern Colorado. It is also the present home of Pamela Zoline, notorious New Wave author and designer of ruined sculpture gardens for projected planned communities hidden beyond the rim of the box canyon in which Telluride nests. Each time I've visited Pamela and her husband, John Lifton, I've been struck by the community's yeasty brew of onetime mining families, genuine hippies who sought refuge here from the expected apocalypses of the sixties, and the bright young corporate men and women who are here to administer the town's one true industry, the Telluride Ski Area. The town became an actual "new-age" community about six years ago when the hippies took over the local government in a peaceful political offensive. The single image I now associate most with Telluride is the town marshal, a tall, windburned Marlboro Man, with a quite serviceable automatic holstered on his hip, and a single gold earring in one lobe.

I think of Telluride as a rather more vital Vermilion Sands. Naturally I wanted to write stories set in the town. "Thermals" is the first of what will probably be a series. I could not resist writing about hang gliders after I first watched the butterfly-patterned craft drift down to the valley floor from Prospect Point, two thousand feet above Telluride. I stood on the ground entranced, mouth open. Only last week, a friend sent me a newspaper clipping about a hang-gliding accident in Telluride. Evidently one wing collapsed, much like the initial event in "Thermals." The pilot died. I had an awful sense of literary déjà vu. There are times such as this when I don't want SF to even smack of being a predictive medium.

"Hayes and the Heterogyne" is a section from *Cinnabar*, my series of tales about a city remote from the here and now, a city in which technology is sufficiently advanced to be virtually indistinguishable from magic. Cinnabar is a place where individuals can do—and *be*—virtually anything or anyone they wish. This power leads, of course, to problems—and that's precisely why the stories are worth writing.

It seemed appropriate in this story to bring onstage a twentieth-century-American-viewpoint character to take a look around Cinnabar. This was a gentle nod toward the devices of the nineteenth-century Utopian novels. It was no accident that I created a protagonist who was an unwordly, insecure, not-too-mature college freshman who had just entered a large university in 1963 when he was snatched up to Cinnabar. Strangely, *I* was a callow freshman myself in 1963. Not that fictional constructs are one hundred percent accurate reflections of real people—they cannot be—but both Harry Vincent Blake and I have felt a certain identification with the character Toad in *American Graffiti*. . . .

Some readers have called "Teeth Marks" a Bert Lance story, a Richard Nixon story, or a Kennedy story. It was intended to be rather less specialized than any of those. I simply wanted to write about people coming home after long absences. I wished to write about a person confronting his past. Specific elements that triggered the story? I can credit arts administrator Paula Barta with telling me of the affluent Aspen family for whom she once baby-sat. The nursery contained imposing playground equipment designed to make three-year-olds very tough, very fast. I can also credit Quincy Burton, ace creator of fine dolls and stuffed animals, whom I once commissioned to create a "Teddyshark" as a Christmas gift. Quincy worked the best part of a year getting the critter right, tailoring a meter-long Great White out of two shades of gray plush. The mouth was the finest touch, gaping open and lined with black leather. I had brought back a large assortment of shark teeth from Los Angeles. Quincy drilled a hole in each tooth, then sewed each from the rear into the jaws. The Teddyshark had genuine teeth. Some time later, I looked across my room at my own Teddybear and wondered why most kids' bears are constructed with closed mouths. . . .

A note to bibliographers: "Teeth Marks" reflects two stories published in my collection *Among the Dead*. Senator Frank Alessi appeared as a second-lead character in "Tactics." His daughter, Connie Alessi, had a brief cameo in "Adrift on the Freeway."

There really isn't much to say about "Winslow Crater"

other than to note that it may well be the last of the concrete school of poetics. I could mention that it recaps a school science lesson that includes at least three basic facts about meteors. But as a poet, I make a competent house painter.

A real poet named Dina Vaughan read "Precession" and wrote me in a letter, "You must have loved her very much." I still do. I could say that I wanted to write a story about the application of the second law of thermodynamics to love. What I will say is that I wrote a downbeat love story that is not without a note of peace.

"Stone" was filmed not long ago as a big-budget movie starring Bette Midler and called *The Rose*. Just kidding, folks. Well, almost. Despite my knowledge that I could pick critical holes in *The Rose* as a film, I have seen it six times. Each time I watch the final concert scenes, I am reminded of "Stone." This sense of correspondence is not derived from ego or pretension. It's because both the moviemakers and I took our material from the same source: Janis Joplin's life, and her life as filtered through Myra Friedman's biography, *Buried Alive*. It's now a decade after her death. She is still loved and remembered, and has now been transmuted to a modern myth. I feel both *The Rose* and "Stone" work because neither tries to set down *the story* of Janis Joplin. Working with myth is something else entirely. . . .

Close to fifteen years ago, I stood entranced at the edge of the stage at a rock club in Denver and watched Janis Joplin perform. I suppose the hypnosis has never completely worn off. A little more than a decade ago, I slept a night in my car at an Interstate 80 rest area just outside of Des Moines. In the morning I brushed my teeth with water from the jug I was saving to fill the radiator and turned on the radio. That night, the announcer said, Janis was to sing in Des Moines. I was tempted . . . but I had hundreds of miles to cover that day. Places to go. I should have stayed.

Earlier in the introduction, I said I had two favorites in this book. Actually I have three, and the third is "Strata." Here is a case where I can trace a story back to a single image. I'd known for several years that I wanted to build something out of an observation from central Wyoming: in scenic Wind River Canyon, the Highway Department has posted signs informing travelers through which particular geological epoch they're driving. Traversing the length of the canyon involves a journey through between four and five hundred million years. It's a particularly subtle form of time travel that I thought deserved investigation.

The characters in "Strata" began to generate in spring 1979 one night after a psychopath with KILL and HATE amateurishly tattooed on his knuckles tried to terrorize me in the Conquistador Cafe in Laramie. The psychopath didn't make it into the story (he'll have his own someday). But he did delay me sufficiently that I was later at the right time and in the right place to meet some people whose appearance and conversation started to jell the relationships I was looking for for the people in "Strata." If you're trying to follow all that, just remember that literary footnotes from real life are often harder to edit into simplicity than are bits of fiction.

I am unabashedly a Western chauvinist: presently I will not entertain the idea of living on either coast because the density of population oppresses me. I love wide horizons with cities hundreds of miles apart. I glory in the sweep of plains and mountain ranges. I don't think I'm blindly uncritical of the Rocky Mountain West—that's why "Strata" is not completely a love letter to the region. But increasingly I am fascinated by the West's place in determining America's course during the remainder of the century. Excitement? I see it generating indirectly from coal, oil shale, petroleum, uranium, wind, solar power, gas. The direct excitement rises from a volatile brew of politicians, environmentalists, energy corporations, ranchers, transient workers, farmers, Native Americans, social engineers, artists, townspeople, terrorists, hippies, mountain men, and labelless human beings who are simply looking for a way to survive the twentieth century. True, futures in science fiction often translate as L-5 colonies, Lunar domes, Mars settlements, cities on the fourth planet of the Proxima Centauri system, and shuttles to Andromeda. But our futures also are Craig, Billings, Casper, and Denver.

I believe "The *Hibakusha* Gallery" took longer to write than any other of my short stories. All told, the gestation period lasted through about two and a half years and several major rewrites. There's always a considerable pressure on full-time writers to finish the stories they have started; then get the work out to market as soon as possible in order to return income. I couldn't do that with "The *Hibakusha* Gallery." When I first invented the peculiarly perverse gallery of the title, I knew I had an effective device around which to set my story. But the characters and their relationships were tortuously difficult in defining themselves. You would not believe some of the clumsy constructions that lurched onstage at first (for instance, a warped governmental scheme to use gamma radiation to make beautiful young people prematurely old and wrinkled, and ultimately to kill them). I have been tempted to burn early drafts; but, with my pack-rat mentality, I'm still filing these alternative pages as a possible future tax-deductible donation.

At any rate, it took two and a half years to come to a realization who my characters were and *why* they were on a collision course. Even finally calling it good and seeing the story published in *Penthouse* wasn't the end. I've since refined the story again in a film script. Maybe one of these days I'll decide I'm finally done writing the damned thing. Writers find with most stories that there is a point of diminishing returns beyond which it's not only useless, it's absolutely harmful to keep tinkering.

Two and a half years to write a story is not exactly cost-effective. But it is satisfying; it *is* necessary.

"giANTS" started as a joke. Finally, only a little more than the title remained of the original intent. I was startled and pleased when Orson Scott Card pegged the story's evolution with absolute accuracy in a column in *Science Fiction Review:* "It ['giANTS'] could have been written on a bet—'Hey, Ed, betcha can't write a giant ant story that doesn't violate the square-cube law'—but it is a witness of Bryant's caliber as a writer that he was incapable of treating it as a joke. Instead, while he wins the bet, he also creates a strong character, and the climax of the plot is actually overshadowed by the character climax—a little matter of a broken stained-glass window." Naturally a writer likes praise for his work, and I blush a bit at Scott's assessment. But I laud him for picking out the key: I started writing a simple, short, one-punch story. When I became aware that I truly liked my characters, I realized they would not allow me to end the story either quickly or easily. Bless them. Bless my unconscious.

"To See" is a love letter.

It is short in inverse proportion to the subject matter.

Whether you love it or hate it, "To See" is the note on which I wish to end this book.

Now. It will not have escaped readers with normal attention spans that up until now, I have not made reference to the title of this introduction: "The Legacy of Hans Christian Sauropod." Some time ago, I read that a survey of adult science-fiction readers (and by extension, writers) had discovered a common factor, two recurring areas of interest to SF people when they were children: dinosaurs and fairy tales. I can vouch for the validity of that theory. I have fond memories of books such as Roy Chapman Andrews' *All About Dinosaurs*. For years I wanted to be a paleontologist, traveling to the steppes of Central Asia to dig up dinosaur bones and eat disgusting concoctions of sheep's eyes. Then there were the Brothers Grimm, Hans Christian Andersen, and the lesser compilers of fairy tales. I possess vivid memories of poisoned apples, enchanted castles, and terrible things happening to the eyes of miscreants falling into blackberry bushes. When I still needed the services of a pediatrician, I recall his waiting room in Denver having a splendid wall mural of a magic kingdom.

I've decided to concoct a cockamamie theory about the symbology implicit in those two childhood interests. I suspect future writers of SF who were primarily dinosaur fans grew up to be partisans of shiny, traditional, bolts-and-grommets science fiction—death rays and star cruisers and clanking robots and all that. On the other hand, lovers of fairy tales grew up to write *Dhalgren* and *The Space Merchants* and *Deathbird Stories* and published *New Worlds*.

If you don't buy the simplistic conclusions of my theory, I can't blame you; neither do I. But please let me, just for a little while, cling to the symbols in order to make a point.

I don't intend to launch into an essay on the evolution of contemporary science fiction. I will assert, though, that the later 1960s were an innovative time for the field when an accelerating number of writers who were more arts-and-sciences-oriented than technology-based started writing SF. For them, the power of the word was as important as the core idea. A healthy, if strident, dialogue ensued.

A very real theory of mine views the 1970s as a decade of experimentation and consolidation, of innovation and a blending of diverse literary elements. In plainer words, the New Wave people were getting over their knee-jerk dread of all things scientific and technical, and beginning to exercise a natural curiosity about the workings of the physical universe. And the traditionalists discovered that their brilliant ideas were not defused by couching them in sophisticated prose.

I believe the 1980s will see the flowering, a fusion of both elements. Dinosaurs and fairy tales are not incompatible; far from it. Writers of the 1980s are already placing real trachodons in imaginary gardens. I could cite Joan Vinge's *Snow Queen*, *Timescape* by Gregory Benford, Gene Wolfe's *The Book of the New Sun* tetralogy, and a dozen more. The economy and the imminent apocalypse aside, it is a fine time to be writing science fiction.

I am essentially a writer of the 1970s, hoping to continue on as a writer of the 1980s. *Particle Theory* contains much of my best work for the past decade. Presently I'm treading water—it is now July 1980, and I have not completed any new fiction for the new decade. I will.

Here I am, Hans Christian Sauropod, trying to straddle those peculiar literary generations of SF, looking toward the future. I suppose I am an optimist—on good days. And maybe they *won't* find me dying in the gutter. . . .

I'll persevere to the '90s. The dinosaur fairy tales show promise and I don't want to miss the excitement.

—Edward Bryant
Denver

Particle Theory

I see my shadow flung like black iron against the wall. My sundeck blazes with untimely summer. Eliot was wrong: Frost, right.

Nanoseconds . . .

Death is as relativistic as any other apparent constant. I wonder: *Am I dying?*

I thought it was a cliché with no underlying truth.

"Lives *do* flash in a compressed instant before dying eyes," said Amanda. She poured me another glass of Burgundy the color of her hair. The fire highlighted both. "A psychologist named Noyes—" She broke off and smiled at me. "You really want to hear this?"

"Sure." The fireplace light softened the taut planes of her face. I saw a flicker of the gentler beauty she had possessed thirty years before.

"Noyes catalogued testimonial evidence for death's-door phenomena in the early seventies. He termed it 'life review,' the second of three clearly definable steps in the process of dying; like a movie, and not necessarily linear."

I drink, I have a low threshold of intoxication, I ramble. "Why does it happen? How?" I didn't like the desperation in my voice. We were suddenly much farther apart than the geography of the table separating us; I looked in

Amanda's eyes for some memory of Lisa. "Life goes shooting off—or we recede from it—like Earth and an interstellar probe irrevocably severed. Mutual recession at light-speed, and the dark fills in the gap." I held my glass by the stem, rotated it, peered through the distorting bowl.

Pine logs crackled. Amanda turned her head and her eyes' image shattered in the flames.

The glare, the glare—

When I was thirty I made aggrieved noises because I'd screwed around for the past ten years and not accomplished nearly as much as I should. Lisa only laughed, which sent me into a transient rage and a longer-lasting sulk before I realized hers was the only appropriate response.

"Silly, silly," she said. "A watered-down Byronic character, full of self-pity and sloppy self-adulation." She blocked my exit from the kitchen and said, millimeters from my face, "It's not as though you're waking up at thirty to discover that only fifty-six people have heard of you."

I stuttered over a weak retort.

"Fifty-seven?" She laughed; I laughed.

Then I was forty and went through the same pseudomenopausal trauma. Admittedly, I hadn't done any work at all for nearly a year, and any *good* work for two. Lisa didn't laugh this time; she did what she could, which was mainly to stay out of my way while I alternately moped and raged around the coast house southwest of Portland. Royalties from the book I'd done on the fusion breakthrough kept us in groceries and mortgage payments.

"Listen, maybe if I'd go away for a while—" she said. "Maybe it would help for you to be alone." Temporary separations weren't alien to our marriage: we'd once figured that our relationship got measurably rockier if we spent more than about sixty percent of our time together. It had been a long winter and we were overdue; but then Lisa looked intently at my face and decided not to leave. Two months later I worked through the problems in my skull, and asked her for solitude. She knew me well— well enough to laugh again because she knew I was waking out of another mental hibernation.

She got onto a jetliner on a gray winter day and headed east for my parents' old place in southern Colorado. The jetway for the flight was out of commission that afternoon, so the airline people had to roll out one of the old wheeled stairways. Just before she stepped into the cabin, Lisa paused and waved back from the head of the stairs; her dark hair curled about her face in the wind.

Two months later I'd roughed out most of the first draft for my initial book about the reproductive revolution. At least once a week I would call Lisa and she'd tell me about the photos she was taking river-running on an icy Colorado or Platte. Then I'd use her as a sounding board for speculations about ectogenesis, heterogynes, or the imminent emergence of an exploited human host-mother class.

"So what'll we do when you finish the first draft, Nick?"

"Maybe we'll take a leisurely month on the Trans-Canadian Railroad."

"Spring in the provinces . . ."

Then the initial draft was completed and so was Lisa's Colorado adventure. "Do you know how badly I want to see you?" she said.

"Almost as badly as I want to see you."

"Oh, no," she said. "Let me tell you—"

What she told me no doubt violated state and federal laws and probably telephone-company tariffs as well. The frustration of only hearing her voice through the wire made me twine my legs like a contortionist.

"Nick, I'll book a flight out of Denver. I'll let you know."

I think she wanted to surprise me. Lisa didn't tell me when she booked the flight. The airline let me know.

And now I'm fifty-one. The pendulum has swung and I again bitterly resent not having achieved more. There is so much work left undone; should I live for centuries, I still could not complete it all. That, however, will not be a problem.

I am told that the goddamned level of acid phosphatase in my goddamned blood is elevated. How banal that single fact sounds, how sterile; and how self-pitying the phraseology. Can't I afford a luxurious tear, Lisa?

Lisa?

Death: I wish to determine my own time.

"Charming," I had said. "End of the world."

My friend Denton, the young radio astronomer, said,

"Christ almighty! Your damned jokes. How can you make a pun about this?"

"It keeps me from crying," I said quietly. "Wailing and breast-beating won't make a difference."

"Calm, so calm." She looked at me peculiarly.

"I've seen the enemy," I said. "I've had time to consider it."

Her face was thoughtful, eyes focused somewhere beyond this cluttered office. "*If* you're right," she said, "it could be the most fantastic event a scientist could observe and record." Her eyes refocused and met mine. "Or it might be the most frightening; a final horror."

"Choose one," I said.

"If I believed you at all."

"I'm dealing in speculations."

"Fantasies," she said.

"However you want to term it." I got up and moved to the door. "I don't think there's much time. You've never seen where I live. Come"—I hesitated—"visit me if you care to. I'd like that—to have you there."

"Maybe," she said.

I should not have left the situation ambiguous.

I didn't know that in another hour, after I had left her office, pulled my car out of the Gamow Peak parking lot, and driven down to the valley, Denton would settle herself behind the wheel of her sports car and gun it onto the Peak road. Tourists saw her go off the switchback. A Highway Department crew pried her loose from the embrace of Lotus and lodgepole.

When I got the news I grieved for her, wondering if this were the price of belief. I drove to the hospital and, because no next of kin had been found and Amanda intervened, the doctors let me stand beside the bed.

I had never seen such still features, never such stasis short of actual death. I waited an hour, seconds sweeping silently from the wall clock, until the urge to return home was overpowering.

I could wait no longer because daylight was coming and I would tell no one.

Toward the beginning:

I've tolerated doctors as individuals; as a class they terrify me. It's a dread like that of shark attacks or dying by fire. But eventually I made the appointment for an examination, drove to the sparkling white clinic on the appointed day, and spent a surly half hour reading a year-old issue of *Popular Science* in the waiting room.

"Mr. Richmond?" the smiling nurse finally said. I followed her back to the examination room. "Doctor will be here in just a minute." She left. I sat apprehensively on the edge of the examination table. After two minutes I heard the rustling of my file being removed from the outside rack. Then the door opened.

"How's it going?" said my doctor. "I haven't seen you in a while."

"Can't complain," I said, reverting to accustomed medical ritual. "No flu so far this winter. The shot must have been soon enough."

Amanda watched me patiently. "You're not a hypochondriac. You don't need continual reassurance—or sleeping pills, anymore. You're not a medical groupie, God knows. So what is it?"

"Uh," I said. I spread my hands helplessly.

"Nicholas." Get-on-with-it-I'm-busy-today sharpness edged her voice.

"Don't imitate my maiden aunt."

"All right. *Nick*," she said. "What's wrong?"

"I'm having trouble urinating."

She jotted something down. Without looking up: "What kind of trouble?"

"Straining."

"For how long?"

"Six, maybe seven months. It's been a gradual thing."

"Anything else you've noticed?"

"Increased frequency."

"That's all?"

"Well," I said, "afterwards, I, uh, dribble."

She listed, as though by rote: "Pain, burning, urgency, hesitancy, change in stream of urine? Incontinence, change in size of stream, change in appearance of urine?"

"What?"

"Darker, lighter, cloudy, blood discharge from penis, VD exposure, fever, night sweats?"

I answered with a variety of nods and monosyllables.

"Mmh." She continued to write on the pad, then snapped it shut. "Okay, Nick, would you get your clothes off?" And when I had stripped: "Please lie on the table. On your stomach."

"The greased finger?" I said. "Oh, shit."

Amanda tore a disposable glove off the roll. It crackled as she put it on. "You think I get a thrill out of this?" She's been my GP for a long time.

When it was over and I sat gingerly and uncomfortably on the edge of the examining table, I said, "Well?"

Amanda again scribbled on a sheet. "I'm sending you to a urologist. He's just a couple of blocks away. I'll phone over. Try to get an appointment in—oh, inside of a week."

"Give me something better," I said, "or I'll go to the library and check out a handbook of symptoms."

She met my eyes with a candid blue gaze. "I want a specialist to check out the obstruction."

"You found something when you stuck your finger in?"

"Crude, Nicholas." She half-smiled. "Your prostate is hard—stony. There could be a number of reasons."

"What John Wayne used to call the Big C?"

"Prostatic cancer," she said, "is relatively infrequent in a man of your age." She glanced down at my records. "Fifty."

"Fifty-one," I said, wanting to shift the tone, trying, failing. "You didn't send me a card on my birthday."

"But it's not impossible," Amanda said. She stood. "Come on up to the front desk. I want an appointment with you after the urology results come back." As always, she patted me on the shoulder as she followed me out of the examination room. But this time there was slightly too much tension in her fingers.

I was seeing grassy hummocks and marble slabs in my mind and didn't pay attention to my surroundings as I exited the waiting room.

"Nick?" A soft Oklahoma accent.

I turned back from the outer door, looked down, saw tousled hair. Jackie Denton, one of the bright young minds out at the Gamow Peak Observatory, held the well-thumbed copy of *Popular Science* loosely in her lap. She honked and snuffled into a deteriorating Kleenex. "Don't get too close. Probably doesn't matter at this point. Flu. You?" Her green irises were red-rimmed.

I fluttered my hands vaguely. "I had my shots."

"Yeah." She snuffled again. "I was going to call you later on from work. See the show last night?"

I must have looked blank.

"Some science writer," she said. "Rigel went supernova."

"Supernova," I repeated stupidly.

"Blam, you know? *Blooie.*" She illustrated with her hands and the magazine flipped onto the carpet. "Not that you missed anything. It'll be around for a few weeks—biggest show in the skies."

A sudden ugly image of red and white aircraft warning lights merging in an actinic flare sprayed my retinas. I shook my head. After a moment I said, "First one in our galaxy in—how long? Three hundred and fifty years? I wish you'd called me."

"A little longer. Kepler's star was in 1604. Sorry about not calling—we were all a little busy, you know?"

"I can imagine. When did it happen?"

She bent to retrieve the magazine. "Just about midnight. Spooky. I was just coming off shift." She smiled. "Nothing like a little cosmic cataclysm to take my mind off jammed sinuses. Just as well; no sick leave tonight. That's why I'm here at the clinic. Kris says no excuses."

Krishnamurthi was the Gamov director. "You'll be going back up to the peak soon?" She nodded. "Tell Kris I'll be in to visit. I want to pick up a lot of material."

"For sure."

The nurse walked up to us. "Ms. Denton?"

"Mmph." She nodded and wiped her nose a final time. Struggling up from the soft chair, she said, "How come you didn't read about Rigel in the papers? It made every morning edition."

"I let my subscriptions lapse."

"But the TV news? The radio?"

"I didn't watch, and I don't have a radio in the car."

Before disappearing into the corridor to the examination rooms, she said, "That country house of yours must really be isolated."

The ice drips from the eaves as I drive up and park beside the garage. Unless the sky deceives me there is no new weather front moving in yet; no need to protect the car from another ten centimeters of fresh snow.

Sunset comes sooner at my house among the mountains; shadows stalk across the barren yard and suck heat from my skin. The peaks are, of course, deliberate barriers blocking off light and warmth from the coastal cities. Once

I personified them as friendly giants, amiable *lummoxen* guarding us. No more. Now they are only mountains again, the Cascade Range.

For an instant I think I see a light flash on, but it is just a quick sunset reflection on a window. The house remains dark and silent. The poet from Seattle's been gone for three months. My coldness—her heat. I thought that transference would warm me. Instead she chilled. The note she left me in the vacant house was a sonnet about psychic frostbite.

My last eleven years have not been celibate, but sometimes they feel like it. Entropy ultimately overcomes all kinetic force.

Then I looked toward the twilight east and saw Rigel rising. Luna wouldn't be visible for a while, so the brightest object in the sky was the exploded star. It fixed me to this spot by my car with the intensity of an aircraft landing light. The white light that shone down on me had left the supernova five hundred years before (a detail to include in the inevitable article—a graphic illustration of interstellar distances never fails to awe readers).

Tonight, watching the hundred-billion-degree baleful eye that was Rigel convulsed, I know *I* was awed. The cataclysm glared, brighter than any planet. I wondered whether Rigel—unlikely, I knew—had had a planetary system; whether guttering mountain ranges and boiling seas had preceded worlds frying. I wondered whether, five centuries before, intelligent beings had watched stunned as the stellar fire engulfed their skies. Had they had time to rail at the injustice? There are one hundred billion stars in our galaxy; only an estimated three stars go supernova per thousand years. Good odds: Rigel lost.

Almost hypnotized, I watched until I was abruptly rocked by the wind rising in the darkness. My fingers were stiff with cold. But as I started to enter the house I looked at the sky a final time. Terrifying Rigel, yes—but my eyes were captured by another phenomenon in the north. A spark of light burned brighter than the surrounding stars. At first I thought it was a passing aircraft, but its position remained stationary. Gradually, knowing the odds and unwilling to believe, I recognized the new supernova for what it was.

In five decades I've seen many things. Yet watching the sky I felt as if I were a primitive, shivering in uncured furs. My teeth chattered from more than the cold. I wanted to hide from the universe. The door to my house was unlocked, which was lucky—I couldn't have fitted a key into the latch. Finally I stepped over the threshold. I turned on all the lights, denying the two stellar pyres burning in the sky.

My urologist turned out to be a dour black man named Sharpe who treated me, I suspected, like any of the other specimens that turned up in his laboratory. In his .early thirties, he'd read several of my books. I appreciated his having absolutely no respect for his elders or for celebrities.

"You'll give me straight answers?" I said.

"Count on it."

He also gave me another of those damned urological fingers. When I was finally in a position to look back at him questioningly, he nodded slowly and said, "There's a nodule."

Then I got a series of blood tests for an enzyme called acid phosphatase. "Elevated," Sharpe said.

Finally, at the lab, I was to get the cystoscope, a shiny metal tube which would be run up my urethra. The biopsy forceps would be inserted through it. "Jesus, you're kidding." Sharpe shook his head. I said, "If the biopsy shows a malignancy . . ."

"I can't answer a silence."

"Come on," I said. "You've been straight until now. What are the chances of curing a malignancy?"

Sharpe had looked unhappy ever since I'd walked into his office. Now he looked unhappier. "Ain't my department," he said. "Depends on many factors."

"Just give me a simple figure."

"Maybe thirty percent. All bets are off if there's a metastasis." He met my eyes while he said that, then busied himself with the cystoscope. Local anesthetic or not, my penis burned like hell.

I had finally gotten through to Jackie Denton on a private line the night of the second supernova. "I thought last night was a madhouse?" she said. "You should see us now. I've only got a minute."

"I just wanted to confirm what I was looking at," I said. "I saw the damn thing actually blow."

"You're ahead of everybody at Gamow. We were busily

focusing on Rigel—" Electronic *wheeps* garbled the connection. "Nick, are you still there?"

"I think somebody wants the line. Just tell me a final thing: Is it a full-fledged supernova?"

"Absolutely. As far as we can determine now, it's a genuine Type II."

"Sorry it couldn't be the biggest and best of all."

"Big enough," she said. "It's good enough. This time it's only about nine light-years away. Sirius A."

"Eight-point-seven light-years," I said automatically. "What's that going to mean?"

"Direct effects? Don't know. We're thinking about it." It sounded as if her hand cupped the mouthpiece; then she came back on the line. "Listen, I've got to go. Kris is screaming for my head. Talk to you later."

"All right," I said. The connection broke. On the dead line I thought I heard the twenty-one-centimeter basic hydrogen hiss of the universe. Then the dial tone cut in and I hung up the receiver.

Amanda did not look at all happy. She riffled twice through what I guessed were my laboratory test results. "All right," I said from the patient's side of the wide walnut desk. "Tell me."

"Mr. Richmond? Nicholas Richmond?"

"Speaking."

"This is Mrs. Kurnick, with Trans-West Airways. I'm calling from Denver."

"Yes?"

"We obtained this number from a charge slip. A ticket was issued to Lisa Richmond—"

"My wife. I've been expecting her sometime this weekend. Did she ask you to phone ahead?"

"Mr. Richmond, that's not it. Our manifest shows your wife boarded our Flight 903, Denver to Portland, tonight."

"So? What's wrong? Is she sick?"

"I'm afraid there's been an accident."

Silence choked me. "How bad?" *The freezing began.*

"Our craft went down about ten miles northwest of Glenwood Springs, Colorado. The ground parties at the site say there are no survivors. I'm sorry, Mr. Richmond."

"No one?" I said. "I mean—"

"I'm truly sorry," said Mrs. Kurnick. *"If there's any change in the situation, we will be in touch immediately."*

Automatically I said, "Thank you."

I had the impression that Mrs. Kurnick wanted to say something else; but after a pause, she only said, "Good night."

On a snowy Colorado mountainside I died.

"The biopsy was malignant," Amanda said.

"Well," I said. "That's pretty bad." She nodded. "Tell me about my alternatives." *Ragged bits of metal slammed into the mountainside like teeth.*

My case was unusual only in a relative sense. Amanda told me that prostatic cancer is the penalty men pay for otherwise good health. If they avoid every other health hazard, twentieth-century men eventually get zapped by their prostates. In my case, the problem was about twenty years early; my bad luck. *Cooling metal snapped and sizzled in the snow, was silent.*

Assuming that the cancer hadn't already metastasized, there were several possibilities; but Amanda had, at this stage, little hope for either radiology or chemotherapy. She suggested a radical prostatectomy.

"I wouldn't suggest it if you didn't have a hell of a lot of valuable years left," she said. "It's not usually advised for older patients. But you're in generally good condition; you could handle it."

Nothing moved on the mountainside. "What all would come out?" I said.

"You already know the ramifications of 'radical.' "

I didn't mind so much the ligation of the spermatic tubes—I should have done that a long time before. At fifty-one I could handle sterilization with equanimity, but—

"Sexually dysfunctional?" I said. "Oh, my God." I was aware of my voice starting to tighten. "I can't do that."

"You sure as hell can," said Amanda firmly. "How long have I known you?" She answered her own question. "A long time. I know you well enough to know that what counts isn't all tied up in your penis."

I shook my head silently.

"Listen, damn it, cancer death is worse."

"No," I said stubbornly. "Maybe. Is that the whole bill?"

It wasn't. Amanda reached my bladder's entry on the list. It would be excised as well.

"Tubes protruding from me?" I said. *"If* I live, I'll have to spend the rest of my life toting a plastic bag as a drain for my urine?"

Quietly she said, "You're making it too melodramatic."

"But am I right?"

After a pause, "Essentially, yes."

And all that was the essence of it; the *good* news, all assuming that the carcinoma cells wouldn't jar loose during surgery and migrate off to other organs. "No," I said. The goddamned lousy, loathsome unfairness of it all slammed home. "Goddamn it, no. It's my choice; I won't live that way. If I just die, I'll be done with it."

"Nicholas! Cut the self-pity."

"Don't you think I'm entitled to some?"

"Be reasonable."

"You're supposed to comfort me," I said. "Not argue. You've taken all those death-and-dying courses. *You* be reasonable."

The muscles tightened around her mouth. "I'm giving you suggestions," said Amanda. "You can do with them as you damned well please." It had been years since I'd seen her angry.

We glared at each other for close to a minute. "Okay," I said. "I'm sorry."

She was not mollified. "Stay upset, even if it's whining. Get angry, be furious. I've watched you in a deep-freeze for a decade."

I recoiled internally. "I've survived. That's enough."

"No way. You've been sitting around for eleven years in suspended animation, waiting for someone to chip you free of the glacier. You've let people carom past, occasionally bouncing off you with no effect. Well, now it's not some*one* that's shoving you to the wall—it's some*thing*. Are you going to lie down for it? Lisa wouldn't have wanted that."

"Leave her out," I said.

"I can't. You're even more important to me because of her. She was my closest friend, remember?"

"Pay attention to her," Lisa had once said. *"She's more sensible than either of us."* Lisa had known about the affair; after all, Amanda had introduced us.

"I know." I felt disoriented; denial, resentment, numbness—the roller coaster clattered toward a final plunge.

"Nick, you've got a possibility for a healthy chunk of life left. I want you to have it, and if it takes using Lisa as a wedge, I will."

"I don't want to survive if it means crawling around

as a piss-dripping cyborg eunuch." The roller coaster teetered on the brink.

Amanda regarded me for a long moment, then said earnestly. "There's an outside chance, a long shot. I heard from a friend there that the New Mexico Meson Physics Facility is scouting for a subject."

I scoured my memory. "Particle-beam therapy?"

"Pions."

"It's chancy," I said.

"Are you arguing?" She smiled.

I smiled too. "No."

"Want to give it a try?"

My smile died. "I don't know. I'll think about it."

"That's encouragement enough," said Amanda. "I'll make some calls and see if the facility's as interested in you as I expect you'll be in them. Stick around home? I'll let you know."

"I haven't said yes. We'll let each other know." I didn't tell Amanda, but I left her office thinking only of death.

Melodramatic as it may sound, I went downtown to visit the hardware stores and look at their displays of pistols. After two hours, I tired of handling weapons. The steel seemed uniformly cold and distant.

When I returned home late that afternoon, there was a single message on my phone-answering machine:

"Nick, this is Jackie Denton. Sorry I haven't called for a while, but you know how it's been. I thought you'd like to know that Kris is going to have a press conference early in the week—probably Monday afternoon. I think he's worried because he hasn't come up with a good theory to cover the three Type II supernovas and the half dozen standard novas that have occurred in the last few weeks. But then nobody I know has. We're all spending so much time awake nights, we're turning into vampires. I'll get back to you when I know the exact time of the conference. I think it must be about thirty seconds now, so I—" The tape ended.

I mused with winter bonfires in my mind as the machine rewound and reset. Three Type II supernovas? One is merely nature, I paraphrased. Two mean only coincidence. Three make a conspiracy.

Impulsively I dialed Denton's home number; there was

no answer. Then the lines to Gamow Peak were all busy. It seemed logical to me that I needed Jackie Denton for more than being my sounding board, or for merely news about the press conference. I needed an extension of her friendship. I thought I'd like to borrow the magnum pistol I knew she kept in a locked desk drawer at her observatory office. I knew I could ask her a favor. She ordinarily used the pistol to blast targets on the peak's rocky flanks after work.

The irritating regularity of the busy signal brought me back to sanity. Just a second, I told myself. Richmond, what the hell are you proposing?

Nothing, was the answer. Not yet. Not . . . quite.

Later in the night, I opened the sliding glass door and disturbed the skiff of snow on the second-story deck. I shamelessly allowed myself the luxury of leaving the door partially open so that warm air would spill out around me while I watched the sky. The stars were intermittently visible between the towering banks of stratocumulus scudding over the Cascades. Even so, the three supernovas dominated the night. I drew imaginary lines with my eyes; connect the dots and solve the puzzle. How many enigmas can you find in this picture?

I reluctantly took my eyes away from the headline phenomena and searched for old standbys. I picked out the red dot of Mars.

Several years ago I'd had a cockamamie scheme that sent me to a Mesmerist—that's how she'd billed herself—down in Eugene. I'd been driving up the coast after covering an aerospace medical conference in Oakland. Somewhere around Crescent City, I capped a sea-bass dinner by getting blasted on prescribed pills and proscribed Scotch. Sometime during the evening, I remembered the computer-enhancement process JPL had used to sharpen the clarity of telemetered photos from such projects as the Mariner flybys and the Viking Mars lander. It seemed logical to me at the time that memories from the human computer could somehow be enhanced, brought into clarity through hypnosis. Truly stoned fantasies. But they somehow sufficed as rationale and incentive to wind up at Madame Guzmann's "Advice/Mesmerism/Health" establishment across the border in Oregon. Madame Guzmann had skin the color of her stained hardwood door; she

made a point of looking and dressing the part of a stereotype we *gajos* would think of as Gypsy. The scarf and
crystal ball strained the image. I think she was Vietnamese.
At any rate she convinced me she could hypnotize, and
then she nudged me back through time.

*Just before she ducked into the cabin, Lisa paused and
waved back from the head of the stairs; her dark hair
curled about her face in the wind.*

I should have taken to heart the lesson of stasis; entropy
is not so easily overcome.

What Madame Guzmann achieved was to freeze-frame
that last image of Lisa. Then she zoomed me in so close
it was like standing beside Lisa. I sometimes still see it
in my nightmares: Her eyes focus distantly. Her skin has
the graininess of a newspaper photo. I look but cannot
touch. I can speak but she will not answer. I shiver with
cold—

—and slid the glass door farther open.

There! An eye opened in space. A glare burned as cold
as a refrigerator light in a night kitchen. Mars seemed to
disappear, swallowed in the glow from the nova distantly
behind it. Another one, I thought. The new eye held me
fascinated, pinned as securely as a child might fasten a
new moth in the collection.

Nick?

Who is it?

Nick . . .

You're an auditory hallucination.

There on the deck the sound of laughter spiraled around
me. I thought it would shake loose the snow from the
trees. The mountain stillness vibrated.

The secret, Nick.

What secret?

You're old enough at fifty-one to decipher it.

Don't play with me.

Who's playing? Whatever time is left—

Yes?

*You've spent eleven years now dreaming, drifting, let-
ting others act on you.*

I know.

Do you? Then act on that. *Choose your actions. No
lover can tell you more. Whatever time is left—*

Shivering uncontrollably, I gripped the rail of the deck.
A fleeting pointillist portrait in black and white dissolved

into the trees. From branch to branch, top bough to bottom, crusted snow broke and fell, gathering momentum. The trees shed their mantle. Powder swirled up to the deck and touched my face with stinging diamonds.

Eleven years was more than half what Rip Van Winkle slept. "Damn it," I said. "Damn you." We prize our sleep. The grave rested peacefully among the trees. "Damn you," I said again, looking up at the sky.

On a snowy Oregon mountainside I was no longer dead. And yes, Amanda. Yes.

After changing planes at Albuquerque, we flew into Los Alamos on a small feeder line called Ross Airlines. I'd never flown before on so ancient a DeHavilland Twin Otter, and I hoped never to again; I'd take a Greyhound out of Los Alamos first. The flight attendant and half the other sixteen passengers were throwing up in the turbulence as we approached the mountains. I hadn't expected the mountains. I'd assumed Los Alamos would lie in the same sort of southwestern scrub desert surrounding Albuquerque. Instead I found a small city nestled a couple of kilometers up a wooded mountainside.

The pilot's unruffled voice came on the cabin intercom to announce our imminent landing, the airport temperature, and the fact that Los Alamos has more Ph.D.'s per capita than any other American city. "Second only to Akademgorodok," I said, turning away from the window toward Amanda. The skin wrinkled around her closed eyes. She hadn't had to use her airsick bag. I had a feeling that despite old friendships, a colleague and husband who was willing to oversee the clinic, the urgency of helping a patient, and the desire to observe an exotic experiment, Amanda might be regretting accompanying me to what she'd termed "the meson factory."

The Twin Otter made a landing approach like a strafing run and then we were down. As we taxied across the apron I had a sudden sensation of déjà vu: the time a year ago when a friend had flown me north in a Cessna. The airport in Los Alamos looked much like the civil air terminal at Sea-Tac where I'd met the Seattle poet. It happened that we were both in line at the snack counter. I'd commented on her elaborate Haida-styled medallion. We took the same table and talked; it turned out she'd heard of me.

"I really admire your stuff," she said.

So much for my ideal poet using only precise images. Wry thought. She was—is—a first-rate poet. I rarely think of her as anything but "the poet from Seattle." Is that kind of depersonalization a symptom?

Amanda opened her eyes, smiled wanly, said, "I could use a doctor." The flight attendant cracked the door and thin New Mexican mountain air revived us both.

Most of the New Mexico Meson Physics Facility was buried beneath a mountain ridge. Being guest journalist as well as experimental subject, I think we were given a more exhaustive tour than would be offered most patients and their doctors. Everything I saw made me think of expensive sets for vintage science-fiction movies: the interior of the main accelerator ring, glowing eggshell white and curving away like the space-station corridors in 2001; the linac and booster areas; the straightaway tunnel to the meson medical channel; the five-meter bubble chamber looking like some sort of time machine.

I'd visited both FermiLab in Illinois and CERN in Geneva, so I had a general idea of what the facilities were all about. Still I had a difficult time trying to explain to Amanda the Alice in Wonderland mazes that constituted high energy physics. But then so did Delaney, the young woman who was the liaison biophysicist for my treatment. It became difficult sorting out the mesons, pions, hadrons, leptons, baryons, J's, fermions, and quarks, and such quantum qualities as strangeness, color, baryonness, and charm. Especially charm, that ephemeral quality accounting for why certain types of radioactive decay should happen, but don't. I finally bogged down in the midst of quarks, antiquarks, charmed quarks, neoquarks, and quarklets.

Some wag had set a sign on the visitors' reception desk in the administration center reading: Charmed to meet you. "It's a joke, right?" said Amanda tentatively.

"It probably won't get any funnier," I said.

Delaney, who seemed to load every word with deadly earnestness, didn't laugh at all. "Some of the technicians think it's funny. I don't."

We rehashed the coming treatment endlessly. Optimistically I took notes for the book: The primary problem with a radiological approach to the treatment of cancer is that *hard radiation not only kills the cancerous cells, it also irradiates the surrounding healthy tissue. But in the mid nineteen seventies, cancer researchers found a more promising tool: shaped beams of subatomic particles which can be selectively focused on the tissue of tumors.*

Delaney had perhaps two decades on Amanda; being younger seemed to give her a perverse satisfaction in playing the pedagogue. "Split atomic nuclei on a small scale—"

"Small?" said Amanda innocently.

"—smaller than a fission bomb. Much of the binding force of the nucleus is miraculously transmuted to matter."

"Miraculously?" said Amanda. I looked up at her from the easy cushion shot I was trying to line up on the green velvet. The three of us were playing rotation in the billiards annex of the NMMPF recreation lounge.

"Uh," said Delaney, the rhythm of her lecture broken. "Physics shorthand."

"Reality shorthand," I said, not looking up from the cue now. "Miracles are as exact a quality as charm."

Amanda chuckled. "That's all I wanted to know."

The miracle pertinent to my case was atomic glue, mesons, one of the fission-formed particles. More specifically, my miracle was the negatively charged pion, a subclass of meson. Electromagnetic fields could focus pions into a controllable beam and fire it into a particular target—me.

"There are no miracles in physics," said Delaney seriously. "I used the wrong term."

I missed my shot. A gentle stroke, and gently the cue ball rolled into the corner pocket, missing the eleven. I'd set things up nicely, if accidentally, for Amanda.

She assayed the table and smiled. "Don't come unglued."

"That's very good," I said. Atomic glue does become unstuck, thanks to pions' unique quality. When they collide and are captured by the nucleus of another atom, they reconvert to pure energy; a tiny nuclear explosion.

Amanda missed her shot too. The corners of Delaney's mouth curled in a small gesture of satisfaction. She leaned across the table, hands utterly steady. "Multiply pions, multiply target nuclei, and you have a controlled aggregate explosion releasing considerably more energy than the entering pion beam. *Hah!*"

She sank the eleven and twelve; then ran the table. Amanda and I exchanged glances. "Rack 'em up," said Delaney.

"Your turn," Amanda said to me.

In my case the NMMPF medical channel would fire a directed pion beam into my recalcitrant prostate. If all went as planned, the pions intercepting the atomic nuclei of my cancer cells would convert back into energy in a series of atomic flares. The cancer cells being more sensitive, tissue damage should be restricted, localized in my cancerous nodule.

Thinking of myself as a nuclear battlefield in miniature was wondrous. Thinking of myself as a new Stagg Field or an Oak Ridge was ridiculous.

Delaney turned out to be a pool shark *par excellence*. Winning was all-important and she won every time. I decided to interpret that as a positive omen.

"It's time," Amanda said.

"You needn't sound as though you're leading a condemned man to the electric chair." I tied the white medical smock securely about me, pulled on the slippers.

"I'm sorry. Are you worried?"

"Not so long as Delaney counts me as part of the effort toward a Nobel Prize."

"She's good." Her voice rang too hollow in the sterile tiled room. We walked together into the corridor.

"Me, I'm bucking for a Kalinga Prize," I said.

Amanda shook her head. Cloudy hair played about her face. "I'll just settle for a positive prognosis for my patient." Beyond the door, Delaney and two technicians with a gurney waited for me.

There is a state beyond indignity that defines being draped naked on my belly over a bench arrangement, with my rear spread and facing the medical channel. Rigidly clamped, a ceramic target tube opened a separate channel through my anus to the prostate. Monitoring equipment and shielding shut me in. I felt hot and vastly uncomfortable. Amanda had shot me full of chemicals, not all of whose names I'd recognized. Now dazed, I couldn't decide which of many discomforts was the most irritating.

"Good luck," Amanda had said. "It'll be over before you know it." I'd felt a gentle pat on my flank.

I thought I heard the phasing-up whine of electrical equipment. I could tell my mind was closing down for the duration; I couldn't even remember how many billion

electron volts were about to route a pion beam up my
backside. I heard sounds I couldn't identify; perhaps an
enormous metal door grinding shut.

My brain swam free in a chemical river; I waited for
something to happen.

*I thought I heard machined ball bearings rattling down
a chute; no, particles screaming past the giant bending
magnets into the medical channel at three hundred thousand kilometers per second; flashing toward me through
the series of adjustable filters; slowing, slowing, losing
energy as they approach; then through the final tube and
into my body.*

Inside . . .

*The pion sails the inner atomic seas for a relativistically
finite time. Then the perspective inhabited by one is inhabited by two. The pion drives toward the target nucleus.
At a certain point the pion is no longer a pion; what was
temporarily matter transmutes back to energy. The energy
flares, expands, expends, and fades. Other explosions det-
onate in the spaces within the patterns underlying larger
patterns.*

Darkness and light interchange.

*The light coalesces into a ball; massive, hot, burning
against the darkness. Pierced, somehow stricken, the ball
begins to collapse in upon itself. Its internal temperature
climbs to a critical level. At six hundred million degrees,
carbon nuclei fuse. Heavier elements form. When the fuel
is exhausted, the ball collapses further; again the temperature is driven upward; again heavier elements form and
are in turn consumed. The cycle repeats until the nuclear
furnace manufactures iron. No further nuclear reaction
can be triggered; the heart's fire is extinguished. Without
the outward balance of fusion reaction, the ball initiates
the ultimate collapse. Heat reaches one hundred billion
degrees. Every conceivable nuclear reaction is consummated.*

*The ball explodes in a final convulsive cataclysm. Its
energy flares, fades, is eaten by entropy. The time it took
is no more than the time it takes Sol-light to reach and
illuminate the Earth.*

"How do you feel?" Amanda leaned into my field of
vision, eclipsing the fluorescent rings overhead.

"Feel?" I seemed to be talking through a mouthful of cotton candy.

"Feel."

"Compared to what?" I said.

She smiled. "You're doing fine."

"I had one foot on the accelerator," I said.

She looked puzzled, then started to laugh. "It'll wear off soon." She completed her transit and the lights shone back in my face.

"No hand on the brake," I mumbled. I began to giggle. Something pricked my arm.

I think Delaney wanted to keep me under observation in New Mexico until the anticipated ceremonies in Stockholm; I didn't have time for that. I suspected none of us did. Amanda began to worry about my moody silences; she ascribed them at first to my medication and then to the two weeks' tests Delaney and her colleagues were inflicting on me.

"To hell with this," I said. "We've got to get out of here." Amanda and I were alone in my room.

"What?"

"Give me a prognosis."

She smiled. "I think you may as well shoot for the Kalinga."

"Maybe." I quickly added, "I'm not a patient anymore; I'm an experimental subject."

"So what do we do about it?"

We exited NMMPF under cover of darkness and struggled a half kilometer through brush to the highway. There we hitched a ride into town.

"This is crazy," said Amanda, picking thistle out of her sweater.

"It avoids a strong argument," I said as we neared the lights of Los Alamos.

The last bus of the day had left. I wanted to wait until morning. Over my protests, we flew out on Ross Airlines. "Doctor's orders," said Amanda, teeth tightly together, as the Twin Otter bumped onto the runway.

I dream of pions. I dream of colored balloons filled with hydrogen, igniting and flaming up in the night. I dream of

Lisa's newsprint face. Her smile is both proud and sorrowful.

Amanda had her backlog of patients and enough to worry about, so I took my nightmares to Jackie Denton at the observatory. I told her of my hallucinations in the accelerator chamber. We stared at each other across the small office.

"I'm glad you're better, Nick, but—"

"That's not it," I said. "Remember how you hated my article about poetry glorifying the new technology? Too fanciful?" I launched into speculation, mixing with abandon pion beams, doctors, supernovas, irrational statistics, cancerous nodes, fire balloons, and gods.

"Gods?" she said. "*Gods? Are you going to put that in your next column?"

I nodded.

She looked as though she were inspecting a newly found-out psychopath. "No one needs that in the press now, Nick. The whole planet's upset already. The possibility of nova radiation damaging the ozone layer, the potential for genetic damage, all that's got people spooked."

"It's only speculation."

She said, "You don't yell 'Fire!' in a crowded theater."

"Or in a crowded world?"

Her voice was unamused. "Not now."

"And if I'm right?" I felt weary. "What about it?"

"A supernova? No way. Sol simply doesn't have the mass."

"But a nova?" I said.

"Possibly," she said tightly. "But it shouldn't happen for a few billion years. Stellar evolution—"

"—is theory," I said. "*Shouldn't* isn't *won't*. Tonight look again at that awesome sky."

Denton said nothing.

"Could you accept a solar flare? A big one?"

I read the revulsion in her face and knew I should stop talking; but I didn't. "Do you believe in God? Any god?" She shook her head. I had to get it all out. "How about concentric universes, one within the next like Chinese carved ivory spheres?" Her face went white. "Pick a card," I said, "any card. A wild card."

"God damn you, shut up." On the edge of her desk, her knuckles were as white as her lips.

"Charming," I said, ignoring the incantatory power of words, forgetting what belief could cost. I do not think she deliberately drove her Lotus off the Peak road. I don't want to believe that. Surely she was coming to join me.

Maybe, she'd said.

Nightmares should be kept home. So here I stand on my sundeck at high noon for the Earth. No need to worry about destruction of the ozone layer and the consequent skin cancer. There will be no problem with mutational effects and genetic damage. I need not worry about deadlines or contractual commitments. I regret that no one will ever read my book about pion therapy.

All that—maybe.

The sun shines bright— The tune plays dirgelike in my head.

Perhaps I am wrong. The flare may subside. Maybe I am not dying. No matter.

I wish Amanda were with me now, or that I were at Jackie Denton's bedside, or even that I had time to walk to Lisa's grave among the pines. Now there is no time.

At least I've lived as long as I have now by choice.

That's the secret, Nick. . . .

The glare illuminates the universe.

The Thermals of August

I see the woman die, and the initial beauty of the event takes away my breath. Later I will feel the sickness of pain, the weakness of sorrow. But for the moment I sit transfixed, face tilted toward the irregular checkerboard of cumulus. The drama of death has always seemed to me the truest element in life.

The other diners see what I had detected a moment before: a tiny irregularity in the smooth sweep of the newly launched kite. The kite is cobalt blue and dart-shaped, apparently a modified Rogallo wing—not one of the Dragons we'll all be flying later in the week.

Having come to the outdoor cafe by Bear Creek for a late breakfast, I'd hoped simply to satisfy a necessary but unwanted need. Now, however, the bite of croissant lies dry in my mouth and the cup of coffee cools undrunk. Perhaps I did not really see the minute lurch in the kite's path. I allow myself that one brief luxurious hope, staring at the kite and its pilot more than two thousand feet above the valley floor. The kite is a vivid midge against the lighter blue of the sky.

Then the kite falls.

I see the craft first slip into a stall, then nose downward—no problem for even a moderately experienced pilot. But suddenly half the wing folds back at an unnatural

53

angle. In a little more than a second, we on the ground hear the twang and snap of breaking control wires and twisting aluminum frame.

The kite tumbles.

I am surrounded by babble and one of the other diners begins to whimper.

It seems to take forever to fall.

My brain coolly goes to work and I know that the descent is far more rapid in terms of feet per second than appears to our eyes.

At first the kite fell like a single piece of confetti pitched from a Wall Street window. Now the collapsed portion of the wing has wrapped around pilot and harness, and the warped mass rotates as it appears to us to grow larger.

The crippled kite twists and spins, flutters and falls like a leaf of aspen. I think I see the shrouded form of the pilot, a pendulum flung outward by centrifugal force.

The kite's fall seems to accelerate as it nears ground, but that also is illusion. Someone screams at us to take cover, evidently thinking that the kite will plunge into the midst of the outdoor diners. It doesn't. The kite makes half a final revolution and spins into the corner of the Conoco Building. The cocooned pilot slams into the brick with the flat smack of a beef roast dropped onto kitchen tile. The wreckage drapes over the temporary barbed-wire fence protecting this building under perpetual reconstruction.

The bit of croissant still lies on my tongue. I feel every sharp edge. I gag and taste bitterness coat my throat.

The dead-moth corpse of the kite is not more than fifty feet away, and the crowd slowly begins to close the distance. I am among them. The others grant me a wide path because most recognize that I too am a pilot. "Let the woman through." Gingerly I approach my fallen comrade.

Her body is almost totally swathed in the cobalt fabric of the kite. I can see her face; her eyes stare open and unpeacefully. The concealed contours of her body are smooth. I suspect most of the bones of her body are splintered.

When I softly touch one of her shoulders, I inadvertently drag one tightly folded flap of kitewing against a steel barb. Pooled blood bursts forth in a brief cataract. Mixed with the scent of her blood is the odor of urine.

This is not death; it is indignity.

My nylon windbreaker is composed of my colors: gold

and black. I take it off and cover the dead woman's face. Then I glare around the circle of onlookers. Most of them stare at the ground and mumble, then turn and leave.

I draw back the jacket for a moment and lightly kiss the dead woman's lips.

I love this town between festivals. Living among the stable population of two thousand refreshes me after months of engulfment in the cities of the coasts. I am pleased by the ambivalent socialness of friendly greetings on the street, but without anyone pushing me to respond further. Warm people who hold a fetish of privacy are an impossible paradox elsewhere. This town prides itself on paradox.

The rules do not always hold true in the public downtown, particularly during the festivals. The outsiders flood in at various times of the year for their chamber music and jazz festivals, art symposiums, video circus, and other, more esoteric gatherings.

Although the present festival will not begin until tomorrow at dawn, the town is crowded with both participants and spectators. Tonight people fill the bars downtown and spill out onto the sidewalks along both sides of Main. Though August is not yet ended, the cold crisps the night. The town is at nearly nine thousand feet, and chill is to be expected; but the plumes of breath billow more than one would expect. The stars are clear and icy tonight; I see clouds scudding up the valley from the west.

There is a shifting, vibrant energy in the crowds that runs like quicksilver. I can feel it. The moon tonight is new, so I can't ascribe anything to lunar influence. The magic must generate from the gestalt interaction of the flyers and the watchers. Or, more likely, from the ancient mountains that ring us on three sides.

The air seems most charged in the Club Troposphere, the street-front bar on the ground floor of the Ionic Hotel. I have a table in one of the Trope's raised bay display windows overlooking the sidewalk. The crowd flux continually alters, but at any given moment, at least a dozen others share the table with me. Some stand, some sit, and in the crowd din, body language communicates at least as much as words. I'm stacking empties of imported beers in front of my glass. This early in the evening, my pyramid looks more Aztec than Egyptian.

I continue to taste blood; the thick, dark ale won't wash it away. Before I truly realize what I'm doing, I grasp the latest empty by the neck and slam it down on the hardwood. "God *damn!*" Amber glass sprays across the table and I raise the jagged edges of the neck to the level of my eyes.

"Mairin!" Across the table I see Lark look up from nuzzling Haley's throat. "Mairin, are you all right?" he says. Haley stares at me as well. Everyone at the table is staring at me.

"I dropped it," I say. I set the severed neck down beside my glass.

Lark gets up from Haley's lap and comes around the table to me. I stare from one to the other of the vertices of my present triangle. Lark is small, compact, and dark, with the sense of spatial orientation and imagination and the steel muscles, all of which make him a better Dragon pilot than anyone else here. With the probable exception of me. Haley is tall and light, a woman of the winter with silky hair to her waist and eyes like ice chipped from inaccessible glaciers. But when she smiles, the ice burns.

"Are you okay?" Lark places his fingers lightly on the hand with which I smashed the bottle. I move the hand and pick up my glass. A barmaid hovers beside us, wiping shards into a paper towel.

I nod. "It was an accident."

Lark puts his face very close to mine. "The rookie who died today—you saw the whole thing, right?"

"I saw her get into the truck for the ride up to the point. She was very young. I didn't know her."

"She was good," Lark says. "I know people who flew with her in the Midwest. Today she was very unlucky."

"Obviously."

"That's not what I meant." Lark smiles in the way I've learned to interpret during the long years of competition as all teeth and no mirth. "After the medics took her body away from you practically at gunpoint, I went over her equipment with the officials. She committed a beginner's error, you know—dipped a wingtip when she went off. Clipped an outcropping."

"I saw," I say. "She recovered."

"We did X rays. There was a flaw in the metal. That's why the one wing buckled."

"God." I feel sick, dizzy, as though I'm whirling around

in that bright cobalt body bag, waiting for the ground to smash out my life.

"Whoever," Lark says. "Just bad luck." He hesitates. "I keep thinking about all the times I've inspected my own equipment. You can only check so much."

Haley has come around the table too and stands close to Lark. "I wonder what it felt like."

"I know," I say. I look at Lark's face and realize he knows too. Haley is an artist and photographer who sticks close to her gallery here in town. She has never flown. She can never know.

I'm really not sure how many beers I've drunk tonight. It must be more than I think I've counted, because I do and say what is uncharacteristic of me. With Lark and Haley both standing there, I look into Haley's winter eyes and say, "I need to be with someone tonight."

"I— Mairin—" Haley almost stutters. She gentles her voice. "Lark asked me already. . . ."

"Lark could unask you," I say. I know that's unfair, but I also know my need. Lark is staring studiously out the window, pretending to ignore us both.

Haley says, "Lark was there too. He needs—"

"*I* need." They both stare at me uncomfortably now without speaking. Individually I know how stubborn each can be. Three springs tauten. I want to reach out and be held, to thaw and exhaust myself with body warmth. I want to reach out with the shattered bottleneck and rip both of them until I bathe in steaming blood. Then it all goes out from me and I sink back in my chair. I am so goddamned suspicious of the word *need* and I have heard it too many times.

"I'm sorry," I say. "I'm behaving badly."

"Mairin—" both start to say. Lark touches my shoulder. Haley reaches out.

I shove back my chair and get up unsteadily. My head pounds. Nausea wracks my belly and I am glad there is no competition for me tomorrow. "I'm going to my room. I don't feel . . ." I let the words trail off.

"Do you need help?"

"No, Haley. No, love. I can make it." I push past and leave them at the table. I hope I'm leaving my self-pity there too. The lobby of the Ionic is another zoo of milling humans. I make it to the lone elevator where luck has brought the cage to the first floor. As I enter the car, a bearded flyer-groupie in a yellow down jacket unwisely reaches in from the lobby and grabs my wrist.

"Lady, would you like a drink?" he says.

The spring, still taut, ratchets loose. Luckily for him my knee catches him only in the upper thigh and he flails backward into the lobby as spectators gape. The doors close and the elevator climbs noisily toward my floor. Two young men stand nervously in the opposite corner, just as far from me as four feet will allow.

I'll regret all this tomorrow.

I know the woman who comes to me that night.

I am she.

The cotton sheet slides coolly, rustling, as I restlessly change position. I've pushed the down comforter to my knees. It's too hot for that. The cold will come later, past midnight when the hotel lowers all the thermostats.

Finally I despair of sleeping, lie still, lie on my back with my hands beside me. I can see dimly in the light from the frosted-glass transom, as well as the white glow from the hotel neon outside the single window. I hear the muffled sounds of celebration from the street below.

Then I see the woman standing silently at the foot of the bed. I know her. She is short—five four without shoes. Her body is slender and muscular. The shadows shift as she moves around to the side of my bed. Darkness glides across her eyes, her neck, between her breasts, on her belly and below. Her breasts are small, with dark, prominent nipples. Her muscles, when she moves, are not obtrusive but are clearly delineated.

She steps into the light from the street. There are no crow's-feet visible in chiaroscuro. Her face is delicately boned, heart-shaped, with a chin that misses sharpness by only a degree. Her eyes are wide and as dark as her close-cut hair. In the semidarkness I know I am seeing her as she was when she was twenty and as she will be when she is forty.

I slip the sheet aside as she silently lies in my bed. Slowly, delicately, I slide the fingers of one hand along the side of her face, down the jawline, across her lips. Her lips part slightly and one fingertip touches the firm, moist cushion of her tongue.

Then even more gently I cup her breasts, my palms

feeling their warmth long before the skin touches the tips of each erect nipple.

It takes a thousand years.

My hands slide down her flanks and touch all that is moist and warm between her legs. I know what to seek out and I find it. The warmth builds.

I think of Haley. I think of Lark. I blink him out. Haley leaves of her own accord and abandons me pleading. My pleading, her leaving.

My finger orbits and touches, touches and orbits, touches. The warmth builds and builds, is more than warmth, builds and heats, the heat— The heat coils and expands, ripples outward, ripples across my belly, down my thighs. For a moment, just a bare moment, something flickers like heat lightning on the horizon—

—but it is not sufficient. I am not warm enough.

Heat radiates and is lost, spent. I see Lark and Haley again in my mind and blink away the man. But Haley leaves too.

Only I am left.

I wish the woman would sleep, but I know her too well.

I wish I could sleep, but I know me so well.

Dragon Festival.

It is nearly dawn and the roar of dragons splits the chilly air. The tongues of propane burners lick the hearts of twenty great balloons. The ungainly shapes bulk in the near darkness and slowly come erect. The crews hold tight to nylon lines.

As the sun starts to rise above the peaks beyond the two waterfalls, I see that snow dusted the San Juans sometime past midnight. The mountains are topped with were-snow—a sifting that came in the night and will shortly vanish with morning sun. The real storms are yet to come with the autumn.

Mythic creatures rear up in the dawn. These are nothing so simple as the spherical balloons of my childhood. Laboratory-bred synthetics have been sculpted and molded to suggest the shapes of legend. A great golden gargoyle hunches to the east. To the west, a hundred-foot-tall gryphon strains at its handlers' lines. The roaring, rushing propane flames animate a sphinx, a satyr, a kraken with basket suspended from its drooping tentacles, a Cheshire cat, and chimeras of every combination. The giants bob and dip as they distend, but it is a perfect morning with no wind.

I find a perverse delight in not feeling as wretched as I anticipated last night. My mind is clear. My eyes do not ache. Though I was not able to cope with breakfast food, I did manage to drink tea. I realize I'm being caught up in the exhilaration of the first festival day. I know that within the hour I will be flowing with the wind, floating with the clouds.

"How do you feel this morning?" A familiar voice.

"Did you get any rest?" Another familiar voice.

I turn to greet Haley and Lark. "I feel fine. I got some sleep." I determine to leave any qualifications behind.

"I'll see you on the ground," says Lark.

Haley looks at me steadily for several seconds, a time that seems much longer. Finally she draws me close and says, "Good luck. Have a fine flight." Her lips are cool and they touch my cheek briefly.

Lark and she walk toward the balloon called *Cheshire*. I hear fragmented words from a portable public-address system that tell me all flyers should be linking their craft to their respective balloons. I walk across the meadow to *Negwenya*. *Negwenya* is the Zulu word for dragon. *Negwenya* is a towering black-and-scarlet balloon owned by a man named Robert Simms. Robert's eight-times-removed grandparents were Zulu. Robert is a great believer in the mystique of dragons and sees an occult affinity between *Negwenya* and the Dragon Five flyers he ferries up to the sky.

I walk between the serpentine legs of *Negwenya* and feel the sudden chill of entering shadow. The people holding *Negwenya*'s lines, mostly local volunteers, greet me and I answer them back. From where he waits beside my Dragon Five, Robert raises a broad hand in welcome. My gold-and-black glider looks as fragile on the wet grass as it did in the electric glow when I left to watch the coming dawn.

"You ready?" Robert's voice is permanently hoarse from a long-ago accident when a mooring line snapped and lashed around his throat.

"I'm ready." I check the tough lightweight lines that will allow my Dragon to dangle below *Negwenya* as the balloon takes us up to twelve thousand feet. The ends of the lines tuck into safety pressure catches both on the underside of *Negwenya*'s gondola and on my craft's keel tube and wing braces. Either Robert or I can elect at any time to release the catches. Once that happens, *Negwenya* will go on about its own business and I will describe the great descending spiral that eventually brings me back to earth.

More orders blare from the bullhorn across the field. It doesn't matter that none of us can understand the words; we all know what happens next.

"Let's link up," says Robert.

I nod and climb into my harness under the Five as Robert and a helper hold the wings steady on the support stands. It isn't like getting ready to fly a 767; just a few metallic clicks and the appropriate straps are secured. I pull on my helmet and check the instrumentation: the microprocessor-based unit in the liner records air speed, ground speed, and altitude. The figures appear on a narrow band along the inside of the transparent visor. There is an audible stall warning, but I rarely activate that; I'd rather gauge stability directly from the air flutter on the wing fabric.

"Okay, just a few more minutes," says Robert.

I'm glad the Five is resting on the supports. The entire craft may weigh only sixty pounds, but that's half what I weigh. My flight suit feels sticky along the small of my back; I'm sweating. I hear the amplified words of the pageant director continue to fragment on the leading edge of the mountain.

"Time to do it," says Robert. He climbs up to the launch ladder and steps into the gondola. Then he looks back over the edge—I see the reflection in the bulge of my visor—and grins. "Good luck, lady." He displays an erect thumb. "Break a leg."

With a rush and a roar, the twenty lighter-than-air craft embark. The paradox is that with all the fury and commotion, the score of balloons rises so slowly. Our ascension is stately.

Excited as ever by the sight, I watch the images of ground things diminish. I see the takeoff field swarm with video people; the insect eyes of cameras glitter. From beyond the ropes, the sustained note of the crowd swells with the balloons' first rising.

Harpies, genies, furies all, we soar toward a morning clear but for high cirrus. I fill my lungs with chill clean air and feel the exuberance, the climactic anticipation of that moment when each of us cuts loose the tether from our respective balloons and glides into free flight.

Free is the word, free is the key. I know I'm smiling; and then I feel the broad, loose grin. My teeth ache with the cold, but it doesn't matter. I want to laugh madly and I restrain myself only because I know I can afford to waste none of the precious oxygen at this altitude.

The weather's fine!

I raise a gloved hand to Lark as *Cheshire* slowly rises past *Negwenya*. His brown-and-yellow wings bob slightly as he waves back. The grin on *Cheshire's* cat doesn't seem nearly so wide as mine.

The valley town is a parti-colored patchwork. I glance up and scan the line of red figures along my visor. I'm a thousand feet above the meadow. I look from the comfortable brick and frame of the old town to the newer, wooden, fake Victorian homes rising from the mountain's skirts. Now I'm level with the end of the trees and the beginning of bare rock. To the east I look beyond the old Pandora Mill and see the sun catch the spray from Ingram Falls and Bridal Veil. The waterfalls have not yet been turned off for the winter.

Toward the top of the canyon, light crosswinds buffet the balloons slightly as I expected they would. *Negwenya* rotates slowly and I concentrate on feeling no vertigo. We sweep past a sheer rock face to the waves and shouted greetings of a party of climbers strung like colored beads from their ropes. The balloon pilots yell back.

I can intellectually understand the attraction of technical climbing, but I was never able to appreciate it on a gut level. And I tried. Perhaps the only level on which it communicates to me is: *because it's there. Haley.* I wonder if I should desire Haley so intensely if she were more accessible. Even the anticipation of the coming long flight cannot erase the chill and heat of her from my mind.

"Mairin!"

I hear Robert's shout above the rushing-wind sound of the burner.

"Mairin, are you watching your gauge?"

I hadn't been. *Negwenya's* at twelve-seven and it won't be long before we're thirteen thousand feet above sea level. While I was thinking about sapphire eyes, like a rank amateur, the other flyers had been cutting loose from their balloons. Below me I see the looping, swarming flight of Dragons.

I glance at the readouts again. Robert has assured my wind direction. I drop.

My Dragon Five drops away from the gondola and *Negwenya*'s roar grows faint; then is gone. The silence of my flight enfolds me. I lie prone in my harness, nothing else between me and the valley but air.

I fly for this moment.

The microprocessor's electronic senses tell me hard information: I am two thousand nine hundred and sixty-two feet above the valley floor. My air speed is twenty-two miles per hour, only slightly less than my ground speed. My Dragon Five presently travels nearly twelve feet horizontally for every foot it drops. In a minute I will lose about two hundred feet. Without searching out the thermal currents, I'll reach the ground in about fifteen minutes.

I pay no attention to the readouts. For the moment, the silence and openness, the caress of air on my face, all stir a complex reaction in my mind and body. I feel the throbbing start, far inside.

The slight shift of my body affects the attitude of my flight. The Dragon responds and I sweep into a wide, shallow turn.

No women or men have given me this feeling so fully as has the sky. I spiral down above the land and desire this to last forever. Gravity is the enemy of my love. As well I remind myself that I am part of the pageant; that just as the balloons are now drifting eastward, engaged in their slow-motion behemoth race, so it's demanded of the flyers that all land at about the same time in a live simulation of wide-screen spectacle. The cameras whir. The broadcasts fan out from microwave towers. The spectators watch.

But I want to make it last.

And I realize, first shocked, then amused, how many minutes it's been since I've held Haley's image in my mind.

I wheel the Dragon around in a descending spiral, as silent and graceful as any gull. Catching up with the other Dragons, I hear the mutter of wind rippling the fabric ever closer to the wing's trailing edge. I recognize the proximity of a stall and moderate slightly the angle of the warperons.

There are times when I have thought of gently and irrevocably slipping into the tightest of spirals and hurling myself blackly through the heart of the air. I cannot count the times I have skirted that final edge. Always I've refrained.

The air touches my cheekbones with the soft, tickling touch of Haley's cloudy hair.

There are times . . .

Death in triplicate stands by my elbow at the bar. Three tall shapes in black hooded robes have stepped to the brass rail. Skull faces, obviously sculpted with care, grin from cowled shadows. They say nothing. The trio reminds me of participants in a Mexican holy-day parade.

Two deaths stare around the crowded Trope. The other looks at me. With my beer, I toast it back silently.

"Hey! You people want anything?" The barman tonight is one of the Trope's owners. With the Dragon Festival now started, all possible personnel are needed to service the crowds.

Three bony grins turn to smile at him. There are no words.

After a pause the owner says, "Listen, this is for paying customers. You want something?"

Three shrouded figures lean across the bar toward him. The owner draws back. "Drink," he says, "or get out."

Dead silence.

He apparently decides he's outnumbered. "Shit," the owner mutters, and goes off to wait on newcomers at the end of the bar. I think I hear a giggle from the death figure farthest from me. The nearest turns again to face me. Again I raise a glass in toast.

The figure reaches, hand ivory with makeup, into a pocket beneath the robes and withdraws an object. Then it extends the hand toward me. I accept a small skull made of spun sugar, another relic of Mexican religious celebrations. I incline my head gravely and set the candy skull beside my glass.

The nearest figure turns back to its fellows. I hear a whispered consultation. Then all three leave the bar together. As they reach the door, the barman shouts, "Good goddamn riddance!" He walks past me on the way to the cash register and I hear him say in a lower voice, "Give me the creeps."

"Friends of yours?"

I turn to face Haley and Lark. I hadn't seen them coming. "Friends of ours." I shrug.

"Spooky," says Haley.

"Striking masks," says Lark.

"Want a beer?"

"We're already set," says Lark. "We've got a table back behind the grove of rubber plants. Do you want to join us?"

I toss down the final swallow of beer. "Thanks, no. Not yet. I'm going to get some fresh air before I do any more drinking. You want to come along?"

Lark shakes his head. "We've got to do some drinking before we get some more fresh air."

"Then I'll see you both later. I need the air." I pick up the spun-sugar skull and gnaw on the jaw region as I push through the crowd.

Outside it's warmer than it was last night. There is cloud cover; I suspect the San Juans will be solidly snow-capped by morning. I zip the front of my flight jacket and stick my balled fists into the pockets. Turning right, I head along Main toward the landing meadow. I see the amber lights of trucks still bringing in and unloading the deflated forms of the racing balloons. I heard earlier that Robert Simms and *Negwenya* won. I decide that's a good omen.

"Girl? Hey, stop a moment, girl."

I turn and look toward the source of the voice. I'm in front of the Teller House, the town's lone real department store. I look into the display window and see the life-sized image of an elderly ragged woman staring back at me. It's an argee screen—the name comes from the initials of the people who started setting up these synchronous video arrangements back in the late seventies. One enormous complex of electronic art, the argee screens are spotted in cities and towns around the globe. Each screen shows a live, life-sized, simultaneous transmission of a street scene somewhere else in the world. Sound and video equipment beam my voice and image back to the linked screen. A computer randomly changes the linkages.

Right now the old woman sees and hears me. I see and hear her. I have no idea where she really is. The scene behind her is dark and obviously urban. It could be any nighttime city.

"I'm in Baltimore," she says. "Where are you?"

I tell her.

"Oh, yeah," she says. "I heard about you people. Saw you on the news. Bunch of fools who jump off cliffs on kites."

I laugh. "Condors launch from cliffs."

"Birds aren't too smart."

"But they fly."

"Yeah." She inspects me seriously. "You one of them?"

"Do I fly?" I nod. "Not exactly on a kite, though."

Her voice is thirsty. "Tell me about it."

For some reason I cannot ignore the imperative in her voice. I tell her about flying. I describe my Dragon Five as the combination of a high-winged monoplane and a bat. I talk of tomorrow's competition. I paint with words the colors of the long, gliding dragon kite I will tow behind my Five. I tell her of the *manjha*, the razor-sharp cutting line with which I will attempt to sever the towline of my opponent's kite. And with which he or she will try to sever mine. But most of all, I describe the flying. I talk religiously of fighting maneuvers in the sky.

And when I pause for breath, she says, "Girl, God bless you." Her image flickers.

The argee screen relinks. I blink a moment at the light. I see a daylight scene under bright sun. In the background is something that looks vaguely like the Taj Mahal. A man in a white linen suit looks out of the screen at me. He inspects me and stares at the colors of my jacket. Slowly he nods his head as though comprehending something. He says, *"Woh kata hai?"*

I smile, spread my hands helplessly, and walk on.

Woh kata hai. I believe that's an Indian kite fighter's challenge.

Dreaming.

It's called a *pench* and I love it more than either soccer or skiing. Each of us stands in a circle about three yards in diameter; the circles are approximately twenty feet apart. The officials have limed the circles on the grass as they would stripe the yard lines for a football game. The breeze is light this morning, but it may kick up. I have brought several different sizes of fighting kites. When I look around at my competition, I generally have to tilt my head back. I am eleven years old.

My gear litters the close-cropped grass around my feet: kites, extra lines, a spare spool. My little brother, eight, sits boredly reading a science-fiction paperback just inside my circle. If I need it, he'll help with the launching.

I love Saturday mornings in general, but this particular one is the Michael Collins Annual Kite Fly. It's the second Saturday in September and it delights everyone except the high-school football coach who wanted to use this field for a practice scrimmage. Luckily the principal has an autographed picture of the Apollo 11 crew and is an old kite fighter himself, so that was that.

The kite-fighting contest isn't the only event today, but it's the only one that interests me. The *pench* should start in a few minutes, at nine, and will continue until noon. Since I've got some sort of reputation, I'm one of the flyers who get to start. Anyone who wants can take a turn standing in the opponent circle. If he loses, someone else takes his place. And if I lose, I'm out. Then I get to stand in line, waiting to challenge the current champions. I don't plan to spend a lot of time waiting in line.

This is an average Indian summer morning. It's cool now, but I'm guessing it's going to get very hot by midday. The nearest referee—Mr. Schindler, the junior-high shop teacher—tells us through his bullhorn that each contestant should be ready. My first opponent steps into the next circle. I don't know his last name, but his first name is Ken and he's really sure of himself. I tell him I wish him luck. Ken snickers. He's in at least eighth grade.

"You want help launching?" says my little brother.

"I can do the first one myself." I adjust the bridle on a middle-sized kite. The breeze is gentle but steady.

"Okay." His attention returns to his Robert Heinlein novel.

Ken's kite looks fourteen inches by a foot—too small. He's overestimating the wind velocity. Too bad.

"Launch 'em," says the referee.

I lightly throw my gold-and-black fighter into the air and pump the cotton string with my right hand: pull in, let out, pull in, let out, until the diamond-shaped kite gains lift in the breeze and begins to climb. I sneak a glance at Ken. His fighter autumnleafs into the ground. I catch his eye and smile. He glares before picking up his kite to launch again.

My kite is solidly airborne. I continue the rhythm of launch; now the pumping motions are longer, smoother, slower. With one handle of the spool anchored at my feet, I stand at an angle to the nine-pound control line. String sings between thumb and forefinger of my left hand at shoulder level. I brake with right hand at right hip. My fighting kite soars. My mind goes with it and, for a moment, I look down at the field and see myself distantly below. I recognize me because of the colors of my jacket.

Ken has finally launched his kite, and is trying to gain altitude with brute force rather than subtlety. I pay out another hundred feet of line and feel the knot that signals I'm at the preagreed altitude. I practice wind-current turns with my kite and look bored. I know Ken's looking at me, but I studiously ignore him.

"Okay," says the referee. "You both got the altitude? Go to it."

The strategy is fairly simple. Each of us has a flying line of five hundred feet. Then there's one hundred feet of cutting line between that and the kite. The cutting line is *manjha,* ordinary four-stranded string coated with a mixture of egg, starch, and powdered glass. I mixed mine myself. The rules allow us to double-coat the line so that when it's dry, it can slice an opponent's line either from above or below. The winner of the competition is the flyer who has cut loose the greatest number of opponents' kites.

Ken opens the battle ferociously and heavy-handedly, diving his fighter at cross-angles to my string. I dive mine to compensate and am slightly faster. Ken cancels the tactic. That's a mistake too. I see his kite lurch sluggishly for just a moment. I pay out line and let my string rise into his. My index finger detects the slight vibration as the lines touch. I pull in and my fighter rises, tugging the cutting line against Ken's. His kite, severed, spins down with the wind while he reels in loose string. He does not look happy as my next competitor steps up to replace him.

"Good flight," says my little brother, and I'm not sure whether he's being sarcastic to Ken or to me.

My new opponent is a girl in the seventh grade who has just taken up fighting. She has promise, but very little experience. Her kite doesn't fly long after reaching fighting altitude.

It keeps going like that. In the first hour, I destroy five opponents. Next hour, six more. I let the competition keep their defeated kites if they can find them. Where would I store them all in my room?

Each hour we're allowed fifteen minutes out of competition. I use my time to change lines on my kite. Every time I cut someone else's line, my string loses some of its abrasive. I also adjust the bridle angle because the breeze continues to pick up.

The third and final hour gives me some better competition, but no one all that challenging. Not until Lark steps into the circle. He's even smaller than I am, but he's really tough. He's my age. We've grown up in the same small town and gone to school together from the first grade. We both started flying kites about the same time. Lark is the only one whose fighting ability I respect.

He nods to me and smiles, but says nothing as he launches his fighter. Even my little brother is interested in this contest, so he puts his paperback down for the while. "Mairin hasn't lost yet," he says to Lark.

"I'd hate to spoil her morning," Lark says, "but I'm feeling pretty good."

His kite soars on the late-morning heat. Lark's fighter is brown with bright yellow birdwings inset. "Okay," says Mr. Schindler, the referee. "This is the last one. It's almost noon."

At first Lark fights conservatively, not actively countering my spectacular strategies. The trouble is that my kite is all color. I dive on him like a falcon, swoop up from beneath, twirl my fighter across his like the blade of a buzz saw. Nothing happens. I know that much of the abrasive has been scraped from my cutting line by the seven competitions of the past hour. But I'm sure that at least a few feet of cutting edge remain on the line. It's a matter of finding it.

Lark realizes my problem and bides his time.

"Hey," says Mr. Schindler. "I want to go to lunch."

Lark makes his move. His brown-and-yellow fighter crosses the angle of my own string, then drops. My index finger feels the slight vibration as his line touches mine. Lark starts rolling his kite sideways. I compensate by letting out more string and somehow neither line cuts. What does happen, though, each of us discovers simultaneously through fingertips. Our lines have become entangled. Lark's expression is grim.

"Don't worry," I call. I pay out more string as I simultaneously give the line a series of small tugs. Instead of rotating my kite so as to unwind our lines, I rotate to wrap them tighter. Then I pull.

I cut Lark's string, and capture his kite because the upper line is still entwined with mine, all at the same time.

"Mairin!" He sounds furious. My eyes are on the two fighters.

"What?"

His voice moderates as I begin to reel in the kites. "It was a good contest."

I'll keep his kite in my room. For now, I lower my gaze to him and say, "Yes, it was very good." Unaccountably I want to run across to his circle and hug him. I would like to kiss him.

Hug Lark? Kiss him? I sit upright suddenly, supported on my elbows, and stare confusedly at the curtained light. My room in the Ionic Hotel takes on a dawn reality. I glance to the side. Beside me, a humped form snores beneath the comforter. It's not Lark; I know that.

Lark? I didn't grow up with him; we come from opposite sides of the continent. We did not match our kites in childhood. My disorientation causes me to touch my face gently with my fingers to see if I am still who I think I am.

I try to recapture something of the dream. There is an elusive truth I'm missing.

Skyfighters.

We spend our lives riding the thermals, those great columns of heated air that lend lift to our machines and spirits. The thermals rise because they are warmer than the surrounding air. We look for the clues and seek them out, using them as elevators to the sky.

The best thermals generate in this valley from mid to late afternoon. Since there are two competitors remaining in the Dragon Festival contests, that time has been reserved for them. The sun has begun its descent into the open western end of the valley and the colors are, as always, spectacular. Crimson tongues lick through the cumulus.

Lark is one competitor; I am the other. All but we have seen our towed dragon kites spin down the long drop into mountainside, forest, or town, where the children vie to find the many-colored dragons and rip them to shreds.

Our duel will climax the festival.

Negwenya and *Cheshire* are waiting to ferry us both to a minimal fighting altitude. Then we will ride the thermals. Today Haley walks with me across the staging meadow. Her hand is in mine.

"You do talk in your sleep, you know," Haley says. "Do you know that?" Without an answer, she continues, "Some of the time the words are clear. Sometimes you simply make sounds and your body moves. You're a restless sleeper. I sleep like a lizard on a hot rock." She laughs. "Did you notice?"

I nod.

Her expression turns serious. "I know last night was important to you—at least it was before last night." Her smile is indecipherable. "Now isn't the time to ask you things, I suppose." She hesitates, and her grip tightens in mine. "People don't work well as goals for you. That's my game." Now I see sadness in her face. "You love the sky more."

We have reached *Negwenya*. Robert Simms waits with his assistants by my Dragon Five. Haley enfolds me in her arms and kisses me a long time on the lips. "Fly well," she whispers, then turns and walks across the field toward *Cheshire*.

I realize I'm crying, and I'm not sure yet why.

"Time to link up," says Robert, and his harsh, rope-scarred voice sounds to me softer than usual. I fasten myself into the harness of the Dragon Five. I check to make sure the bridle of my fighting kite is securely fastened to the winch post projecting downward from the Five's keel tube, just behind the point to which my legs extend. The fighting kite is a long, serpentine dragon of mylar, painted in my colors. It has the oval face and trailing, snakelike body characteristic of dragon kites. The only differences are the additional lifting surfaces and stabilizing fins.

The flight is ready to begin. I look across to *Cheshire*. Lark gives me a thumbs-up sign and Haley waves. At *Negwenya*, Robert offers me a brilliant smile and his ritual "Break a leg, lady." And we launch.

*   *   *

At twelve thousand feet, *Negwenya* floats almost directly above the immense tailings pond of the moribund Pandora Mine. The bright white tailings heap looks like some malignant thing beached between creek and trees. I think of kids singing their technological jingles when the wind rises and sifts white dust from the tailings down across the town: "Hexa, hexa, hexa-valent chromium!"

I notice that the aspen on the steep sides of the valley are starting to turn prematurely. Great slashes of golden yellow have suddenly appeared within twenty-four hours. No aspen is an island. The root systems of groves are interconnected. When the chlorophyll breaks down in one tree's leaves in the autumn, so goes its extended family.

I had seen broken cumulus above the valley when I linked up to *Negwenya*. Scattered puffy formations are the giveaway signs of thermals, since condensation forms atop the pillars of warm air. The problem is that clouds move with the wind and usually only indicate where the thermals *were*. Extrapolation and a few good guesses should gain my ride up.

At twelve-five, I release the pressure catches and the Five drops away from *Negwenya*. I crane my neck and see that Lark has also dropped. In terms of radiated heat, both of us are more likely to find thermals over the tailings pond or the rooftops of town than above the darker fields or forest. Lark seems to be making for the pond. I stretch my body, feel the muscles loosen, and wheel my Dragon toward the center of town.

The scarlet sunset momentarily dazzles my eyes. I guessed correctly. I feel the left wing rise slightly, indicating I am skirting a thermal. I bring the nose down and turn into it; then feel the mild confirming bump that I am all the way in. Now what I have to do is stay inside the current in a gentle ascending spiral until I've reached the prearranged altitude. In this case, that is fifteen thousand feet. Neither Lark nor I want to try for altitude records today, though kite pilots here have gone above eighteen thousand without oxygen.

Up, up, and the readout on my visor lists off the numbers. As I rise in the thermal column, I touch the button on my control bar that unreels the line tethering my fighter. The black-and-gold dragon shape drops below and behind my Five. The lift ratio of the kite with its fins is excellent, so it takes only a few moments before it is

gliding behind the Dragon. I pay out the entire hundred
feet of line. Dragon follows Dragon like an offspring trailing the parent.

I am allowed fifty feet, half the tether, to be cutting
line. But where the abrasive lengths are placed, and indeed *what* lengths are made abrasive, are up to me. Equipment officials carefully checked before launch to ensure
that no more than fifty percent of the Dragon's towline is
a cutting surface. Like shagreen, the surface cuts only
in one direction.

As I swing back across the town, I see that Lark is
ascending above the tailings pond. I see his Dragon followed by the brown-and-yellow fledgling that is his fighter.

At fifteen thousand feet, the air is thin and painfully
crisp. The sunlight feels as if it's striking my eyes with
sharp edges until I polarize my visor. Now that it's time to
leave the thermal. I exit on the upwind side to minimize
altitude loss in the cooler surrounding air.

Lark and I stalk each other like soaring birds. These
Dragons are not the Indian fighting kites of childhood.
There are no sudden moves—or rarely. Maneuvers tend
to be graceful and conservative, to minimize loss of altitude.

We sweep by each other in a wide pass and I estimate
I'm about one hundred feet higher than Lark. From one
point of view, we might seem to be tracing arabesques
across the sky. From a more realistic referent, we circle
each other like hungry, cautious predators.

Lark loops back in a figure eight and sails along still
below, but parallel to me. I assume he is offering bait and
try to guess how many moves ahead he's thinking. My
craft and I are slightly heavier than he and his; my sink
rate is higher and so I'm gradually descending to his altitude. I'm in a position to wing over and pounce, but
that's the expectable thing. Lark doesn't expect me to do
the expected; so I do it.

I hit the warperons hard; the ends of my wings deform
and peel me into a steep, descending bank. I'm losing vertical advantage fast, but my Dragon is cutting down hard
behind Lark's tail. It should have been an easy victory
except that Lark reacts as though anticipating me—and I
have the bemused thought that he probably was. The
brown-and-yellow Dragon matches me move for move. If

he's not duplicating the exact angle of bank and degree of dive, I can't tell the difference.

Damn it! Frustration moderates my caution as I slam the Dragon into a reverse-angle bank. Stabilized fabric crackles like firecrackers; the aluminum skeleton groans.

Lark predicted that one too. I know the long lenses on the ground are taking all this in. I hope the viewers are enjoying it.

The hell with this. I tighten my downward spiral, knowing that sooner or later I'll suck him out of the tactic. Either that or we'll hit the ground together.

Any others would have pulled out of this falling-moth spiral in some sort of sane maneuver that should have allowed me to use the slim remaining margin of altitude to cross their fighter's tether with my cutting line. At times I must remind myself that Lark is no saner than I. One moment I'm aware that I'm still sinking closer to Lark and in a relatively short time am going to be right on top of him. The next moment Lark reverses the pitch of his spiral in an aching, crushing maneuver that neither rips off his wings nor puts him into a stall. I see brown fabric rush past my right eye, so close that I recoil slightly. *Jesus!* One track of my mind wonders how close his cutting line came to severing my wing—or my head.

I don't know what he's planning, but I won't equal his suicide maneuver. As I level off less precipitously, I see Lark to my right, apparently fleeing. I look beyond his Dragon and know this is not an abdication of the field. Lark is making for what appears to be a great funnel of birds soaring upward. They're in a thermal.

Rather than seek out my own thermal, I pursue Lark, hoping to catch him before he reaches the elevator. The epinephrine surge from Lark's spectacular maneuver starts to abate, leaving tinglings in my chest and hands. I will the Dragon to fly faster; other than that I can do nothing but let the craft sail serenely along. I enjoy the silence. I remember the network coverage of a previous Dragon tourney in which, as a novelty, audio technicians had dubbed in the wasp-buzz sounds of old, piston-engined fighter planes. It was amusing at first, but ultimately offensive.

I am close to Lark, but not close enough as he enters the thermal and begins his ascent. I glance at my altimeter readout: ten-seven. That means we were about a thousand feet above the town when Lark pulled out of the spiral. I trust all the groundlings were suitably thrilled. At a thousand feet, people truly *do* look like ants.

The gentle bump of entering the warmer air rocks the Dragon's nose and I start to follow Lark vertically. As I go into the ascending bank, I sneak a look behind and see that my black-and-gold fighter is still trailing. Good. It hasn't occurred to me in these past minutes to check. It's an article of faith that I won't lose the dragon kite through mechanical accident or chance.

Again because he's lighter, Lark rises faster in the thermal than I. I resign myself fatalistically to the ride up and start to think like a tourist. I never, *never* think like a tourist. But now I look at the aspen, or I stare down at the checkerboard town, or I think about the act of flight rather than feeling it. Or something.

Something!

I look up and stare and react—try to do all those things at once. Lark hasn't done as I anticipated. He has not waited until achieving the fighting altitude. No need —no rule that says he must. Instead he swoops upon me like a hawk at prey.

His Dragon grows in my vision. I watch. I know I must choose a maneuver, but something else bids me wait. By now I should be reacting unconsciously. If my conscious is at work, it's now too late. There are several possible defensive maneuvers. So far today, Lark has correctly anticipated my every movement.

—large, so large. Brown and—

I must choose, I must— I do nothing.

That is my choice.

Lark does not anticipate it. Our vectors merge. His Dragon slams into mine with a force I could probably calculate, except—except I cannot think. I don't know if I'm hurt or if I'm in shock. I feel nothing. I simply know a buffeting like a great wind has seized us. I realize we are flying a ragged craft composited of bits and pieces of our two Dragons: snapped, flailing wires, twisted tubing, rent fabric. Lark hangs in his harness only a few feet from me, but he doesn't look up.

My vision skips like the frames in a badly spliced film. I see the golden aspen and the town spread out in the valley below us. I see Lark start to raise his head. Blood covers one side of his face. Droplets fly backward from his head like a fan.

I see the truth in that scarlet spray.

It is a long moment suspended in time.

Then it falls.

We fall—as bits of shattered Dragon spin away from us like colored confetti. I try to reach out toward Lark, but I can move only one arm. He stares back at me and I think he's alive. The sky, I try to tell him. At least we're in the sky. There could have been so many other ways. But the sky— Those who fly there are more important than any others.

Wind sucks the breath from my lungs. Lark, I try to say. Friend. I was wrong. I think Haley knows. Lovers. I should have—

I see green fields below.

Lark, it should have been us. We know the sky—

And the ground rises up like a fist.

Hayes and the Heterogyne

On November 22, 1963, a sixteen-year-old University of Denver student was run down and metaphorically killed by a speeding time machine. By "killed," it is not meant he suffered a condition either literal or permanent. The student, whose name was Harry Vincent Blake, was effectively severed from his own here-and-now and transferred somewhere else. Somewhen else. That's death.

The odor of insulation burning.

A metallic, acid taste in the back of his throat.

The sound of a ripsaw biting and binding in wet lumber.

He hadn't really been aware of the library's hushed ambiance. The musty scent of the stacks was too familiar to consciously note. Vince Blake had been preoccupied, mentally reviewing again his notes in preparation for a quiz in his zoology lab. He stepped into the revolving door and put out his hands. His fingers touched nothing; he fell forward . . . and forward . . .

More like rubber tires aflame, the smell.

The taste in his throat was vomit.

The ripsaw whine found a companion set of harmonics.

Back in the Mary Reed Library, no one had looked at the revolving door; no one had marked the entrance, or the lack of an exit. The girl at the checkout desk thumbed

up the volume on the radio and startled faces turned toward her. "Oh, my God!" someone said.

Tourmaline Hayes and Timnath Obregon had recently
finished making love in the latter's laboratory. They lay
loosely entwined on one of the broad tables in the experimental section, with the gear scooted down to one end to
make a comfortable space. Obregon and Hayes were old
friends who valued their intermittent, if often stormy,
periods of companionship.

"Tired?"

"Sex with you is always such a celebration," said Obregon.

"That's what makes me a star," Tourmaline said. "Is it
a criticism?"

"No, just a comment. Maybe a codification and reaf-
firmation."

"All that?" Her laugh was low and musical. She lightly
ran her fingernails down the taut skin of his rib cage.

"Don't do that. I still have work to do."

"What's the project?"

"This week I'm inventing time travel."

She trailed her nails lower, along his belly. "Sometimes
you're one of the most grandiose people with whom I've
ever made love. You like to astonish me with revelations.
Time travel, really?"

Obregon moaned something that could either have been
assent or pleasure. He carefully detached her hand.
"Really."

She replaced her fingers and exerted small pressures.
"Once, in one of my bored periods, I took an early-morn-
ing Network course in temporal physics. The professor
pretty much destroyed the case for practical time travel."

Obregon said distractedly, "That's the problem with
popular science. No imagination." Again he brushed away
her hand.

And again she replaced it. "I know. That's why my
curiosity occasionally brings me here to the Institute. Did
you think I come merely for the benefit of your flaccid
attentions?"

They both laughed. Obregon said, "Time travel exists.
You see evidence of it all around you in Cinnabar."

"*I* do?"

He suddenly sat up, levering himself on bony elbows.

"Look at the very nature of the vortical time streams that converge on the city. In City Center the time belts move appreciably faster than the belts farther out toward the suburbs. The city is so huge, one doesn't always notice. But the difference becomes apparent when one moves from one belt to another."

"Don't lecture me," Tourmaline said, giving him a cautionary squeeze. "That I can get from the Network."

Obregon winced. "Sorry. Sometimes I forget I'm not a pedant anymore."

"Not officially. I suspect you amuse yourself in private by devising declamations."

"Listen, do you want to know about time travel or not?"

Mock-chastened: "Yes, I want to know about time travel."

"Then consider this. A person moving toward City Center on a straight line would effectively be approaching the future. Each concentric time belt toward the center would accelerate him forward."

"Toward what?"

"That's theoretical. At the precise center, presumably the final collapse and regeneration of the universe."

"All right, but that's not *time travel*. I'm talking about someone actually traveling into her own past or future."

"What I'm talking about is a matter of perspective," said Obregon. "I'm merely pointing out that time distortions exist right here at home where we can observe them."

"Don't be sulky," Tourmaline said. She bent forward and let her blue hair sweep slowly across his upper thighs.

Obregon mumbled something.

"What?"

"I suspect you're not really interested in time travel."

"But I am, Timnath." She put her hands on his shoulders and drew him inexorably down beside her. "I would enjoy traveling through time. How long before your vehicle is perfected?"

"I have no vehicle."

"Then—?" She straddled him carefully.

With resignation he said, "I'm running a time-trawling experiment. This is the initial phase; actual time-traversing gadgets will come later. It takes time to erect a program."

"Doesn't it, though," said Tourmaline, situating herself. Obregon put his hands on her waist. "I'm disappointed.

Then there's no beautiful gingerbread machine like the one about which I read in that marvelous Mr. Wells?"

"No." He let his fingers stroke along her flanks. "It's as though I've encountered a wide river but haven't invented the boat. I'm standing on the bank with ropes and grappling hooks. I can see debris washing by, and some of it I can retrieve from the shore. But I still can't venture out in my own craft."

Tourmaline contracted her muscles and felt his back arch in response. "That's an awful metaphor. The professor on the Network program said that comparing time to a river was the oldest cliché in temporal mechanics."

Obregon made gasping, pleasured noises.

"Articulate, Timnath."

"I said use any simile you like. Time fits almost any image you can think of. Oh. *Ohhh*."

"Time is like . . . the water vanishing down a sink drain."

"Banal." He lifted his hands to cup her breasts. "Basically correct, but too ordinary."

"Time is like . . . a ripe, spotted banana."

"Don't be silly."

She began to laugh. "Time is like . . . a frog's tongue."

Obregon's distracted features composed for a moment. "That's right. That's truly accurate. How did you know?"

"Know—what?" said Tourmaline. Her eyes looked at him but they were not focused.

Obregon rocked beneath her. "You know," laughing, breath hissing between clenched teeth, "you know you know."

Beyond them, a bell chimed softly.

"It worked!" Obregon tried to sit up, bumping his forehead against Tourmaline's chin. His expression was suddenly intent.

"What are you doing?"

The bell chimed again, three times. "It *worked*." Obregon disengaged himself, swinging one leg down off the table.

"Timnath, you—" Her voice shook. "You *fool*! What—"

He grabbed her hand and nearly dragged her from the table. "Come on, it's the alarm. Something in the time stream—my devices have locked onto it."

"Timnath!" Her voice approached a wail.

They stumbled across the laboratory. "We may have captured the first time traveler," said Obregon.

"Fuck," said Tourmaline.

Vince Blake fell through the pearl-gray medium which had no other identifying sensory characteristics. It was neither warm nor cold, with no odors and no sounds. The only thing to watch was his companion, the two-by-three-foot breadboard assemblage, winking and sparkling its circuitry atop a cubical black box. Vince had no idea what the machine was, though he'd spent considerable time speculating. The machine orbited him slowly; but its perigee was about a yard, and that was not close enough for Vince to reach across the intervening space.

Subjective time dilated.

27. (Q) The process of sexual reproduction in the genus Paramecium is called ——————.
    (A) Conjugation.

His spatial orientation was minimal; confusion stymied attempts to assign labels to up or down or sidewise. Yet Vince knew he fell. He had tried sky-diving the previous summer and this was how it felt, though without the rush of wind tearing at his clothing. *Free fall*, he thought. *Is this how it was for Colonel Glenn?* But free fall in—what? English 412, last quarter. He recalled Alice's interminable tumble down the rabbit hole.

79. (Q) Why does the male opossum have a forked penis?
    (A) Because the female has two vaginas,

Vince's sense of time was stalled. Occasionally he checked his watch, but the hands remained poised invariably at 11:28. He couldn't remember whether it had been morning or evening.

192. (Q) The primary male hormones are called ———————.
     (A) Androgens.

Something important remained with him—the constant, nagging knowledge of the importance of this afternoon's

zoology test. He had slacked off the past few weeks . . .
Karen . . . his grade hung in precarious balance. In his
mind he created questions and answered them. Endlessly.

460. (Q) **What characteristic do female cats and
female rabbits have in common when they
are in heat?**
(A) **They are both spontaneous ovulators.**

And all the while, farther back toward the rear of his
skull, mental Muzak endlessly replayed the Cascades singing: "Listen to the rhythm of the falling rain." He specu-
lated whether he might have died and gone to hell.

1,386. (Q) **True or false: a male porcupine must
urinate on the female to make her sexually receptive.**
(A) **"True,"** he said aloud, but heard the sound
only because the vibrations traveled from his larynx to his
ears via the intervening tissues and bones. Sounds coming
from his mouth were damped as soon as they tried to
penetrate the gray space. It gave him a spooky feeling.

1,387. (Q) ——

Piss on it, he thought—and remembered question 1,386.
He grinned, and then thought of Karen, and then dove
headlong into depression. It was not a novelty. Karen had
sat beside him in the afternoon functional anatomy section
for nearly a quarter now. He had hardly dared speak to
her except for the Friday she forgot her pen and asked to
borrow one of his. Karen was beautiful, nineteen, and,
for Vince, unapproachable. For the entire quarter she had
starred in his masturbatory fantasies. Virgin dreams.

Before Karen there had been a round-faced brunette
with slow, sleepy eyes named Angela. English 412. Vince
had hesitantly asked her to accompany him to the Home-
coming Dance. She had turned him down ungracefully.
She had laughed. *Would I date my little brother?* To her
it was a minor matter and she never noticed when Vince
moved for the remainder of the quarter to another row.
Vince remembered and brooded and hurt. Increasingly he
regretted his being sixteen and precocious. Pubescence was
difficult.

Vince wondered what it was like to make out.

It seemed to be infinite, the number of Friday nights he had walked through the dormitory lobby on the way to see a movie alone. The lobby was always crowded with guys waiting to pick up their dates. All the swim-team jocks from New York and the baseball jocks from Southern California. Vince watched them laugh and be cool and he wondered what it was like. This fall the big catchword in from the coasts was "bitchin'." Whenever Vince tried to use topical jargon he sounded unsure and pretentious. But since he talked to few people, perhaps it really didn't matter.

Bitchin'.

He was aware of a change in motion. He had the feeling that the alteration had been building up for some time before it was sufficiently large to notice. He still fell, but now there was a lateral force; it tugged with a steady, insistent gentleness. Physics 532, but before that, of course, Cherry Creek Junior High general science: *A body in motion tends to remain in motion unless a force is applied.* Simple. He could detect no cause for the new force. The machine with its breadboard components still circled him silently, no change in its measured orbit.

Vince felt a wave of nausea. He shut his eyes and swallowed and when he opened his eyes again, he stared. He was circling the lip of a cosmic funnel.

He felt as though he were looking miles down the inside wall of the funnel. No longer uniform, the gray lightened to a metallic sheen as it descended, then brightened to a point of painful brilliance far below in the center. Vince's eyes skipped across that point; it was like looking at the sun. His eyes watered with dazzle images.

English 412 again; Edgar Allan Poe. This was the brink of the Maelstrom. He felt himself to be an infinitesimal chip about to launch into the huge whirlpool. There were no referents; he realized he could not realistically estimate the size of the vortex below.

He saw a few dark dots on the near side of the funnel; they moved clockwise, relative to his own position. *Other flotsam?* He wondered whether they were people or machines or something else.

The lateral force pulled harder. Pain cramped his belly. He cried out and, as before, the sound died at his lips. He felt a wave of vertigo and knew he was sliding into the pit.

And it was at that point that the pain blossomed out like a metastasis and the gray darkened to black.

When Vince awoke, two nude people were standing over him. It was the first time he'd ever seen a naked woman in the flesh.

Obregon hunkered down and touched the boy's right wrist with his fingers, seeking the pulse. "How are you— do you feel all right?"

"My stomach . . . hurts." The boy's eyes focused on Tourmaline for a moment, then looked quickly away.

"This is a time traveler?" said Tourmaline. "He's so young."

"Nausea?" said Obregon.

The boy nodded.

"With luck, that will be the worst of it." Obregon obtained a glass of effervescent liquid from the chemical console and returned to the boy's side. Tourmaline helped prop the boy's head so he could drink. Obregon took the empty glass away. "What's your name?"

"Vince. Harry Vincent Blake. Where am I?" He struggled to sit upright. "Is this a hospital?"

"This is a research laboratory at the Tancarae Institute."

"Where's that?"

"Near the suburbs of Cinnabar."

Vince said confusedly, "I was in Denver. What happened? Where's Cinnabar?"

"Timnath," said Tourmaline, "he won't look at us. What's wrong?"

Obregon said, "I think we've snagged a prude out of the time stream. Vince, does it upset you that we're naked?"

Vince's face was fiery. He mumbled something.

"How strange," said Tourmaline. "I'd better get our clothing."

Vince glanced at her and his flush improbably deepened. Tourmaline shook her blue mane in disbelief and walked away. Vince watched her swaying hips retreat. Turning back to Obregon, he repeated, "What's happened?"

"I'd hoped you'd be able to supply me with some of those details," said Obregon. "You've been traveling." He pointed toward the black box crowned with the breadboard circuitry. "That brought you."

"What is it? When I started—it just seemed . . . to appear."

"It's your time machine, of course."

Vince looked bewildered. "It's not mine. I don't know what it is."

"I just told you—it's a time machine. Didn't you build it?"

"No."

"Were you merely an experimental subject for the inventor?"

"No. I told you I—"

"—am quite ignorant, I'm sure. This is indeed strange," Obregon said.

Tourmaline reentered the laboratory clad in a knee-length sapphire shift. "I hope this is modest enough." She tossed Obregon a brown, rough-woven garment.

Obregon wound the fabric around his waist and tucked in the loose end. "Do you know what a time machine is?" he said to Vince.

"I've read science fiction, but I know time machines are impossible."

"I think we've been through this," said Tourmaline.

"Just accept my word that they're possible," Obregon said. He circled the black box, examining it. "Unsophisticated. Apparently jury-rigged." He bent closer. "There's a metal plate screwed to the top. 'Property of Physics Department, Central Texas College of Science.'" He looked at Vince. "Is that where you came from?"

"I never heard of it. I'm a student at the University of Denver."

"Where's that?"

"Colorado."

"Never heard of it." Obregon probed gingerly at the electronic components. "Surely this must have been a prototype."

Vince took a deep breath. "Is this the future?"

"Not for us."

"You're talking like the people in *Alice in Wonderland*." His voice and body trembling, Vince stared wildly between them. He choked on a sob.

"Baby, poor baby." Tourmaline gathered him into her arms; he pressed his face between her breasts, his back shaking as she soothed him with her fingers. "It's all right, go ahead and cry. You're all right and we're your friends."

She said reproachfully to Obregon, "Give him some simple answers."

"There's no way for him to avoid culture shock." She continued to stare at him and finally Obregon said, "I don't have any simple answers. There's too little data."

Vince blew his nose in the handkerchief Tourmaline gave him. "Have I really traveled through time?"

Obregon nodded. "It's safe to assume you're in a future relative to your embarkation point. How far a journey, I don't know. My instruments still have a limited backtrack capability. Terminex may be able to help me."

"Terminex?"

"The computer."

"I still want to know how I got here."

"As do I. My devices pulled you out of the vortical time streams."

"I remember something like a giant whirlpool." Vince's features set as though he were trying to recall the raveled threads of a nightmare. "It started to suck me down."

"The streams converge," said Obregon, "at the center of all time. And so you're here."

Abruptly, Vince said, "Can I go back?"

"I don't know."

The boy shut his eyes tightly; the muscles of his face tautened in harsh planes. His body again began to shake. Tourmaline reached toward him but Obregon restrained her wrist. After a minute, Vince took several deep, deliberate breaths and opened his eyes. He looked around the laboratory as though seeing it for the first time. "Aren't there any windows?"

"Screened," said Obregon. He clapped his hands twice and sunlight flooded the room, gleaming and glittering on the equipment. Vince stared at the green hillside rolling down to the foot of the towers. "That's more of the Institute there, ahead of us. Off to the left you can see the first houses of Craterside Park. Look farther to the side and you'll see the ocean. The desert's in back of us."

"This is the city," said Tourmaline. "Cinnabar."

Vince said, "I've been to New York and Los Angeles. I've never seen anything like this." He hesitated. "Is this the world? I mean, is this Earth?"

"We call it Earth," said Obregon. "I think home worlds are almost always called Earth."

"I wish I were home." Again, his eyes began to gleam with tears. Tourmaline touched his arm protectively.

"What's that?"

They all three looked around as the hitherto silent black box began to buzz.

"I think I'd better be alone with the time machine," said Obregon. "Will you take care of him for a while?"

Tourmaline said, "Of course."

Obregon ushered them hastily out of the laboratory. "I'll see you both later. Vince, have some food and a rest. Don't worry. Things will be fine." He smiled reassuringly.

Then the laboratory blinked out of existence and Tourmaline and Vince were alone on the hillside.

Vince extended his fingers tentatively, as though the laboratory were still there but now somehow transparent. "Where did he go?"

"Obregon? It's a little trick he uses when there's a dangerous experiment to be performed. Terminex would be extremely upset should the laboratory ever blow up and take half of Craterside Park with it."

"But how does he do it?"

"I'm not a scientist." Tourmaline shrugged. "Just a tourist."

"I don't even know your name."

"It's Tourmaline."

"That's the name of a stone. It's a pretty name."

"Thank you," said Tourmaline. "My friend's name is Timnath Obregon."

"Is he a government scientist?"

Tourmaline looked puzzled. "He's a dilettante," she said. "Just like the rest of us."

"I don't understand."

"Let's go find you a place to rest and something cold to drink." Having firmly changed the subject, Tourmaline took Vince's hand and led him down the grassy slope. Halfway to the towers, a flock of scarlet birds whirred up in their path.

"Cardinals," Vince cried. "I haven't seen any since I was in New York." His voice filled with wonder.

"How old are you?" said Tourmaline.

"Sixteen."

She looked at him sharply. *"Years?"*

"What else? How old are you?"

Tourmaline remembered Timnath's admonition about culture shock. "How old do I look?"

"Oh, maybe twenty."

"Close enough. I'm a little older."

"Twenty-five? You don't look that old."

She smiled. "Sometimes I feel it."

"You remind me of somebody I know."

"Who's that?"

"Nobody. Just a girl named Karen. You wouldn't want to hear about her."

"Of course I would, Vince."

So he told her, surprising himself by the ease with which he talked now to a stranger, especially a female stranger. He talked and she listened attentively and soon they came to a door of oiled mahogany in the base of the first tower.

"We'll go to my apartment," Tourmaline said, holding the door open for him.

Vince balked on the threshold. "It's dark in there."

She took his arm reassuringly and led him inside. "It's perfectly safe."

The disorientation was akin to his wrenching exit from the University of Denver Library. Mercifully, this time the experience was much briefer. Vince had the illusory feeling he was strolling down a long hallway, but that his legs were elastic at the joints and that his feet were preceding him by many yards. Then his feet reached their destination and the rest of his body caught up as though one end of a taut rubber band had been released.

His belly twitched ominously. "My stomach again . . ."

"It's the effect of kleining," said Tourmaline. "Take a deep breath. You'll be fine."

There was no dark room and no dim hallway. They stood again in sunlight, this time dappled by leaf shadows. The tree spread its branches around and above them. They were evidently in the middle of a copse; Vince could see the rounded green crowns of other trees surrounding them, but generally lower than the platform on which they stood. The platform, sawn from rough planks, was a disc about ten yards across. Nested in the crotch of three limbs, each several times as thick as Vince's body, the platform was pierced in the center, allowing the major trunk to pass through. Several black wrought-metal ladders and staircases evidently led to the upper reaches of the tree.

It was the most elaborate treehouse Vince had ever seen and he said so.

"I've used it for quite a while," said Tourmaline, "but I've never grown bored with it." She led the way to the staircase which spiraled up around the central trunk. "Let's go to the kitchen."

The kitchen was an oval platform projecting far enough to bathe one end in undiluted sunshine. "Would you like something to eat?" said Tourmaline.

"No, my stomach . . ." Vince started to say automatically, then reconsidered, realizing he was, indeed, hungry. "Yes, please."

Tourmaline slid open a panel in the trunk and extracted a bowl of fresh fruit. "What would you like to drink?"

"Milk, please."

She obtained a tumbler from the same panel. Looking around, she said, "Oh, I'm sorry," and a set of mushroom-like stools and table sprang up from the floor.

A small heap of peelings and fruit cores stacked quickly in front of Vince. "Do you live here all the time?"

Tourmaline shook her head. "I stay a number of places; but this is one of my favorites. I love to switch the screens off and sleep in the open on one of the upper platforms."

"This must cost a lot," said Vince. "Are you rich?"

Again she shook her head. "Only in the sense that considerable numbers of people enjoy my talents. The Network arranges these homes for me."

He looked at her inquiringly.

"My employer. It's basically an entertainment medium."

"You're in show business?"

"I'm an entertainer."

Vince finished the final orange.

"More?"

"I'd better not," he said wistfully.

She looked at him speculatively for a few seconds. "Would you like to go for a ride?"

"Where?"

"Over parts of Cinnabar."

"Why not?" He spread his hands. "As long as I'm here I might as well see the sights. Can Mr. Obregon get in touch with us?"

"Call him Timnath. If he has anything to tell us, he can reach us." Tourmaline realized Vince was smiling for the first time since he had arrived in Cinnabar, as though it were only now that he had begun to enjoy the adventure.

"How will we go?" said Vince. "Not that—hallway; I've eaten too much."

"I've another vehicle," Tourmaline said. "It's perfect for sightseeing." She spread the remnants of Vince's meal out on the platform for the birds to pick. Then the two of them climbed stair after stair to the top of the tree.

When they emerged from the last branches of the crown, Vince sucked in his breath. "Wow!" He stared at the eighty-foot, cigar-shaped bag. "A balloon?"

"It's a helium blimp," said Tourmaline.

The metal stairs wound up around the pylon which served as a mooring tower. The blimp was painted bright blue, darker than the sky. About two-thirds of the way back along the stubby body of the gas bag, two pods with four-bladed propellers were suspended. Behind them were steering vanes.

"Where do we ride?" said Vince.

"There's a passenger platform ahead of the engines. It's transparent now."

"I'd rather have it opaque, I think."

They came up underneath the shadow of the airship and Tourmaline made a pass with her hand. The passenger platform opaqued—and it was just that: a platform with a single line around the perimeter as a safety railing. Vince cautiously climbed on and was surprised that the platform didn't rock.

"It's perfectly safe," said Tourmaline, following him.

Vince discovered that the platform was upholstered in a soft. comfortably deep pile. On his hands and knees, he carefully looked over the leading edge. The trees swayed below.

"Do you mind if I take this off?" said Tourmaline. "When I fly I don't like anything on my skin but the air and sun."

Vince said, "It's your dirigible."

"Blimp." She pulled the shift over her head and tossed it over the side. The dress fluttered down and hung like a blue pennant on one of the upper branches. "You ought to try this."

"I'm very comfortable," said Vince.

"You can look at me," said Tourmaline. "I'll be very

upset if you continue to pretend there's a blind spot in your eye every time you look at my body."

Vince's face flushed again.

Tourmaline cast off the mooring line. The twin propellers began to revolve. With a gentle whir, the airship launched into the skies above Cinnabar.

Tourmaline waved her arm in a lazy circle. "This is basically all there is to the world: the desert, the greenbelt, the city, and the sea."

"Aren't there any other cities?" said Vince.

"Not that I know of. Maybe one. Can you see that?" She pointed out toward the tan waste of the desert; Vince sighted along her forearm.

"What is it, a road?"

"It's the remnant of an elevated train track. I've seen the near terminus. The rails are ancient and corroded."

"Where does it go?"

"I have no idea. I've heard stories that it eventually crosses the desert and leads to a city called Els. No one I know can remember ever having seen a train arrive from Els."

"Haven't you ever tried going there?"

"Never," said Tourmaline. "The desert makes me uncomfortable." She considered. "Perhaps someday, if I get bored enough, I'll try."

"I'd try it."

"You've enough to explore here in Cinnabar." She turned back toward the city and began to point out local sights: "The Tancarae Institute, Craterside Park, the Neontolorium, Serene Village—that's where the unredeemable elderly live—the Klein Expressway, the Balloon Works—"

"Where they made your blimp?"

She nodded. "There's the Natural History Club, that long, low building. And on beyond, if you shade your eyes, you can see the red bluffs; below them is Tondelaya Beach."

"What's that?" Vince pointed to an ovoid structure gleaming like a giant aluminum egg.

"That's a biogenesis center."

"I'm a zoo major." He added, "I haven't decided how I'm going to specialize, but I know I want to be a biologist."

"The center would probably interest you," she said. "Would you like to investigate?"

"Sure," said Vince. "Do they really create life there? Where I came from, we're still trying to synthesize a virus."

"Virtually anything can be accomplished in a biogenesis center. They cater to all individual options."

"Even test-tube babies?" said Vince.

Tourmaline looked puzzled.

Vince struggled to recall the term. "Uh, ectogenesis. Growing a human embryo outside its mother's body."

Shocked, Tourmaline said, "How else?"

"You know—the natural way."

"In the mother's own womb?"

"Sure."

"That's disgusting," said Tourmaline. "Barbaric. It's Neo-Creelist dogma."

"Where I come from," said Vince, taken aback, "mothers have children."

"Not here," Tourmaline said. "Not if they have any sense."

"Were you—"

"I was decanted. So was my mother and my mother's mother."

"That's really spooky," said Vince.

"In fact, the only one of my friends I can ever recall actually bearing a child in their own body was Timnath."

It was Vince's turn to display puzzlement. "He's a man, isn't he?"

"Don't put stock in superficial genotypes. Somatics can be altered as well. Timnath went to the center and had a uterus implant performed. He carried the child for nearly a full term." She paused reflectively. "Timnath has a more curious bent than anyone else I know, but even he didn't want to carry it through. He had the fetus transferred to a host mother."

"A woman?"

"No, a cow."

Vince attempted to digest all this. "Are you kidding me?"

"Of course not."

"But a cow?"

"Animals are very loving mothers." She added soberly, "Since the biological freeing of the rest of us, I sometimes suspect animals have become the new oppressed class."

Vince said skeptically, "What about the maternal instinct?"

"There's no such thing."

"Well, there *was*."

"Let's be precise," said Tourmaline. "There is a biological basis for the sex drive and for the caring for the young of any species. As for a specific drive toward pregnancy —probably once there was one. But after technology liberated us, we acculturated it out of existence."

"You sound like one of my professors at D.U."

"I studied this when I did some Network propaganda shows. You see, not everybody's liberated—" She stopped as a rock arced over the platform, narrowly missing Vince's head.

The airship had descended toward the biogenesis center in a gentle spiral. Vince peered over the edge of the passenger platform. About thirty feet below, a dozen men and women dressed in somber clothing gesticulated upward angrily. Some threw more stones. Several carried placards:

THERE'S ONLY ONE WAY—NATURALLY

"What's happening?" said Vince.

"Neo-Creelists. I don't think we'll be visiting the center today."

"Who are they?"

"They term themselves creative anachronists. They're misguided romantics trying to capture a past that never existed."

MOTHERHOOD IS SACRED

Several of the women were visibly pregnant.

"They oppose ectogenesis as historically unnatural," said Tourmaline.

"Can't they have children as they want?"

"Of course."

"Then why are they throwing stones?"

"Having found their truth, they worry it like an animal with a bone. They want to force their sick nostalgia on the rest of us."

TWO SEXES! NO MORE, NO LESS!

A furious voice carried up to them: "Down with the heterogyne's whore!"

"They recognize me," said Tourmaline. "Another benefit of being a star."

"Heterogyne?"

"Timnath. They're offended by his bearing of his own child."

The voices grew fainter as the airship ascended above the surly crowd.

"We can try the center again tomorrow. The anachronists are likely to become bored and leave. They're more unpleasant than dangerous." She adjusted the airship's controls and then yawned, stretching her arms wide.

Vince watched her breasts rise with the motion and furiously willed himself not to blush, knowing he had no control over the blood rushing to his face. "Now where are we going?"

"I've parked us against the wind." A pair of gray gulls circled the platform curiously and then flew on. Tourmaline moved closer to Vince. "I'm slowly deducing things about your culture," she said. "As with the Neo-Creelists, I'm afraid I'm a little appalled."

"I'm sorry," Vince said automatically.

"There's nothing for you to be sorry for. What appalls me is the thought of a world in which biological options are so limited. It's hard for me to imagine a culture in which progeny are automatically equivalent with the pain and discomfort of mandatory childbirth. Have you ever thought of what it really must feel like to give birth?"

"No," said Vince.

"I suppose not. You're locked into your own role."

"But if you haven't had a baby," said Vince defensively, "how do you *know?*"

"I can extrapolate," said Tourmaline. "Besides that, I've experienced sensory recordings of childbearing. The Network runs them as part of their horror-show series." She took his hand. "You must think I'm quite a coward— well, I am. But it isn't just the pain. I've got a feeling that the months of discomfort would breed in me a vested interest in the child—as if it owed me something. I hate possessiveness." Guiding his fingers, she continued, "My cunt was never intended for that sort of abuse."

Vince tensed, but let himself touch her.

"The girl Karen," she said. "What did you want her to do with you?"

Vince thought. "I wanted her to like me."

Tourmaline laughed. "Be specific."

"To—kiss me."

"Is that all?"

"No."

"Tell me all the things."

He told her; and she did them.

The declining afternoon brought a chill to the shaded platform below the airship. Tourmaline stirred restlessly and woke Vince up. "It's getting cold now. Let's start back."

"I really feel relaxed," said Vince.

"You should." She fed power to the blimp's engines and took manual control of the steering vanes. "Would you like to stop by Timnath's and see how he's proceeding?"

"I thought the same thing," said Vince. "Sure." The airship began to drone across the sky. With seeming nonchalance, Vince put his hand on the pilot's upper thigh.

"All of a sudden you're a cauldron of energy," she said, laughing. "Were you really a virgin?"

He nodded and took his hand away.

"It's not an insult," she said. "I just have grave reservations about a culture that forces a sixteen-year-old to keep those tensions bottled up. It must be very uncomfortable."

"It's awful. You know, I used to sit in the dorm and listen to guys when they came in after a date, and sometimes I knew they were lying, but sometimes they were telling the truth. And even if I was really young, I used to wonder how long it would take for me, or even if I ever would. Then I'd try to study for an exam or something, but I'd finally give up and lock the door and go to bed; and then I'd—I'd beat off."

Tourmaline listened to the torrent sympathetically, trying to remember how it had been to be young. Her memories of the time were sketchy and approximate. She kissed him and let her head tuck into the juncture between his chin and neck.

"Look!" said Vince. "I can see the lab, and there's smoke—"

The laboratory was a two-storied white structure perched at the top of its hill. Dense black smoke poured from the lower floor. They could see human figures milling about outside.

"There must have been an accident," said Tourmaline. She touched the controls and the pitch of the propellers whined up the scale.

"It was the time machine," said Vince. "Maybe it blew up."

The airship angled lower toward the dark plume. One of the capering figures beside the burning lab looked into the sky and began to shout something indistinguishable. They were close enough to hear the crackling flames.

"Those aren't firemen."

"Damn them to hell," said Tourmaline. "They're Neo-Creelists." The airship's engines began to strain against the updraft of heat. The fire had the odor of overdone barbecue. "Timnath—"

Vince pointed. "He's on the roof!"

The swirling smoke parted for a moment and she saw Obregon waving his arms frantically. Below, the Neo-Creelists set up a howl and began to hurl rocks and bottles. The airship settled ponderously toward the roof.

"Wow, it's like a movie," Vince said. "The good guys to the rescue."

Tourmaline said, "Don't be a romantic. The Neo-Creelists are romantics enough."

Obregon didn't wait for the airship to touch down. When the passenger platform was level with his head, he jumped and caught hold of the safety line. Vince and Tourmaline hauled him onto the platform. Gasping for breath, he hugged them. "Good timing," he said. "Get out of here."

The airship began to rise. "The updraft will compensate for the extra weight," said Tourmaline. "We'll get enough altitude; we'll easily make it back to the tree."

From the ground, shrill cries of chagrin trailed after them.

"Did the Neo-Creelists do that?"

Obregon nodded. "One of the most amazing things that's ever happened to me. I'd brought the lab back from klein space and had taken the time machine up to the second level. Meanwhile, the Neo-Creelists sneaked around and threw an incendiary into the downstairs—I suspect they devised a pressure bomb out of an aerosol can of liquid fuel. There's not much on the second level but storage space, so I climbed up to the roof. But I was getting worried; I was afraid I'd have to jump and take my chances reasoning with those people."

"Aren't there any police?" said Vince.

"If a district wants rules, it makes up its own. For instance, Craterside Park's big on law and order; but their jurisdiction doesn't extend this far. Besides, no one suspected that the Neo-Creelists were capable of violence."

Tourmaline told him about the mob besieging the biogenesis center.

"They're certainly getting restive," commented Obregon. "I'll be glad when this nostalgia craze ends."

"They wanted to kill you."

"That occurred to me. I might even have accepted, had I not wanted to be able to continue the time-travel experiments."

"The time machine!" Vince said.

Obregon said, "No problem. The buzzing was merely an internal alarm indicating that the fuel supply was exhausted."

"No, the fire—"

Obregon looked uncomfortable. "That was the unfortunate thing. By now the machine has almost certainly been destroyed."

"What'll happen?"

"I don't know."

"Am I stuck here?"

"That, also, I'm afraid I don't know."

"Your clothing stinks of smoke," Tourmaline said to the two of them. "Throw it over the side; we don't need the weight." Both obliged; Vince, hesitating momentarily.

The bright bits of fabric sailed down, disappearing into the dusk shadows before they hit the ground. Vince watched them fall and fade; he felt as lost.

On their level, the trunk of the tree rippled with a tawny firelight effect. Vince remembered the traditional Christmas tree he had never actually seen, but as his grandmother had described it: decorated with flickering candles attached to the live branches. He looked upward through the leafy canopy and could not tell where the candles stopped and the stars began.

Live grass carpeted the deck. To one side, the covering had been built up so that a shallow pool could be sunk. Water bubbled over the inboard lip from a concealed pump. The overflow cascaded off the deck in a thin sheet;

long before reaching the forest floor, it dissipated into a fine mist.

Obregon sat between two lily pads, scrubbing his sooty arms. "I feel like I've been running races all day. Do you mind rubbing my back?"

"No," said Vince. He knelt on the bank behind Obregon.

"A little higher," Obregon directed.

"This morning," said Vince, "when you took the laboratory—away. Did you find out anything?"

"I've been debating whether to tell you. I discovered a number of things."

"I want to know."

Tourmaline descended the spiral stairs from the kitchen bower. Carrying a tray, she padded across the grass toward them. "I went to lengths with the soup," she said. "This is not a programmed recipe."

"I'm ravenous," said Obregon. He splashed onto the bank like a clumsy otter.

The wooden bowls contained a thick stew of meat and vegetables. There were serving dishes filled with fruits and finger-sized loaves of dark bread and bundles of string cheese. A flagon brimmed with a clear, effervescent liquid. Tourmaline filled three tumblers.

Vince sipped cautiously and said, "It's like licorice ginger ale." He raised the glass to drink again, but Tourmaline put cautioning fingers on his wrist.

"Slowly . . . it's to be enjoyed."

"A toast!" said Obregon. Their glasses clinked dully together. "To you and your contemporary, Mr. Herbert George Wells."

"Really?" Tourmaline said to Vince, "I think that's exciting."

"H. G. Wells? He died before I was born."

"Close enough," said Obregon, "when you're considering all the recorded history of all recorded worlds. I took phrases like 'Denver University' and 'Central Texas College of Science' and your name and programmed a wide-range, random association inquiry of Terminex."

"The computer?"

Obregon nodded smugly. "The results came from one of Terminex's most isolated random-information vaults. I discovered a six-hundred-and-forty-year 'gramed run of something called the *New York Times*."

"It was a newspaper—"

"Apparently a compilation of all trivial knowledge for an entire culture. But I found a number of references to you. I also discovered what may be a pertinent cross-reference to the Central Texas College of Science. It figured in the news on twenty-two November 1963, according to your calendar."

"That's today," said Vince.

"I found the reference in a small item on an interior page. It was the report of the deaths of two physicists in a small school in a province called Texas. Rather strangely, according to the reporter, the laboratory had imploded rather than exploded. An investigation was evidently launched, but I couldn't find any other references when I tracked ahead. In any case, the lone report was overshadowed by other news of the day."

"That must be where the time machine came from."

"At a guess, yes."

"But how did I get into this?"

"I very specifically checked, but there were no items about people mysteriously vanishing from a library in Denver."

"You said you found references to me."

"They were later."

"What kind of references?"

"Well," said Obregon uncomfortably. "One thing I read was your obituary."

Vince stared and started to say something, reconsidered, and then gulped a swallow of liquor.

"That's marvelous," said Tourmaline. "It means you must have returned to your own time." She looked at Obregon. "Isn't that right?"

"I'm cautious when trying to sort out temporal paradoxes."

"Stuff your paradoxes and tell me."

Obregon sighed. "If I can in fact believe the record of the *Times,* Vince did return to his own continuum."

Vince shook his head dazedly. "My obituary? When—"

"It would be unkind to tell you exactly," said Obregon. "But it was substantially later than when you evidently came here."

"My obituary," Vince repeated. "Then I'm dead."

"No," said Obregon. "You will be. That's an important distinction."

"You've got no concept of comfort," Tourmaline said to Obregon.

"I'm okay." Vince raised his glass shakily. "Why didn't you tell me before?"

"Bumbling though I am," said Obregon, "I'm still trying to avoid overloading your mind with shocks."

Tourmaline said, "I think Vince is a much stronger person than we guessed."

Vince sipped his drink. "This is like a roller coaster. The first few hills were scary, but now I guess I'm getting used to it."

"I don't know if it's any comfort, but I'm coming to suspect that the destroyed time machine is immaterial to your return to your own world."

"Did you check time travel in the *Times?*"

"Yes. There was nothing in reference to you."

"I'm not famous for being the first time traveler?"

"No, not for that."

"Something else?"

Obregon smiled. "That's a surprise I'll leave for you to discover."

The candle effects gutted and began to die. A night breeze stirred ripples on the pond.

Tourmaline yawned. "Come to bed."

"Where?" said Obregon.

"The platform with the furs. The night's turning cool."

"The three of us? Or two?"

Vince stared bewilderedly between the two of them.

"Oh," said Tourmaline. "So I'm the one forgetting cultural differences." She thought for a moment. "Two and one now. Maybe three later?"

Obregon nodded. "That kind of comfort will develop."

"Are you guys talking about, uh, sleeping arrangements?" Vince said.

"Yes. For tonight."

"I can sleep anywhere."

"Tonight," said Tourmaline, sounding maternal, "you'll sleep with me."

The soft, thick furs could be pulled over his face for a feeling of warm security; yet it was not stuffy beneath. The low-velocity component of the night wind circulated through the material. Vince cuddled against Tourmaline's body, wondering fleetingly why he hadn't noticed before that she was taller than he.

"I love you."

"You're such a strange mixture of adolescent and adult," she said. "I feel like I'm eating a pie and not knowing what fruit or spice is going to touch my tongue next."

"I do love you."

Tourmaline laughed softly in the darkness. "All the lovers I've had, and none has ever tempted me to become a mother."

"I don't understand."

"I suspect it's the drive I mentioned this afternoon— the one to care for the young of the species."

"Me?"

"Listen," she said. "Don't you know—you're a child I can love." She moved against him, lifting her leg across his body so that his own leg was held tight between her thighs.

"When I said I loved you, I—"

"Hush," she said. "No more of your romance. Love me tangibly."

Later, before they slept, Vince said, "You've done this with lots of men, haven't you?"

"Naturally," said Tourmaline. "And not just men."

He absorbed this information. "I must be really square."

"What does that mean?"

"I'm just not used to all this. Earlier, when you and Timnath were talking about who all were going to bed— was Timnath talking about sex?"

"Partially."

"The three of us together? I mean, having sex?"

"If it were mutually agreed to. Yes."

She felt his head shake slightly from side to side. "Back home—I mean in 1963—that's a perversion. It's against the law."

"You're not home," said Tourmaline reasonably.

"It's what I've been taught."

"You've been taught unbelievable strictures."

"I thought I really questioned things. But not until I got here—this is so wide open. It reminds me of reading about Utopias."

"Cinnabar? It's no Utopia. There are more options here

than you've had before. That's all. There's diversity on an asymptotic curve that never quite touches total breakdown."

"Everything . . ." said Vince. "A heterogyne having his own baby, the ectogenesis center, you, Timnath. I've never seen so much freedom."

Tourmaline's breathing became regular.

"Tourmaline?"

"What."

"I didn't mean to wake you up."

She rested on her elbows. "You started to ask me something."

"I really like Timnath." His voice stumbled. "If—he wants to sleep with us, I don't mind."

"Tomorrow."

"Okay. I mean, I'll try it."

"Fine."

Silence, for a minute.

"Tourmaline?"

"What." She sighed and sat up.

"Has there ever been anything in Cinnabar you couldn't have?"

Tempted to say "sleep," she said instead, "Only boredom."

"Really?"

"I apologize. I'm tired and I was being glib."

"If you really wanted, couldn't you have a child?"

"I suppose. If I really wanted; but I don't. Why are you so persistent?"

"I'm curious," said Vince.

"You know why I won't bear a child. I doubt I'll ever clone an offspring or use any other ectogenetic technique."

"You like to mother," said Vince, "without actually being one."

She considered that. "It's a harmless indulgence. I'm justifiably and unashamedly selfish."

"One thing we learned was that perpetuating the species is a biological truth."

"We learned, we learned," she mocked. "You know so damned much theory."

"Shut up!" He pressed her shoulders down against the furs. "You treat me like—"

"—a child."

"Well, I'm not."

"But you're close." She kissed him. "And you're tired."

He subsided. "I am."

She drew him near and sang soft songs. He fell asleep a few seconds before she did.

In his dream, Vince consummated a quest.

The journey not being easy, Vince was obliged to climb a rocky pinnacle. The mountain rose from the otherwise smooth surface of a tan and desolate plain. Vince was acutely aware of textures. The rock faces he scaled, the ledges he traversed, the steep chimneys he negotiated, did not feel like stone. Surfaces, as soft and resilient as flesh buttressed with bone, sank with his steps. Clambering up an uneven slope that reminded him of a field of shoulder blades, he lost his footing and almost fell. He cried out; his voice, peculiarly muffled, did not echo.

"Where are you?"

Nothing and no one answered him.

"Where are you?"

and stopped, confused because he could not recall whom he was calling.

The air chilled and thickened with a hum. *Keep climbing,* said a voice. Vince stared up the mountainscape but saw no one. *Keep climbing.* He continued to struggle upward.

"Just a little farther." Still no one visible. The voice was a pleasant soprano. "Here I am."

Vince realized he had conquered the peak and there was nowhere more to climb. The summit consisted of a flat, clear area roughly the size and shape of a basketball court. A being appeared.

It took the form of a golden double helix, whose spirals danced and burned with burnished flames. "It's about time."

"It's a tall mountain," said Vince.

"Well, it can't be helped," said the double helix. "Dream quests are noted for their arduousness."

Vince said, "Are you God?"

"Of course not," said the being. "I'm surprised at you."

"Then what are you?"

"Consider me something basic and something utterly human. How arrogant that you think me God."

"Well," said Vince, "I can see that you aren't an old man on a throne ordering the universe."

The double helix said, "It was wrong of you to anthropomorphize."

Vince studied his own toes.

"No matter. I expect you're wondering why I had you climb up here."

Vince looked up; the shimmering strands seemed to tug at his eyes.

"I've something to give you, to take back to the people." A flaming strand of RNA messenger darted out and began to inscribe on the mountaintop between them. The ground trembled as though in torment.

Vince stared at the fiery letters. "I can't read it."

"It is the greatest of my commandments. Remember this. Biologically speaking," said the double helix, "there are no imperatives." The incised letters arranged themselves: NO IMPERATIVES.

"But there *are*," said Vince. "We learned—"

"Are you arguing with life?" said the double helix.

"But—"

"Take my word to the people." The fiery strand withdrew and was rewound by its parent spiral. "Pick it up."

The fire had burned a border around NO IMPERATIVES so as to form a rectangular tablet. Vince bent and picked it up. The stone was soft and the same temperature as his skin. He gripped the tablet tightly and felt a pulse beating within it.

"Go."

For a sacrilegious moment he wished to defy the double helix. Then he turned without a word and began to descend the mountain.

The helix called after him, "Beware the barbarians."

As on cue, the hordes of uncouth barbarians arose from their hiding places among the rocks. They charged up the slope toward him, screaming and rattling their weapons. Their shrill cries filled up his ears as though with blood.

"Vince! There are men—they want to kill us."

"Mmh? Dream . . . Lemme sleep." Submerged in the furs, he drifted in and out of the dream.

"Vince, wake up." She shook him urgently. Then she cried out in pain and fell away from him.

He jerked awake, still hearing the cries of the barbarians. "Tourmaline—"

She crawled back into his field of vision, face bloody, holding a jagged piece of stone half the size of her fist. "They hurt me," she said wonderingly. She leaned over Vince, staring. Blood dripped from her nose to his cheek. "They'll kill us."

"And well you deserve it," said an angry voice.

Vince turned and saw three men standing on the edge of the sleeping platform. All wore the dull blacks of the Neo-Creelists. Each was armed: the first clutched a metal bludgeon, the second held a stiletto with a long blade like a needle, and the third had a pouch filled with stones slung from his waist. The third man looked disgusted and tossed a desultory stone. It struck Tourmaline in the shoulder; she recoiled, but did not cry out.

It was the man with the knife who had spoken. "You must know this is not a personal thing," he said.

The assassin with the bludgeon said, "I always used to catch your shows. I thought you were great."

The man with the stones looked even more sour. "Can't we get this over with?"

"You're all insane," said Tourmaline. She touched her fingers to the cut above her eye and then inspected the blood. Vince scrambled to his feet.

"It was those filthy propaganda shows you did for the Network," said the stiletto man.

"Did they harm you?" said Tourmaline.

"Not me. I was already sure of the truth. But I can imagine the effect on more impressionable people."

"I was only trying to educate—"

"To evil," said the stiletto man. "Against nature."

"Nature is healthy when it's diverse. That's all I—"

"Trash," said the bludgeon man. "Sick, perverted trash."

The three assassins moved apart from one another as they advanced slowly across the platform.

Vince cursed his nakedness. "Get behind me," he said to Tourmaline. He tried to push her back to what small safety he could offer.

"You're insane too," she said. "This is not a historical romance; you can't save me."

"I can try." He stepped in front of her.

"Please," she said to the assassins. "Don't do this. I haven't interfered with your lives."

The stiletto man said, "You've gone against the truth. That's sufficient."

The man with the stones said, "Some of the women are grumbling."

"Don't kill the boy," said Tourmaline.

"I expect he's tainted," said the stiletto man, as though that settled the issue. "Now let us finish this."

Vince grabbed up one of the rugs at his feet and threw it over the stiletto man. Arms windmilling, the assassin reeled back. Vince leaped at the bludgeon man on his right. The man held his club before him in a clumsy defense; Vince felt his fist sink into the man's solar plexus. He knew amazement; never before had he fought. He brought back his fist again, but someone grabbed him from behind—the man with the pouch of stones. Wiry arms wrapped around his chest, pinning his arms.

The bludgeon man attempted to straighten up; his breath ratcheted in his throat. He raised his head and looked hatefully at Vince.

"Lousy cloned bastard!" Vince recognized the voice of the stiletto man behind him. "This for you, motherless scum."

Vince felt a prick low in his left side; a small cold pain like the stab of a hypodermic needle. He tried to wrench free, but succeeded only in overbalancing his captor and they both toppled to the soft floor. Then he heard low wounded-animal cries and realized after a seeming eternity that they were his.

Another cry in the background—Tourmaline. Again he attempted to free himself, but he had no strength. He tried to yell and there was no sound.

Am I dying? he thought. *It doesn't hurt.*

But soon enough it did, and that is when the darkness bore him away in a soft rush of silence.

This time there was no bright dream; only the feel of textures. His boyhood fever fantasies replayed: a tactility both smooth and sticky. Things slid across his skin, yet simultaneously clung. The paradox stirred a core of nausea. The moment stretched . . .

He awoke into a gentle white light. Vince opened his eyes and discovered he was lying recumbent, naked, on a cushioned table. The man standing over him had a familiar face. "Timnath?"

The man shook his head. "Gerald. I'm his son." He wore a pale green smock.

"Are you a doctor?"

"That, too. I'm a healer."

"What happened?"

"You want a catalogue?" Gerald ticked off the items on his fingers: "Two skewered kidneys, complete renal failure, massive shock, a torn aorta, a punctured inferior vena cava. Those are the major items. Would the complete list interest you?"

"No, I don't think so." Vince closed his eyes.

"What amazes me," said Gerald, "is that all your wounds came from a thrust and twist of that meat-skewer of a knife."

"Those men! Where's Tourmaline?"

"Here, of course."

Vince opened his eyes and saw Tourmaline bending down to kiss him. She wore a black choker. "Really, you're all right?"

"Look for yourself." She pirouetted. There was no bruise on her shoulder, no scar above her eye.

"How long have I been asleep?"

"Three days," Gerald said. "You required some effort."

Vince moved his arm experimentally.

"Go ahead. You can sit up."

He did so gingerly. "I can really move like this three days after getting stabbed?"

Behind him, Timnath entered the room. "Remember the *New York Times*? You'll live to fill your obituary yet."

Vince swung his legs down off the table and sat on the edge. "Timnath, you're all right too?"

Tourmaline said, "He's fine; who do you think wandered down from his own sleeping platform and tossed those three assassins off ours?"

"I didn't mean to be quite so extreme," said Obregon. "It was reflex action, and I had the element of surprise."

"The tree needs the compost," said Tourmaline.

Vince said, "I was mostly asleep; I don't remember much. How'd they get up there?"

"Climbed," said Obregon. "Ropes, hooks, bark pitons. I found their gear on the lower porch."

"I've installed some precautions." She smiled grimly.

"Will there be more trouble?"

"I don't know," said Obregon. "I'm afraid they'll continue with their historical fantasies."

"As long as they keep their fantasies exactly that," said Tourmaline.

"Incidentally," said Obregon to Vince. "I've used the last three days to advantage in my temporal researches. My colleagues at Tancarae graciously helped outfit a new laboratory."

"What happened? Have you rebuilt the time machine?"

"No, I recovered your old machine from the remains of my former laboratory. I'm afraid that all that was left was a fused mass of glass and metal. A pity." He shook his head. "No, I've spent my time reasoning out a likely hypothesis for your return to your own time."

"Are you going to build a new machine?"

"I probably could, but I won't. There's a simpler and safer method for your return. In temporal mechanics there are specialized laws of matter and energy conservation. The physical fact that you and the machine are here in Cinnabar and not in 1963 creates a sort of gap in your proper continuum.

"When the machine brought you here, its self-contained power source provided the energy to maintain the time transfer. The residual effect kept you here after the machine was incapacitated in the fire, so your presence now is an indeterminate condition. There is a faint trail of dissipating energy leading from Cinnabar back to 1963. I call it a T-line. When the residual effect from the time machine can no longer stably maintain you here, you'll be pulled back along the T-line to your origin. Like nature, time abhors a vacuum."

"How long?" Tourmaline and Vince echoed each other.

Obregon said, "I don't know. If theory's correct, it could be anytime."

"Do I have to go back?" said Vince soberly. "Isn't there any way to stabilize me here?"

"I could apply energy indefinitely to keep the T-line open," said Obregon. "But I run into the problem of temporal paradoxes. You have a destiny back in your own continuum. I doubt it would be wise, attempting to fool with that."

"Bitchin'," said Vince.

"What?"

"Nothing. I just realized how much I've been trying to forget 1963."

Tourmaline put her arms around his shoulders and held him tightly.

Gerald Obregon produced a tray of instruments. "Temporal mechanics is fascinating, but there are a few more tests before I can let this person go."

Vince saw a sheen of tears in Tourmaline's eyes. She said, "We'll wait for you outside in the park." She turned and Obregon and she left.

"You owe her quite a lot," said Gerald, lightly touching Vince's abdomen with a cold silver rod.

"I know."

"You don't." Gerald poked hard enough to make him wince. "You didn't listen when I told you you'd suffered total renal failure. She gave you one of her kidneys. Not that it's anything momentous, but it's a very nice gesture."

Vince swallowed dryly, without saying anything.

"The organ is gerontologically stable," continued Gerald. "It should certainly function longer than your own body. My father told me about your culture."

"We've had kidney transplants in 1963," said Vince, "but they don't work if they're not between blood relatives. There's a natural rejection syndrome."

Nonplused, Gerald said, "I've already ensured that your body will accommodate the kidney with a temporary oversupply of one-handed antibodies. Your body cannot recognize the new organ as foreign. There will be no problem with either two-handed antibodies or blood complement."

Vince looked thoughtful. "You heard what Timnath said about the T-line and my returning to my own time. Even if the kidney's in me, isn't it still Tourmaline's tissue and doesn't it belong here in Cinnabar? It's going to be rough on me if it vanishes and comes back here along its own T-line."

"Timnath thought of everything." Pride tinged Gerald's voice. "He gave me a subminiature energy supply to implant in the kidney; it's only about as large as a few thousand nephrons; you'll never notice. It will last as long as the kidney."

"I'm a cyborg," said Vince.

"So? There's no social stigma."

"That was sort of a joke."

"Mmph." Gerald made a few concluding prods and

replaced the rod on the tray. "I'd say you're quite ready. You can even drink all the liquids you wish."

Vince climbed off the table carefully, finding that his legs were weak.

"Get some exercise." Gerald smiled for the first time. "Enjoy your stay."

With some modification of the frame and skin, and the addition of another helium compartment for increased lift, Tourmaline's airship accommodated three easily. The wind thrummed between the struts supporting the engine pods and brought the salt smell from the ocean. Gulls curiously orbited the craft. Momentarily cold, the three passengers drew around them one of the broad furs borrowed from the sleeping platform.

"What will it be like?" said Vince.

"Sudden," Obregon said. "No suspenseful blurrings in and out of reality, with a final slow fade. Very neat and clean."

"That's a relief."

The airship sailed on toward the red bluffs overshadowing Tondelaya Beach. The gulls, bored, veered back toward the sea.

"My time here's been good," said Vince. He sat between Tourmaline and Obregon. Their arms were around his shoulders. "I know that's a dumb way to say it, but I wanted to try and say how I feel."

"You sound like you're saying good-bye," said Tourmaline. "You don't know that it's time yet."

"I feel like it is."

All three sat silently for a while, watching Cinnabar's towers glide by beneath.

"I've really come to love both of you," said Vince.

"I think the feeling's reciprocated," Obregon said.

"Whatever happens when I get home, I won't forget all this."

Tourmaline, smiling, laid a slender finger across his lips.

"I won't," he repeated. "I can't."

The airship cleared the bluffs and they saw the sand and the steady slow waves.

Vince said, "I don't want to leave. You know, I never—"

He vanished. Air rushed together, filling the space where he had been with an audible *plock*.

"I imagine," said Obregon, "that those kilos of slagged time machine in my laboratory have also plocked out of existence." He wiped tears from his face.

Tourmaline looked away, down toward the clean sand. She said, "I feel very sad."

"—this morning in Dallas," said the radio.

In varying degrees of shock, students and library personnel gathered around the desk.

"—apparently fired from an upper floor of the Texas Book Depository. At this time, no one—"

A whisper of disturbed air swirled behind him. No one noticed.

Vince Blake stumbled forward, fingers pressed against the cold metal reality of the bar of the revolving door. Disoriented, he emerged into the open air where two coeds, climbing the steps, giggled at his dazed look.

He shook his head and decided that today was one day he could afford to cut his zoology quiz. That evening he returned to the library to research the current state of immunology in regard to the rejection problems of organ transplants.

"Do you suppose he's all right?" said Tourmaline.

Obregon said, "I know he is."

They lay in a striped red-and-blue hammock strung between two of the topmost boughs in Tourmaline's tree. It was a place to listen to the busy insect noises in the leaves around them. The afternoon sun burned their skins a richer brown.

Tourmaline trailed her fingernails down Obregon's chest. "Will you tell me now about his obituary?"

"It wouldn't depress you?"

She shook her head.

Obregon said, "He won a Nobel Prize."

"Is that good?"

"Apparently the best of his time. It was awarded for his achievements in genetics and human reproductive biology."

"Then he remained in the life sciences as his chosen field. That's good."

Obregon nodded. "He became known as the so-called father of the biological revolution, a title that evidently afforded him great amusement. It was an odd achievement to gain that distinction. He was a strong individualist in a time noted for team approaches to scientific research."

"Did he remain unmarried?"

"Yes. Why?"

She laughed. "I was afraid I'd find out that he had lived a long and monogamous life with someone named Karen."

"He was mourned by his own descendants."

"That's good."

Obregon paused. "Vince was also reviled by most of his own generation. In the last years of his life he was popularly termed a traitor to his species."

"Tell me," said Tourmaline.

"Vince pioneered in ectogenesis."

Tourmaline slowly began to smile.

"He had a flare for the propaganda value of public exposure. When he entered his maturity, he bore a child. The cultural impact was incalculable; he was the first woman-alternate, the first heterogyne."

"Magnificent," said Tourmaline.

"There's more. Receiving the first rejectionless implant of a uterus was only half the experiment. The other half was the embryo's origin; it was cloned from Vince's own body tissue."

Her eyes widened and she opened her mouth to speak.

"The tissue came from his kidney. He named his daughter Tourmaline."

Tourmaline was speechless.

"One could say that at long last you're a mother," said Obregon.

"And a father."

He said. "And that."

"Is there a happy ending?"

"I hesitate to tell you," said Obregon. "He was assassinated by persons unknown. His martyrdom aided the movement his supporters founded."

She stared away toward the trees below. "Was he old, by then?"

"He was old."

"I don't know whether to laugh or cry."

"Whichever," he said. "It was a good ending."

"Then I'll smile," said Tourmaline.

Their bodies touched and, for a moment, they were three together. Then only two again, and the two wept because they felt the loss.

Teeth Marks

My favorite vantage has always been the circular window at the end of the playroom. It is cut from the old-fashioned glass installed by Frank Alessi's father. As a young man, he built this house with his own hands. The slight distortions in the pane create a rainbow sheen when the light is proper. I enjoy the view so much more than those seen through the standard rectangular windows on the other floors, the panes regularly smashed by the enthusiasms of the younger Alessis through the years and duly replaced. The circular window is set halfway between the hardwood floor and the peak of the gabled ceiling, low enough that I can watch the outside world from a chair.

Watching window scenes with slight distortions and enhanced colors satisfies my need for stimulation, since I don't read, nor go out to films, nor do I ever turn on the cold television console in the study. Sometimes I see jays quarreling with magpies, robins descending for meals on the unkempt lawn, ducks in the autumn and spring. I see the clouds form and roil through a series of shapes. The scene is hardly static, though it might seem such to a less patient observer. Patience must be my most obvious virtue, fixed here as I am on this eternal cutting edge of the present.

I possess my minor powers, but complete foreknowledge

is not numbered among them. Long since taking up residence here, I've explored the dimensions of the house. Now I spend the bulk of my time in what I consider the most comfortable room in the house. I haunt the old-fashioned circular window, and I wait.

Frank Alessi took a certain bitter pleasure in driving his own car. All the years he'd had a staff and driver, he had forgotten the autonomous freedoms of the road. The feel of the wheel in his hands was a little heady. Anytime he wanted, anytime at all, he could twist the steering wheel a few degrees and direct the Ford into the path of a Trailways bus or a logging truck. It was his decision, reaffirmed from minute to minute on the winding mountain highway, his alone: He glanced at the girl beside him, not hearing what she was saying. She wouldn't be smiling so animatedly if she knew he was chilling his mind with an image of impalement on a bridge railing.

Her name was Sally Lakey and he couldn't help thinking of her as a girl even though she'd told him at least three times that she had celebrated her twentieth birthday the week before.

". . . *that* Alessi?" she said.

He nodded and half-smiled.

"Yeah, really?" She cocked her head like some tropical bird and stared from large dark eyes.

Alessi nodded again and didn't smile.

"That's really something. Yeah, I recognize you from the papers now. You're you." She giggled. "I even saw you last spring. In the campaign."

"The campaign," he repeated.

Lakey said apologetically, "Well, actually I didn't watch you much. What it comes down to is that I'm pretty apolitical, you know?"

Alessi forced another half-smile. "I could have used your vote."

"I wasn't registered."

Alessi shrugged mentally and returned his attention to the awesome drop-offs that tugged at the car on Lakey's side. Gravel and raw rock gave way to forest and then to valley floor. Much of the valley was cleared and quilted with irrigated squares. It's a much tamer country than when I left, Alessi thought.

"I'm really sorry I didn't vote."

"What?" Distracted, Alessi swerved slightly to avoid two fist-sized rocks that had rolled onto the right-hand lane, probably during the night.

"I think you're a nice man. I said I'm sorry I didn't vote."

"It's a little late for that." Alessi envenomed the words. He heard the tone of pettiness, recognized it, said the words anyway.

"Don't blame me, Mr. Alessi," she said. "Really, I'm not stupid. You can't blame me for losing . . . Senator."

I'm being reproached, he thought, by a dropout, wet-behind-the-ears girl. Me, a fifty-seven-year-old man. A fifty-seven-year-old unemployable. God damn it! The rage he thought he'd exorcised in San Francisco rose up again. He thought the rim of the steering wheel would shatter under his fingers into jagged, slashing shards.

Lakey must have seen something in his eyes. She moved back across the front seat and wedged herself uneasily into the juncture of bench seat and door. "You, uh, all right?"

"Yes," said Alessi. He willed the muscles cording his neck to relax, with little effect. "I am very sorry I snapped at you, Sally."

"It's okay." But she looked dubious of the sincerity of his apology.

They rode in silence for another few miles. She'll talk, thought Alessi. Sooner or later.

Sooner. "How soon?"

"Before we get to the house? Not long. The turnoff's another few miles." And what the hell, he asked himself, are you doing taking a kid little better than a third your age to the half-remembered refuge where you're going to whimper, crawl in, and pull the hole in after you? It's perhaps the worst time in your life and you're acting the part of a horny old man. You've known her a grand total of eight hours. No, he answered himself. More than that. She reminds me— He tensed. She asked me if she could come along. Remember? She asked me.

I see the dark blue sedan turn into the semicircular driveway and slide between the pines toward the house. Tires crunch on drifted cones and dead leaves; the crisp sound rises toward me. I stretch to watch as the auto nears the porch and passes below the angle of my sight. The engine dies. I hear a car door slam. Another one. For some reason it had not occurred to me that Frank might bring another person with him.

The equations of the house must be altered.

They stood silently for a while, looking up at the house. It was a large house, set in scale by the towering mountains beyond. Wind hissed in the pine needles; otherwise the only sound was the broken buzz of a logging truck downshifting far below on the highway.

"It's lovely," Lakey said.

"That's the original building." Alessi pointed. "My father put it together in the years before the First World War. The additions were constructed over a period of decades. He built them too."

"It must have twenty rooms."

"Ought to have been a hotel," said Alessi. "Never was. Dad liked baronial space. Some of the rooms are sealed off, never used."

"What's that?" Lakey stabbed a finger at the third floor. "The thing that looks like a porthole."

"Old glass, my favorite window when I was a kid. Behind it is a room that's been used variously as a nursery, playroom, and guest room."

Lakey stared at the glass. "I thought I saw something move."

"Probably a tree shadow, or maybe a squirrel's gotten in. It wasn't the caretaker—I phoned ahead last night; he's in bed with his arthritis. Nobody else has been in the house in close to twenty years."

"I did see something," she said stubbornly.

"It isn't haunted."

She looked at him with a serious face. "How do you know?"

"No one ever died in there."

Lakey shivered. "I'm cold."

"We're at seven thousand feet." He took a key from an inside pocket of his coat. "Come in and I'll make a fire."

"Will you check the house first?"

"Better than that," he said, *"we* will check the house."

The buzz of voices drifts to the window. I am loath to leave my position behind the glass. Steps, one set heavier, one lighter, sound on the front walk. Time seems suspended as I wait for the sound of a key inserted into the latch. I anticipate the door opening. Not wanting to surprise the pair, I settle back.

Though they explored the old house together, Lakey kept forging ahead as though to assert her courage. Fine, thought Alessi. If there is something lurking in a closet, let it jump out and get *her*. The thought was only whimsical; he was a rational man.

Something did jump out of a closet at her—or at least it seemed to. Lakey opened the door at the far end of a second-floor bedroom and recoiled. A stack of photographs, loose and in albums displaced from precarious balance on the top shelf, cascaded to her feet. A plume of fine dust rose.

"There's always avalanche danger in the mountains," said Alessi.

She stopped coughing. "Very funny." Lakey knelt and picked up a sheaf of pictures. "Your family?"

Alessi studied the photographs over her shoulder. "Family, friends, holidays, vacation shots. Everyone in the family had a camera."

"You too?"

He took the corner of a glossy landscape between thumb and forefinger. "At one time I wanted to be a Stieglitz or a Cartier-Bresson, or even a Mathew Brady. Do you see the fuzz of smoke?"

She examined the photograph closely. "No."

"That's supposed to be a forest fire. I was not a good photographer. Photographs capture the present, and that in turn immediately becomes the past. My father insistently directed me to the future."

Lakey riffled through the pictures and stopped at one portrait. Except for his dress, the man might have doubled for Alessi. His gray hair was cut somewhat more severely than the senator's. He sat stiffly upright behind a wooden desk, staring directly at the camera.

Alessi answered the unspoken question. "My father."

"He looks very distinguished," said Lakey. Her gaze flickered up to meet his. "So do you."

"He wanted something more of a dynasty than what he got. But he tried to mold one; he really did. Every inch a mover and shaker," Alessi said sardonically. "He stayed here in the mountains and raped a fortune."

"Raped?" she said.

"Reaped. Raped. No difference. The timber went for progress and, at the time, nobody objected. My father taught me about power and I learned the lessons well. When he deemed me prepared, he sent me out to amass my own fortune in power—political, not oil or uranium. I went to the legislature and then to Washington. Now I'm home again."

"Home," she said, softening his word. "I think maybe you're leaving out some things." He didn't answer. She stopped at another picture. "Is this your mother?"

"No." He stared at the sharp features for several seconds. "That is Mrs. Norrinssen; an ironbound, more-Swedish-than-thou, pagan lady who came out here from someplace in the Dakotas before the Depression. My father hired her to—take care of me in lieu of my mother."

Lakey registered his hesitation, then said uncertainly, "What happened to your mother?"

Alessi silently sorted through the remainder of the photographs. Toward the bottom of the stack, he found what he was looking for and extracted it. A slender woman, short-haired and of extraordinary beauty, stared past the camera; or perhaps *through* the camera. Her eyes had a distant, unfocused quality. She stood in a stand of dark spruce, her hands folded.

"It's such a moody picture," said Lakey.

The pines loomed above Alessi's mother, conical bodies appearing to converge in the upper portion of the grainy print. "I took that," said Alessi. "She didn't know. It was the last picture anyone took of her."

"She . . . died?"

"Not exactly. I suppose so. No one knows."

"I don't understand," said Lakey.

"She was a brilliant, lonely, unhappy lady," said Alessi. "My father brought her out here from Florida. She hated it. The mountains oppressed her; the winters depressed her. Every year she retreated farther into herself. My father tried to bring her out of it, but he treated her like a child. She resisted his pressures. Nothing seemed to work." He lapsed again into silence.

Finally Lakey said, "What happened to her?"

"It was after Mrs. Norrinssen had been here for two years. My mother's emotional state had been steadily deteriorating. Mrs. Norrinssen was the only one who could talk with her; or perhaps the only one with whom my mother would talk. One autumn day—it was in October. My mother got up before everyone else and walked out into the woods. That was that."

"That can't be all," said Lakey. "Didn't anyone look?"

"Of course we looked. My father hired trackers and dogs and the sheriff brought in his searchers. They trailed her deep into the pine forest and then lost her. They spent weeks. Then the snows increased and they gave up. There's a stone out behind the house in a grove, but no one's buried under it."

"Jesus," Lakey said softly. She put her arms around Alessi and gave him a slow, warm hug. The rest of the photographs fluttered to the hardwood floor.

I wait, I wait. I see no necessity of movement, not for now. I am patient. No longer do I go to the round window. My vigil is being rewarded. There is no reason to watch the unknowing birds, the forest, the road. The clouds have no message for me today.

I hear footsteps on the stair, and that is message enough.

"Most of the attic," said Alessi, "was converted into a nursery for me. My father always looked forward. He believed in constant renovation. As I became older, the nursery evolved to a playroom, though it was still the room where I slept. After my father died, I moved back here with my family for a few years. This was Connie's room."

"Your wife or your—"

"Daughter. For whatever reason, she preferred this to all the other rooms."

They stood just inside the doorway. The playroom extended most of the length of the house. Alessi imagined he could see the straight, carefully crafted lines of construction curving toward one another in perspective. Three dormer windows were spaced evenly along the eastern pitch of the ceiling. The round window allowed light to enter at the far end.

"It's huge," said Lakey.

"It outscales children. It was an adventure to live here. Sometimes it was very easy for me to imagine I was playing in a jungle or on a sea, or across a trackless Arctic waste."

"Wasn't it scary?"

"My father didn't allow that," said Alessi. Nor did I later on, he thought.

Lakey marveled. "The furnishings are incredible." The canopied bed, the dressers and vanity, the shelves and chairs, all were obviously products of the finest woodcraft. "Not a piece of plastic in all this." She laughed. "I love it." In her denim jeans and Pendleton shirt, she pirouetted. She stopped in front of a set of walnut shelves. "Are the dolls your daughter's?"

Alessi nodded. "My father was not what you would call a liberated man. Connie collected them all during her childhood." He carefully picked up a figure with silk nineteenth-century dress and china head.

Lakey eagerly moved from object to object like a butterfly sampling flowers. "That horse! I always wanted one."

"My father made it for me. It's probably the most exactingly carpentered hobbyhorse made."

Lakey gingerly seated herself on the horse. Her feet barely touched the floor. "It's so big." She rocked back and forth, leaning against the leather reins. Not a joint squeaked.

Alessi said, "He scaled it so it would be a child's horse, not a pony. You might call these training toys for small adults."

The woman let the horse rock to a stop. She dismounted and slowly approached a tubular steel construction. A six-foot horizontal ladder connected the top rungs of two vertical four-foot ladders. "What on earth is this?"

Alessi was silent for a few seconds. "That is a climbing toy for three- and four-year-olds."

"But it's too big," said Lakey. "Too high."

"Not," said Alessi, "with your toes on one rung and your fingers on the next—just barely."

"It's impossible."

Alessi shook his head. "Not quite; just terrifying."

"But why?" she said. "Did you do this for fun?"

"Dad told me to. When I balked, he struck me. When he had to, my father never discounted the effect of force."

Lakey looked disconcerted. She turned away from the skeletal bridge toward a low table shoved back against the wall.

"Once there was a huge map of fairyland on the wall above the table," said Alessi. "Mrs. Norrinssen gave it to me. I can remember the illustrations, the ogres and frost giants and fairy castles. In a rage one night, my father ripped it to pieces."

Lakey knelt before the table so she could look on a level with the stuffed animals. "It's a whole zoo!" She reached out to touch the plush hides.

"More than a zoo," said Alessi. "A complete bestiary. Some of these critters don't exist. See the unicorn on the end?"

Lakey's attention was elsewhere. "The bear," she said, greedily reaching like a small child. "He's beautiful. I had one like him when I was little." She gathered the stuffed bear into her arms and hugged it. The creature was almost half her size. "What's his name? I called mine Bear. Is he yours?"

Alessi nodded. "And my daughter's. His name is Bear too. Mrs. Norrinssen made him."

She traced her fingers along the bear's head, over his ears, down across the snout. Bear's hide was virtually seamless, sewn out of some rich pile fabric. After all the years, Bear's eyes were still black and shiny.

"The eyes came from the same glazier who cut the round window. Good nineteenth-century glass."

"This is wild," said Lakey. She touched the teeth.

"I don't really know whether it was Mrs. Norrinssen's idea or my father's," said Alessi. "A hunter supplied them. They're real. Mrs. Norrinssen drilled small holes toward the back of each tooth; they're secured inside the lining." Bear's mouth was lined with black leather, pliable to Lakey's questing finger. "Don't let him bite you."

"Most bears' mouths are closed," said Lakey.

"Yes."

"It didn't stop my Bear from talking to me."

"Mine didn't have to overcome that barrier." Alessi suddenly listened to what he was saying. Fifty-seven years old. He smiled self-consciously.

They stood silently for a few seconds; Lakey continued to hug the bear. "It's getting dark," she said. The sun had set while they explored the house. The outlines of solid shapes in the playroom had begun to blur with twilight. Doll faces shone almost luminously in the dusk.

"We'll get the luggage out of the car," said Alessi.

"Could I stay up here?"

"You mean tonight?" She nodded. "I see no reason why not," he said. He thought, did I really plan this?

Lakey stepped closer. "What about you?"

I watch them both. Frank Alessi very much resembles his father: distinguished. He looks harried, worn, but that is understandable. Some information I comprehend without knowing why. Some perceptions I don't have to puzzle over. I know what I see.

The woman is in her early twenties. She has mobile features, a smiling, open face. She is quick to react. Her eyes are as dark as her black hair. They dart back and forth in their sockets, her gaze lighting upon nearly everything in the room but rarely dwelling. Her speech is rapid with a hint of Eastern nasality. Except for her manner of speaking, she reminds me of a dear memory.

For a moment I see four people standing in the playroom. Two are reflections in the broad, hand-silvered mirror above the vanity across the room. Two people are real. They hesitantly approach each other, a step at a time. Their arms extend, hands touch, fingers plait. Certainly at this time, in this place, they have found each other. The mirror images are inexact, but I think only I see that. The couple in the mirror seem to belong to another time. And, of course, I am there in the mirror too—though no one notices me.

"That's, uh, very gratifying to my ego," said Alessi. "But do you know how old I am?"

Lakey nodded. The semidarkness deepened. "I have some idea."

"I'm old enough to—"

"—be my father. I know." She said lightly, "So?"

"So . . ." He took his hands away from hers. In the early night the dolls seemed to watch them. The shiny button eyes of Bear and the other animals appeared turned toward the human pair.

"Yes," she said. "I think it's a good idea." She took his hand again. "Come on; we'll get the stuff out of the car. It's been a long day."

Day, Alessi thought. Long week, long month, longer campaign. A lifetime. The headlines flashed in his mind, television commentaries replayed. It all stung like acid corroding what had been cold, shining, and clean. Old,

old, old, like soldiers and gunfighters. How had he missed being cleanly shot? Enough had seemed to want that. To fade . . . "I *am* a little bushed," he said. He followed Lakey out toward the stairs.

Frank Alessi's father was forceful in his ideal. That lent the foundation to that time and this place. Strength was virtue. "Fair is fair," he would say, but the fairness was all his. Such power takes time to dissipate. Mrs. Norrinssen stood up to that force; everyone else eventually fled.

"Witchy bitch!" he would storm. She only stared back at him from calm, glacial eyes until he sputtered and snorted and came to rest like a great, sulky, but now gentled beast. Mrs. Norrinssen was a woman of extraordinary powers and she tapped ancient reserves.

Structure persists. I am part of it. That is my purpose and I cannot turn aside. Now I wait in the newly inhabited house. Again I hear the positive, metallic sounds of automobile doors and a trunk lid opening and closing. I hear the voices and the footsteps and appreciate the human touch they lend.

She stretched slowly. "What time is it?"

"Almost ten," said Alessi.

"I saw you check your watch. I thought you'd be asleep. Not enough exercise?"

She giggled and Alessi was surprised to find the sound did not offend him as it had earlier in the day. He rolled back toward her and lightly kissed her lips. "Plenty of exercise."

"You were really nice."

Fingertips touched his face, exploring cheekbones, mouth corners, the stubble on the jowl line. That made him slightly nervous; his body was still tight. Tennis, handball, swimming, it all helped. Reasonably tight. Only slight concessions to slackness. But after all, he *was*— Shut up, he told himself.

"I feel very comfortable with you," she said.

Don't talk, he thought. Don't spoil it.

Lakey pressed close. "Say something."

No.

"Are you nervous?"

"No," Alessi said. "Of course not."

"I guess I did read about the divorce," said Lakey. "It was in a picture magazine in my gynecologist's office."

"There isn't much to say. Marge couldn't take the heat. She got out. I can't blame her." But silently he denied that. The Watergate people—*their* wives stood by. All the accumulated years . . . Betrayal is so goddamned nasty. Wish her well in Santa Fe?

"Tell me about your daughter," said Lakey.

"Connie—why her?"

"You've talked about everyone else. You haven't said a thing about Connie except to say she slept in this room." She paused. "In this bed?"

"We both did," said Alessi, "at different times."

"The stuff about the divorce didn't really mention her, at least not that I remember. Where is she?"

"I truly don't know."

Lakey's voice sounded peculiar. "She disappeared, uh, just like—"

"No. She left." Silently: She left me. Just like—

"You haven't heard from her? Nothing?"

"Not in several years. It was her choice; we didn't set detectives on her. The last we heard, she was living in the street in some backwater college town in Colorado."

"I mean, you didn't try—"

"It was her choice." She always said I didn't *allow* her any choice, he thought. Maybe. But I tried to handle her as my father handled me. And *I* turned out—

"What was she like?"

Alessi caressed her long smooth hair; static electricity snapped and flashed. "Independent, intelligent, lovely. I suppose fathers tend to be biased."

"How old is she?"

"Connie was about your age when she left." He realized he had answered the question in the past tense.

"You're not so old yourself," said Lakey, touching him strategically. "Not old at all."

Moonlight floods through the dormer panes; beyond the round window I see starlight fleck the sky. I am very quiet, though I need not be. The couple under the quilted coverlet are enthralled in their passion. I cannot question their motives yet. Love? I doubt it. Affection? I would approve of that. Physical attraction, craving for bodily contact, psychic tension?

I move to my window in the end of the playroom, leaving the lovemaking behind. The aesthetics of the bed are not as pleasing as the placid starfield. It may be that I am accustomed to somewhat more stately cycles and pulsings.

Perhaps it is the crowding of the house, the apprehension that more than one human body dwells within it, that causes me now to feel a loneliness. I wonder where Mrs. Norrinssen settled after the untimely death of her employer. "A bad bargain," he said somberly time after time. "Very bad indeed." And she only smiled back, never maliciously or with humor, but patiently. She had given him what he wanted. "But still a bargain," she said.

I am aware of the sounds subsiding from the canopied bed. I wonder if both now will abandon themselves to dreams and to sleep. A shadow dips silently past the window, a nighthawk. Faintly I hear the cries of hunting birds.

He came awake suddenly with teeth worrying his guilty soul. Connie glared at him from dark eyes swollen from crying and fury. She shook long black hair back from her shoulders. ". . . drove her through the one breakdown and into another." He dimly heard the words. "She's out of it, and good for her. No more campaigns. You won't do the same to me, you son of a bitch." Bitter smile. "Or I should say, you son of a bastard."

"I can't change these things. I'm just trying—" Alessi realized he was shaking in the darkness.

"What's wrong, now what's wrong?" said Connie.

Alessi cried out once, low.

"Baby, what is it?"

He saw Lakey's face in the pooled moonlight. "You." He reached out to touch her cheek and grazed her nose.

"Me," she said. "Who else?"

"Jesus," Alessi said. "Oh, God, God."

"Bad dream?"

Orientation slowly settled in. "A nightmare." He shook his head violently.

"Tell me about it?"

"I can't remember."

"So don't tell me if you don't want to." She gathered him close, blotting the sweat on his sternum with the sheet.

He said dreamily, "You always plan to make it up, but after a while it's too late."

"What's too late?"

Alessi didn't answer. He lay rigid beside her.

I see them in the gilt-framed mirror and I see them in bed. I feel both a terrible sympathy for her and an equally terrible love for him. For as long as I can recall, I've husbanded proprietary feelings about this house and those in it.

Frank Alessi makes me understand. I remember the woman's touch and cherish that feeling, though I simultaneously realize her touch was yet another's. I also remember Frank's embrace. I have touched all of them.

I love all these people. That terrifies me.

I want to tell him, you *can* change things, Frank.

Sometime after midnight he awoke again. The night had encroached; moonlight now filled less than a quarter of the playroom. Alessi lay still, staring at shadow patterns. He heard Lakey's soft, regular breathing beside him.

He lay without moving for what seemed to be hours. When he checked his watch only minutes had passed. Recumbent, he waited, assuming that for which he waited was sleep.

Sleep had started to settle about Alessi when he thought he detected a movement across the room. Part vague movement, part snatch of sound, it was *something*. Switching on the bed-table lamp, Alessi saw nothing. He held his breath for long seconds and listened. Still nothing. The room held only its usual complement of inhabitants: dolls, toys, stuffed creatures. Bear stared back at him. The furniture was all familiar. Everything was in its place, natural. He felt his pulse speeding. He turned off the light and settled back against the pillow.

It's one o'clock in the soul, he thought. Not quite Fitzgerald, but it will do. He remembered Lakey in the car that afternoon asking why he had cut and run. That wasn't the exact phraseology, but it was close enough. So what if he had been forced out of office? He still could have found some kind of political employment. Alessi had not told her about all the records unsubpoenaed as well as subpoenaed—at first. Then, perversely, he had started to catalogue the sordid details the investigating committees had decided not to use. After a while she had turned her head back toward the clean mountain scenery. He continued the list. Finally she had told him to shut up. She had turned back toward him gravely, had told him it was all right—she had forgiven him. It had been simple and sincere.

I don't need easy forgiveness, he thought. Nor would *I* forgive. That afternoon he had lashed out at her. "Damn it, what do you know about these things—about responsibility and power? You're a hippy—or whatever hippies are called now. Did you ever make a single solitary decision that put you on the line? Made you a target for second-guessing, carping analysis, sniping, unabashed viciousness?" The overtaut spring wound down.

Lakey visibly winced; muscles tightened around her mouth. "Yes," she said. "I did."

"So tell me."

She stared back at him like a small surprised animal. "I've been traveling a long time. Before I left, I was pregnant." Her voice flattened; Alessi strained to hear the words. "They told me it should have been a daughter."

He focused his attention back on the road. There was nothing to say. He knew about exigencies. He could approve.

"None of them wanted me to do it. They made it more than it really was. When I left, my parents told me they would never speak to me again. They haven't."

Alessi frowned.

"I loved them."

Alessi heard her mumble, make tiny incoherent sounds. She shifted in her sleep in a series of irregular movements. Her voice rose slightly in volume. The words still were unintelligible. Alessi recognized the tenor; she was dreaming of fearful things. He stared intently; his vision blurred.

Gently he gathered Connie into his arms and stroked her hair. "I will make it right for you. I know, I know . . . I can."

"No," she said, the word sliding into a moan. Sharply: "No."

"I am your father."

But she ignored him.

*　　*　　*

I hear more than I can see. I hear the woman come fully awake, her moans sliding raggedly up the register to screams; pain—not love; shock—not passion. I would rather not listen, but I have no choice. So I hear the desperation of a body whose limbs are trapped between strangling linens and savage lover. I hear the endless, pounding slap of flesh against meat. Finally I hear the words, the words, the cruel words and the ineffectual. Worst of all, I hear the cries. I hear them in sadness.

Earlier I could not object. But now he couples with her not out of love, not from affection, but to force her. No desire, no lust, no desperate pleasure save inarticulate power.

Finally she somehow frees herself and scrambles off the bed. She stumbles through the unfamiliar room and slams against the wall beside the door. Only her head intrudes into the moonlight. Her mouth is set in a rigid, silent oval. The wet blackness around her eyes is more than shadow. She says nothing. She fumbles for the door, claws the knob, is gone. He does not pursue her.

I hear the sound of the woman's stumbling steps. I hear her pound on the doors of the car Alessi habitually locks. The sounds of her flight diminish in the night. She will be safer with the beasts of the mountain.

Alessi endlessly slammed his fist into the bloody pillow. His body shook until the inarticulate rage began to burn away. Then he got up from the bed and crossed the playroom to the great baroque mirror.

"This time could have been different," he said. "I wanted it to be."

His eyes adjusted to the darkness. A thin sliver of moonlight striped the ceiling. Alessi confronted the creature in the mirror. He raised his hands in fists and battered them against unyielding glass, smashed them against the mirror until the surface fragmented into glittering shards. He presented his wrists, repeating in endless rote, "Different, this time, different . . ."

Then he sensed what lay behind him in the dark. Alessi swung around, blood arcing. Time overcame him. The warm, coppery smell rose up in the room.

Perhaps the house now is haunted; that I cannot say. My own role is ended. Again I am alone; and now lonely.

This morning I have not looked through the round window. The carrion crows are inside my mind picking at the bones of memories.

I watch Frank Alessi across the stained floor of the playroom.

The house is quiet; I'm sure that will not continue. The woman will have reached the highway and surely has been found by now. She will tell her story and then the people will come.

For a time the house will be inhabited by many voices and many bodies. The people will look at Frank Alessi and his wrists and his blood. They will remark upon the shattered mirror. They may even note the toys, note me; wonder at the degree of the past preserved here in the house. I doubt they can detect the pain in my old-fashioned eyes.

They will search for answers.

But they can only question why Frank came here, and why he did what he did. They cannot see the marks left by the teeth of the past. Only the blood.

Winslow Crater

```
METEOR
 METEOR
  METEOR
   METEOr
    METEOr
     METEOr
      METEor
       METEor
        METEor
         METeor
          METeor
           METeor
            MEteor
             MEteor
              MEteor
               Meteor
                Meteor
                 Meteor
                  meteor
                   meteorite
```

Shark

The war came and left, but returned for him eighteen years later.

Folger should have known when the clouds of smaller fish disappeared. He should have guessed, but he was preoccupied, stabilizing the cage at ten meters, then sliding out the upper hatch. Floating free, he stared into the gray-green South Atlantic. Nothing. With his tongue, he keyed the mike embedded in his mouthpiece. The sonex transmitter clipped to his tanks coded and beamed the message: "Query—Valerie—location." He repeated it. Electronics crackled in his ear, but there was no response.

Something moved to his right—something a darker gray, a darker green than the water. Then Folger saw the two dark eyes. Her body took form in the murk. A blunt torpedo shape gliding, she struck impossibly fast.

It was Folger's mistake and nearly fatal. He had hoped she would circle first. The great white shark bore straight in, mouth grinning open. Folger saw the teeth, only the teeth, rows of ragged white. "Query—" he screamed into the sonex.

Desperately he brought the shark billy in his right hand forward. The great white shape, jaws opening and closing, triangular teeth knifing, whipped past soundlessly.

Folger lifted the billy—tried to lift it—saw the blood

*and the white ends protruding below his elbow and real-
ized he was seeing surgically sawed bone.*

*The shock made everything deceptively easy. Folger
reached behind him, felt the cage, and pulled himself up
toward the hatch. The shark flowed into the distance.*

*One-handed, it was difficult entering the cage. He was
half through the hatch and had turned the flotation control
all the way up when he blacked out.*

Her name, like that of half the other women in the
village, was Maria. For more than a decade she had kept
Folger's house. She cleaned, after a fashion. She cooked
his two meals each day, usually boiled potatoes or mutton
stew. She loved him with a silent, bitter, unrequited passion. Over all the years, they had never talked of it. They
were not lovers; each night after fixing supper, she returned to her clay-and-stone house in the village. Had
Folger taken a woman from the village, Maria would have
knifed both of them as they slept. That problem had never
arisen.

"People for you," said Maria.

Folger looked up from his charts. "Who?"

"No islanders."

Folger hadn't had an off-island visitor since two years
before, when a Brazilian journalist had come out on the
semiannual supply boat.

"You want them?" said Maria.

"Can I avoid it?"

Maria lowered her voice. "Government."

"Shit," said Folger. "How many?"

"Just two. You want the gun?" The sawed-off twelve-
gauge, swathed in oilcloth, leaned in the kitchen closet.

"No." Folger sighed. "Bring them in."

Maria muttered something as she turned back through
the doorway.

"What?"

She shook her matted black hair. "One is a woman!"
she spat.

*Valerie came to his quarters later in the afternoon. The
project manager had already spoken to Folger. Knowing
what she would say, Folger had two uncharacteristically
stiff drinks before she arrived. "You can't be serious," was
the first thing he said.*

She grinned. "So they told you."

He said, "I can't allow it."

The grin vanished. "Don't talk as though you owned me."

"I'm not, I'm just—" He floundered. "Damn it, it's a shock."

She took his hand and drew him down beside her on the couch. "Would I deny your dreams?"

His voice pleaded. "You're my lover."

Valerie looked away. "It's what I want."

"You're crazy."

"You can be an oceanographer," she said. "Why can't I be a shark?"

Maria ushered in the visitors with ill grace. "Get along," she said out in the hallway. "Señor Folger is a busy man."

"We will not disturb him long," said a woman's voice.

The visitors, as they entered, had to duck to clear the doorframe. The woman was nearly two meters in height; the man half a head taller. Identically clad in gray jumpsuits, they wore identical smiles. They were—Folger searched for the right word—extreme. Their hair was too soft and silkily pale; their eyes too obviously blue, teeth too white and savage.

The pair looked down at Folger. "I am Inga Lindfors," said the woman. "My brother, Per." The man nodded slightly.

"Apparently you know who I am," said Folger.

"You are Marcus Antonius Folger," Inga Lindfors said.

"It was supposed to be Marcus Aurelius," Folger said irrelevantly. "My father never paid close attention to the classics."

"The fortune of confusion," said Inga. "I find Mark Antony the more fascinating. He was a man of decisive action."

Bewildered, Maria stared from face to face.

"You were a component of the Marine Institute on East Falkland," said Per.

"I was. It was a long time ago."

"We wish to speak with you," said Inga, "as representatives of the Protectorate of Old America."

"So? Talk."

"We speak officially."

"Oh." Folger smiled at Maria. "I must be alone with these people."

The island woman looked dubiously at the Lindfors. "I will be in the kitchen," she said.

"It is a formidable journey to Tres Rocas," said Per. "Our airboat left Cape Pembroke ten hours ago. Unfavorable winds."

Folger scratched himself and said nothing.

Inga laughed, a young girl's laugh in keeping with her age. "Marcus Antonius Folger, you've been too long away from American civilization."

"I doubt it," said Folger. "You've obviously gone to a lot of trouble to find me. Why?"

Why?

She always asked him questions when they climbed the rocks above the headland. Valerie asked and Folger answered and usually they both learned. Why was the Falklands' seasonal temperature range only ten degrees; what were quasars; how did third-generation computers differ from second; how dangerous were manta rays; when would the universe die? Today she asked a new question:

"What about the war?"

He paused, leaning into a natural chimney. "What do you mean?" The cold passed into his cheek, numbed his jaw, made the words stiff.

Valerie said, "I don't understand the war."

"Then you know what I know." Folger stared down past the rocks to the sea. How do you explain masses of people killing other people? He could go through the glossary—primary, secondary, tertiary targets; population priorities; death-yields—but so what? It didn't give credence or impact to the killing taking place on the land, in space, and below the seas.

"I don't know anything," said Valerie somberly. "Only what they tell us."

"Don't question them," said Folger. "They're a little touchy."

"But why?"

"The Protectorate remembers its friends," said Per.

Folger began to laugh. "Don't try to snow me. At the peak of my loyalty to the Protectorate—or what the Protectorate was then—I was apolitical."

"Twenty years ago, that would have been treason."

"But not now," said Inga quickly. "Libertarianism has made a great resurgence."

"So I hear. The boat brings magazines once in a while."

"The years of reconstruction have been difficult. We could have used your expertise on the continent."

"I was used here. Occasionally I find ways to help the islanders."

"As an oceanographer?"

Folger gestured toward the window. "The sea makes up most of their environment. I'm useful."

"With your talent," said Per, "it's such a waste here."

"Then, too," Folger continued, "I help with the relics."

"Relics?" said Inga uncertainly.

"War surplus. Leftovers. Look." Folger picked up a dried, leathery rectangle from the table and tossed it to Per. He looked at the object, turning it over and over.

"Came from a killer whale. Got him last winter with a harpoon and shaped charge. Damn thing had stove in three boats, killed two men. Now read the other side."

Per examined the piece of skin closely. Letters and numerals had been deeply branded. "USMF-343."

"See?" said Folger. "Weapons are still out there. He was part of the lot the year before I joined the Institute. Not especially sophisticated, but he had longevity."

"Do you encounter many?" said Inga.

Folger shook his head. "Not too many of the originals."

The ketch had been found adrift with no one aboard. It had put out early that morning for Dos, one of the two small and uninhabited companions of Tres Rocas. The three men aboard had been expecting to hunt seal. The fishermen who discovered the derelict also found a bloody axe and several sections of tentacle as thick as a man's forearm.

So Folger trolled along the route of the unlucky boat in his motorized skiff for three days. He searched a vast area of choppy, gray water, an explosive harpoon never far from his hand. Early on the fourth afternoon a half dozen dark-green tentacles poked from the sea on the port side of the boat. Folger reached with his left hand for the harpoon. He didn't see the tentacle from starboard that whipped and tightened around his chest and jerked him over the side.

The chill of the water stunned him. Folger had a quick, surrealistic glimpse of intricately weaving tentacles. Two eyes, each as large as his fist, stared without malice. The tentacle drew him toward the beak.

Then a gray shadow angled below Folger. Razor teeth scythed through flesh. The tentacle was cut; Folger drifted.

The great white shark was at least ten meters long. Its

*belly was uncharacteristically dappled. The squid wrapped
eager arms around the thrashing shark. The two fish sank
into the darker water below Folger.*

*Lungs aching, he broke the surface less than a meter
from the skiff. He always trailed a ladder from the boat.
It made things easier for a one-armed man.*

"Would you show us the village?" said Inga.

"Not much to see."

"We would be pleased by a tour anyway. Have you
time?"

Folger reached for his coat. Inga moved to help him
put it on. "I can do it," said Folger.

"There are fine experts in prosthesis on the continent,"
said Per.

"No, thanks," said Folger.

"Have you thought about a replacement?"

"Thought about it. But the longer I thought, the better
I got without one. I had a few years to practice."

"It was in the war, then?" asked Inga.

"Of course it was in the war."

On their way out, they passed the kitchen. Maria looked
up sullenly over the scraps of bloody mutton on the cutting board. Her eyes fixed on Inga until the blonde moved
out of sight along the hall.

A light, cold rain was falling as they walked down the
trail to the village. "Rain is the only thing I could do
without here," said Folger. "I was raised in California."

"We will see California after we finish here," said Inga.
"Per and I have a leave. We will get our antirad injections
and ski the Sierras. At night we will watch the Los
Angeles glow."

"Is it beautiful?"

"The glow is like seeing the aurora borealis every
night," said Per.

Folger chuckled. "I always suspected L.A.'s future would
be something like that."

"The half-life will see to the city's immortality," said
Inga.

Per smiled. "We were there last year. The glow appears
cold. It is supremely erotic."

*In the night, in a bed, he asked her, "Why do you want
to be a shark?"*

*She ran her nails delicately along the cords of his neck.
"I want to kill people, eat them."*

"Any people?"

"Just men."

"Would you like me to play analyst?" said Folger. She bit his shoulder hard. *"God damn it!"* He flopped over. *"Is there any blood?"* he demanded.

Valerie brushed the skin with her hand. "You're such a coward."

"My threshold of pain's low," said Folger. *"Sweetie."*

"Don't call me Sweetie," she said. *"Call me Shark."*

"Shark."

They made love in a desperate hurry.

The descent steepened, the rain increased, and they hurried. They passed through a copse of stunted trees and reached the ruts of a primitive road.

"We have flash-frozen beefsteaks aboard the airboat," said Inga.

"That's another thing I've missed," Folger said.

"Then you must join us for supper."

"As a guest of the Protectorate?"

"An honored guest."

"Make mine rare," said Folger. "Very rare."

The road abruptly descended between two bluffs and overlooked the village. It was called simply the village because there were no other settlements on Tres Rocas and so no cause to distinguish. Several hundred inhabitants lived along the curve of the bay in small, one-story houses, built largely of stone.

"It's so bleak," said Inga. "What do people do?"

"Not much," said Folger. "Raise sheep, hunt seals, fish. When there were still whales, they used to whale. For recreation, the natives go out and dig peat for fuel."

"It's quite a simple existence," said Per.

"Uncomplicated," Folger said.

"If you could be anything in the sea," said Valerie, *"what would it be?"*

Folger was always discomfited by these games. He usually felt he chose wrong answers. He thought carefully for a minute or so. "A dolphin, I suppose."

In the darkness, her voice dissolved in laughter. "You lose!"

He felt irritation. "What's the matter now?"

"Dolphins hunt in packs," she said. *"They gang up to kill sharks. They're cowards."*

"They're not. Dolphins are highly intelligent. They band together for cooperative protection."

Still between crests of laughter: "Cowards!"

On the outskirts of the village they encountered a dozen small, dirty children playing a game. The children had dug a shallow pit about a meter in diameter. It was excavated close enough to the beach so that it quickly filled with a mixture of ground seepage and rainwater.

"Stop," said Per. "I wish to see this."

The children stirred the muddy water with sticks. Tiny, thumb-sized fishes lunged and snapped at one another, burying miniature teeth in the others' flesh. The children stared up incuriously at the adults, then returned their attention to the pool.

Inga bent closer. "What are they?"

"Baby sharks," said Folger. "They hatch alive in the uterus of their mother. Some fisherman must have bagged a female sand tiger who was close to term. He gave the uterus to the kids. Fish won't live long in that pool."

"They're fantastic," Per breathed. For the first time since Folger had met him, he showed emotion. "So young and so ferocious."

"The first one hatched usually eats the others in the womb," said Folger.

"It's beautiful," said Inga. "An organism that is born fighting."

The sibling combat in the pit had begun to quiet. A few sand tiger babies twitched weakly. The children nudged them with the sticks. When there was no response, the sticks rose and fell violently, splashing the water and mashing the fish into the sand.

"The islanders hate sharks," Folger said.

She awoke violently, choking off a scream and blindly striking out at him. Folger held her wrists, pulled her against him, and then began to stroke her hair. Her trembling slowly subsided.

"Bad dreams?"

She nodded, her hair working softly against his jaw.

"Was I in them?"

"No," she said. "Maybe. I don't know. I don't think so."

"What happened?"

She hesitated. "I was swimming. They—some people pulled me out of the water. They put me on a concrete slab by the pier. There was no water, no sea—" She swallowed. *"God, I want a drink."*

"I'll fix you one," he said.

"They pulled me out. I lay there and felt the ocean drain away. And then I felt things tear loose inside me. There was nothing supporting my heart and liver and intestines and everything began to pull away from everything else. God, it hurts—"

Folger patted her head. "I'll get you a drink."

"So?" said Per. "Sharks aren't particularly aggressive, are they?"

"Not until after the war," said Folger. "Since then there's been continual skirmishing. Both the villagers and the sharks hunt the same game. Now they've started to hunt each other."

"And," said Inga, "there has been you."

Folger nodded. "I know the sea predators better. After all, that was my job."

The children, bored with the dead shark pool, followed the adults toward the village. They gawked at the Lindfors. One of the more courageous boys reached tentatively toward Inga's hair as it blew back in the wind.

"Vayan!" shouted Folger. "All of you, move!" The children reluctantly withdrew. "They're accustomed to whites," he said, "but blondes are a novelty."

"Fascinating," said Inga. "It is like an enclave of a previous century."

The road widened slightly and became the village's main street, still unpaved, and winding down along the edge of the sea. Folger saw the aluminum bulk of an airboat tied to a pier, incongruous between two fishing ketches. "You come alone?" he said.

"Just the two of us," said Inga.

Per put his hand lightly on her wrist. "We're quite effective as a team," he said.

They passed a dark-stone house, its door swung open to the wind. Rain blew across the threshold.

"Abandoned?" said Inga.

"Quaint old island custom," said Folger. "Catholicism's a little diluted here. Priest only comes twice a year." He pointed at the open door. "The man who lived there died at sea a couple days ago. Family'll keep the door open, no matter what, for a week. It's so his soul can find shelter until it's shunted to heaven or hell."

Per said, "What happened to the man?"

"He was fishing," Folger said. "Friends saw it all. A great white shark got him."

Closer now:

"Dolphin!"

"Shark!"

They lay together.

"I wish we had more time," said Inga. "I should like to hunt a shark."

"Perhaps on some future leave," said Per.

"And that's about it for the village," said Folger. "There isn't much more to see, unless you enjoy native crafts like dipping tallow candles or carding wool."

"It's incredible," said Inga. "The only time I have seen anything remotely like this was in prereconstruction America."

Folger said, "You don't look that old."

"I was barely into puberty. The Protectorate brought our father from Copenhagen. He is a design engineer in hydroelectrics. He worked on the Oklahoma Sea projects."

They stood on a rough plank pier beyond one horn of the crescent of houses. Per tapped a boot on the wood to shake loose some of the mud. "I still can't see how you endure this place, Folger."

Half asleep, Folger said. "Someday when the war is over, we'll get a place by the ocean. There's still some great country north of San Francisco. We'll have a house among the trees, on a mountainside overlooking the beach. Maybe we'll make it a stone tower, like Robinson Jeffers built."

Close to his ear, Valerie said, "A tower would be nice."

"You'll be able to read all day, and swim, and we'll never have any visitors we don't want."

"It's a fine dream for you," Valerie whispered.

"I came as jetsam," Folger said.

The three of them stood silently for a few minutes, watching clouds darker than the water spill in from the west. Triangular shapes took form on the horizon. Folger squinted. "Fishermen are coming in." After another minute he said, "Tour's over."

"I know," said Inga.

"—hoping. I kept hoping." Folger raised himself on one elbow. "You really are going to go through with it."

The fishing boats neared the breakwater. Folger and

the others could hear the faint cries of the crewmen. "Why are you here?" he said.

Per Lindfors laid a comradely hand on Folger's shoulder. "We came here to kill you."

Folger smiled. What other response could there be?

"Tell me how it works," said Valerie.

They paused on a steel catwalk overlooking the catch pens. In the tank immediately below, two divers warily manhandled a five-meter great blue in an oval path. If water weren't forced over the shark's gill surfaces, the fish would suffocate. The water glittered in the glare of arc lights. Beyond the pens, the beacon on Cape Pembroke blinked its steady twelve pulses per minute.

"I know the general techniques," said Folger. "But it's not my specialty. I'm strictly mapping and logistics."

"I don't need apologies," said Valerie.

"Excuse me while I violate the National Security Act." Folger turned to face her. *"Most of the technology is borrowed from the brothers upstairs on the orbital platforms. Everybody's been doing secret work with cyborgs. Somewhere along the line, somebody got the bright idea of importing it underwater."*

"The Marine Forces," said Valerie.

"Right. The bureaucrats finally realized that the best weapons for fighting undersea wars already existed in the ocean. They were weapons which had been adapted for that purpose for more than a hundred million years. All that was needed were guidance systems."

Valerie said wistfully, "Sharks."

"Sharks and killer whales; squid; to a degree, dolphins. We're considering a few other species."

"I want to know how it's done."

"Primarily by direct transplant. Surgical modification. Nerve grafts are partially electronic. Is that what you wanted to know?"

She stared down at the docile shark in the tank. "There's no coming back, is there?"

"We'll probably use your old body to feed the new one."

"So kill me. Do I rate a reason why?"

"Not if your execution had been scheduled now," said Inga. "It would not have been merciful to alert you in advance. Such cheap melodrama is forbidden by Protectorate codes."

Folger snorted. "Isn't all this overly Machiavellian?"

"Not at all. We were given considerable latitude on this assignment. We wished to be sure of doing the right thing."

"*—come down to the point of whether or not I'll stop you from doing this.*" *Wind off the headland deadened his words.*

"*Can you stop me?*" *Valerie's voice was flat, without challenge.*

He didn't answer.

"*Would you?*" *Valerie kissed him gently on the side of the throat.* "*Here's a Hindu proverb for you. The woman you love, you must not possess.*"

He said in a whisper, without looking at her, "*I love you.*"

"If you're not going to kill me," Folger said, "I've got work to do."

"Folger, what is your fondest wish?"

He stared at her with enigmatic eyes. "You can't give it to me."

"Wealth?" said Per. "Recognition? You had a considerable reputation before the war."

"When we leave," said Inga, "we want you to return with us."

Folger looked slowly from one to the other. "Leave the island?"

"A center for deep Pacific studies is opening on Guam," Inga said. "The directorship is yours."

"I don't believe any of this," said Folger. "I'm in my fifties, and even considering the postwar chaos, I'm a decade behind my field."

"Some refresher study at the University of San Juan," said Per.

Inga said, "Reconstruction is not all that complete. Genius is uncommon. You are needed, Folger."

"Death or a directorship," said Folger.

Folger spoke to the project manager in a sterile cubicle off the operating theater. "*What are her chances?*"

"*For survival? Excellent.*"

"*I mean afterwards.*"

The project manager drew deeply on his extinguished pipe. "*Can't say. Test data's been spotty.*"

"*Christ, Danny!*" *Folger swung around.* "*Don't doubletalk me. What's that mean?*"

The project manager evaded Folger's eyes. "A high proportion of the test subjects haven't returned from field trials. The bio boys think it may have something to do with somatic memory, cellular retention of the old, non-human personality."

"And you didn't tell us anything about this?"

"Security, Marc." The project manager looked uncomfortable. "I never know from day to day what's under wraps. You know, we haven't had radio reception for twelve days now. Nobody knows—"

"I swear, Danny, if anything happens to her—"

The pipe dropped from the project manager's open mouth. "But she's a volunteer—"

It was the first time Folger had ever struck another human being.

"Elections are approaching on the continent," said Inga. "Free?"

"Of course," said Per.

"Reasonably," said Inga. 'Within the needs of reconstruction."

A crowd of children scampered past. Further down the beach, the fishermen began to unload the day's catch.

"Do you remember a man named Diaz-Gomide?" said Per.

"No."

"He is a Brazilian journalist."

"Yes," said Folger. "About two years ago, right?"

Per nodded. "He is not only a journalist, but also a higher-up in the opposition party. He is their shadow minister of information."

"Señor Diaz-Gomide has proved a great embarrassment to the present administration," said Inga.

"The same regime that's been in power for a quarter century," said Folger.

Inga made a noncommittal gesture. "Someone had to keep order through the war and after."

"The point is," said Per, "that this Diaz-Gomide has been disseminating historical lies on behalf of his party."

"Let me guess," said Folger. He walked slowly toward the end of the pier and the Lindfors followed. "He has disclosed terrible things about the government in connection with the Marine Institute on East Falkland."

"Among other fabrications," said Per.

Folger stopped with his toes overhanging the water.

"He alleged that inhuman experiments were carried on, that the brains of unwilling or unknowing subjects were transplanted into the bodies of sea creatures."

"Something like that, except he couched it in less clinical language."

"Down the rabbit hole." Folger shook his head slowly. "What do you want from me—a disclaimer?"

Inga said, "We suspect Diaz-Gomide grossly distorted your statements in the interview. It would be well if you set the record straight."

"The Marine Forces experiments have been greatly exaggerated," said Per.

"Probably not," said Folger.

They stared at each other.

Folger floated in the center of the holding tank. The whisper of the regulator sounded extraordinarily loud in his ears. He turned to follow the great white shark as it slowly circled, its eye continually focused on Folger. The shark—he found difficulty ascribing it her name—moved fluidly, weaving, head traveling from side to side slowly with the rhythm of its motion through the water.

She—he made the attempt—she was beautiful; implacably, savagely so. He had seldom been this close to a shark. He watched silently her body crease with a thousand furrows, every movement emphasizing musculature. He had never seen beauty so deadly.

After a time, he tried the sonex. "Valerie—inquiry— what is it like?"

The coded reply came back and unscrambled. "Marc— never know—mass&bulk&security—better."

He sent: "Inquiry—happy?"

"Yes."

They exchanged messages for a few minutes more. He asked, "Inquiry—what will they do with you?"

"Assigned soldier—picket duty—Mariana Trench."

"Inquiry—when?"

"Never—never soldier—run away first."

"So," said Folger. "Recant or die?"

"We would like to see you take the directorship of the research center on Guam," said Inga.

Folger found the paper among other poems scattered like dry leaves in Valerie's room:

> "In the void, inviolate
> from what she was
> is
> and will be"

He went outside to the catch pens. From the catwalk he looked into the tank. The shark circled ceaselessly. She swung around to his side and Folger watched the dark back, the mottled gray-and-white belly slide by. He watched until darkness fell.

"Do I get time to consider the offer?" Folger asked.

The Lindfors looked at each other, considering.

"I was never good at snap decisions."

"We would like to tidy up this affair—" said Per.

"I know." Folger said. "Skiing the Sierras."

"Would twelve hours be sufficient?"

"Time enough to consult my Book of Changes."

"Do you really?" Inga's eyes widened fractionally.

"Treason," Per said.

"No. No more. My mystical phase played through."

"Then we can expect your decision in the morning?"

"Right."

"And now it is time for supper," said Inga. "Shall we go to the boat? I remember, Folger. Very rare."

"No business during dinner?"

"No," Inga promised.

"Your goddamn girl," said the project manager. Soaked through with seawater and reeking of contraband liquor, he sloshed into Folger's quarters. "She got away."

Folger switched on the lamp by the bunk and looked up sleepily. "Danny? What? Who got away?"

"Goddamn girl."

"Valerie?" Folger swung his legs off the bed and sat up.

"Smashed the sea gate. Let loose half the tanks. We tried to head her off in the channel."

"Is she all right?"

"All right?" The project manager cupped his hands over his face. "She stove in the boat. Got Kendall and Brooking. You never saw so much blood."

"Christ!"

"Hell of it was," said the project manager, "we really needed her in the morning."

"For what?"

"Really needed her," the project manager repeated. He staggered out of the room and disappeared in the hall.

Folger answered his own question the following day. Through devious channels of information, he learned that Valerie had been scheduled for vivisection.

That night, Folger climbed the mountain above his house. He felt he was struggling through years as much as brush and mud. The top of the mountain was ragged, with no proper peak. Folger picked a high point and spread his slicker over damp rock. He sat in the cold and watched the dark Atlantic. He looked up and picked out the Southern Cross. A drizzle began.

"Well, hell," he said, and climbed back down the mountain.

Folger took an Institute launch out beyond the cape and anchored. He lowered the cage, then donned his Scuba gear. He said into the sonex: "Query—Valerie—location."

Later that morning, Folger suffered his loss.

Maria shook him awake in the morning. Folger awakened reluctantly, head still full of gentle spirals over glowing coral. The water had been warm; he had needed no suit or equipment. Endless, buoyant flight—

"Señor Folger, you must get up. It has been seen."

His head wobbled as she worried his shoulder with insistent fingers. "Okay, I'm awake." He yawned. "What's been seen?"

"The big white one," Maria said. "The one that killed Manuel Padilla three days ago. It was sighted in the bay soon after the sun rose."

"Anybody try anything?" Folger asked.

"No. They were afraid. It is at least ten meters long."

Folger yawned again. "Hell of a way to start a morning."

"I have food for you."

Folger made a face. "I had steak last night. Real beef. Have you ever tasted beef?"

"No, Señor."

Maria accompanied him down the mountain to the village. She insisted upon carrying some of the loose gear; the mask, a box of twelve-gauge shells, a mesh sack of empty jars. Folger filled the jars with sheep's blood at the village butcher shop. He checked his watch; it was seven o'clock.

The skiff was tied up at the end of the second pier. The aluminum airboat glittered in the sun as they passed it. Inga Lindfors stood very still on the bridge. "Good morning, Folger," she called.

"Good morning," said Folger.

"Your answer?"

Folger appraised her for a moment. "No," he said, walking on.

The carcinogenic spread of the war finally and actively engulfed the Falkland Islands. The systemic integrity of the Institute was violated. Many components scattered; some stayed to fight.

Folger, his stump capped with glossy scar tissue, had already said his good-byes.

Suspended in the cold, gray void, Folger realized he was hyperventilating. He floated free, willing himself to relax, letting his staccato breathing find a slower, smoother rhythm. Beside him, a line trailed up to the rectangular blur of the skiff's hull. Tied to the nylon rope were a net and the unopened jars of sheep's-blood bait.

Folger checked his limited arsenal. Tethered to his left wrist was the underwater gun. It was a four-foot aluminum tube capped with a firing mechanism and a waterproof shotgun shell. A shorter, steel-tipped shark billy was fixed to a bracket tied to the stump of Folger's right arm.

Something intruded on his peripheral vision and he looked up.

Arrogant and sure, the two deadly shadows materialized out of the murk. The Lindfors wore only mask, fins, and snorkel. They appeared armed only with knives.

Folger saw them and raised the shark gun in warning. Per Lindfors grinned, his teeth very white. With slow, powerful strokes, he and his sister approached Folger from either side.

Disregarding Inga for the moment, Folger swung the muzzle of the shark gun toward Per. Per batted it aside with his free hand as Folger pulled the trigger. The concussion seemed to stun only Folger. Still smiling, Per extended his knife hand.

Inga screamed in the water. Per disregarded Folger's weak attempt to fend him off with the billy and began to stroke for the surface. Folger turned his head.

A clownish face rushed at him. Folger stared at the teeth. The pointed nose veered at the last moment as the shark brushed by and struck at Per. The jaws cleanly sliced away Per's left arm and half his chest. The fish doubled back upon itself and made another strike. Per's legs, separate and trailing blood, tumbled slowly through the water.

Then Folger remembered Inga. He turned in the water and saw half her torso and part of her head, a swatch of silky hair spread out fanlike behind the corpse.

He looked back at the shark. It turned toward him slowly and began to circle, eerily graceful for its immense size. A dark eye fixed him coldly.

Folger held the metal billy obliquely in front of his chest. The tether of the shark gun had broken with the recoil.

The shark and Folger inspected each other. He saw the mottled coloration of the shark's belly. He thought he saw a Marine Forces code branded low on the left flank. He keyed the sonex:

"Query—Valerie—query—Valerie."

The shark continued to circle. Folger abruptly realized the shark was following an inexorably diminishing spiral.

"Query—Valerie—I am Folger."

"Folger." An answer came back. "Valerie."

"I am Folger," he repeated.

"Folger" came the reply. "Love/hunger—hunger/love."

"Valerie—love."

"Hunger—love." The shark suddenly broke out of her orbit and drove at Folger. The enormous jaws opened, upper jaw sliding forward, triangular teeth ready to shear.

Folger hopelessly raised the billy. The jaws closed empty and the shark swept by. She was close enough to touch had Folger wished. The shark drove toward the open sea and Folger swam for the surface.

He tossed the yarrow sticks for an hour. Eventually he put them away, along with the book. Folger sat at the table until the sun rose. He heard Maria's footsteps outside on the stone walk. He listened to the sound of her progress through the outside door, the kitchen, and the hall.

"Señor Folger, you didn't sleep?"

"I'm getting old," he said.

Maria was excited. "The great white one is back."

"Oh?"

"The fishermen fear to go out."

"That's sensible."

"Señor, you must kill it."

"Must I?" Folger grinned. "Fix me some tea."

She turned toward the kitchen.

"Maria, you needn't come up tonight to fix supper."

After his usual meager breakfast, Folger gathered together his gear and walked out the front door of the house. He hesitated on the step.

You become what you live.

She lived shark.

He said into the wind, "What do you want me to do? Carve a cenotaph here on the mountain?"

"What, Señor?" said Maria.

"Let's go." They started toward the trail. "Hold it," said Folger. He walked back to the house and opened the front door to wind and rain. He chocked it with a rock. Then he climbed down the path to the sea.

Precession

Broken free from time and space, I grabbed for anchored razor blades. I grimly held on to bits and pieces of continuum. And what if no one touched you again? I thought. I touched no one . . . I lost my concentration and time swung round . . .

I swiveled the chair back from the small, crosshatched panes; the summerscape wavered beyond. I forced my face toward the window. Trees bent nearly double in the sudden storm; branches lashed fitfully. Some broke, the wind whirling green swatches of leaves into the avenue where traffic had slowed to a near-stop. Hail chattered across the glass with each gust. Rain followed, a soft hiss. The late-afternoon sun still shone above the mountains. The range today was blue-gray.

My safe mechanical phase: tracking like the security camera in a department store, my stare returned to the interior of the apartment.

—her eyes were dark blue-gray—

I squinted, soft-focusing on the couch to my left. The topography of the aging green furniture—lumpy cushions reflected the hills and depressions of a form now absent. I panned along the wall to the surrealistic painting of an abandoned oil refinery; blinding white faded to blue, to green, to black. I began to rock back and forth in the chair with my hands in fists. I watched the diffraction-spiral mobile turning in the heat from the table lamp. Rainbow colors glittered. I thought the mobile was slowing. I continued to rock, sensing the proximity of a mood too leaden for directed action to affect. After a very long time I reached for the telephone.

I work with change the only ways I can.

—once—

From outside the noise of the weather ceased in dying whimpers of wind. The air in the apartment was stuffy—I tried to moisten my dry mouth with dry tongue. When I reached to unlatch and open one of the windows, I saw that autumn lay beyond. The sky had darkened. The leaves still hanging from the branches of the nearer elms were parched and brown. Mercury lights came on in the street.

—her hair shone metallic; copper in the street glow, gold in the sun—

I wasn't sure exactly how much time passed before I felt the slick plastic receiver in my hand. I dialed and she answered on the ninth ring. "Hello?" I tried to answer but my throat was still dry. "Who is it?"

"It's me."

"Cal?" Her voice sounded strained.

"Yes. Did I catch you in the tub?"

"No, I was right here by the phone. I'm expecting my parents to call."

"I let it go nine rings—"

"No, one," she said. "I picked it up on the first one."

"I counted. Nine."

"Maybe a bad circuit—"

"Nine," I said determinedly. "Elizabeth—"

"You feel okay? You don't, do you?"

"What do you mean?" I consciously loosened my grip on the receiver.

"I asked how you felt."

"I feel—"

—her flesh always seemed hotter than normal blood temperature. Her heart always beat stronger than mine—

"Okay, you're not all right," said Elizabeth.

"I don't feel—"

—soft voice, her words traced with a light finger against a mat of suede—

I didn't notice how long I said nothing. I concentrated on her presence; imagined the touch, recreated her face, her fingers. I love—

"Cal, are you there? Say something."

"I'm here, I'm here. Are—you?" Dreading the true answer, wondering if tears might be the cheapest release. No solution beyond the immediate. Nothing beyond the now—

"Want me to drive in?" said Elizabeth. "I can be there in half an hour."

"What good . . ."

"Cal? You sound like you're fading."

"I'm here, I'm here, I'm . . ." The words overlapped on the wire, echoed, diminishing.

"I'll come in," she said insistently. "It's no problem; I had the snow tires mounted yesterday."

Winter now? I thought. The phone cord stretched as I swiveled back to the window. Winter. I saw a snowy nimbus surrounding each street lamp. Snow treads crunched on the street; occasional truck chains rattled. "How long's it been snowing?" Silly question.

Elizabeth said, "Here? Just a couple of hours. What's it like in town?"

"I won't—don't know."

Hesitating, "I still don't have a definite answer."

"Okay. I mean yes; come in if you want. But it looks—cold." I saw an image of robins, brittle as the frozen grass, stricken untimely on my lawn.

"It *is* cold—hasn't been above zero all day. No problem. My Volvo's got a good heater. Shall I pick up some wine on the way?"

We should celebrate the passing of seasons? My elbow ached; I transferred the receiver to my left hand.

"Cal?"

It took another conscious decision to answer. "Sure. Make it something cheap and red that I can't spoil with mulled wine mix."

"Okay. See you in an hour."

I said, "It'll be all right?"

She paused too long. "It will. See you, love."

Thirty seconds after the circuit broke, the howler reminded me I was party to a dead line. I replaced the receiver. My apartment lightened. The western clouds reflected the reds and yellows of sunrise; my eyes tried to register the spectrum from ultraviolet to infrared. I reeled before the onslaught of spring as I heard the Easter cry of the robins.

Recall the immutable past?

Certainly I remembered abnormal, unnatural times:

As usual I got up with the alarm at seven, turned on the *Today Show,* immediately poured myself a glass of cold water, added two effervescent tablets, and drank it with six aspirin. My mouth felt the way my rumpled bed looked. I ritualistically flensed my gums with nylon bristles and green gel. My downstairs neighbor always got up before me; I waited for the hot-water tank (only one to the building) to refill so I could shower away the last foggy caul of sleep. I listened to the guest congresswoman on *Today* confidently list syllogistic answers to the food and fuel shortages.

"But are you sure about that?" said the interviewer.

"Logic stands behind us," said the guest. "It enables our system to function."

The interviewer did not look convinced. "Many administration critics seem to feel the present crises will irreversibly worsen."

The guest said, "That violates our national philosophy." She laughed. "In another year, that could qualify as treason."

I was not reassured; then I abandoned myself to shower spray and was grateful the water was at least at room temperature. By the time I'd toweled off, my stomach had settled and I felt like eating something more substantial than Alka-Seltzer and bran flakes. I had grape juice with my bran flakes.

The time and temperature number confirmed what I'd seen in a glance out the window. The late-autumn day would require a heavy sweater. Time to leave; promptness at school counted. I knew the average driving time to campus was seventeen minutes.

At nine-thirty I was in my office at the college. Disgruntled students were already queuing in the hallway. Every term it was the same; I could predict it all. At midterm I'd give them the broad guidelines for the final project. After a week they'd come out of shock and start bitching. It's too demanding, they would say, eyes narrowed, jaws quivering. Well, I'd answer, you're partly right. It's demanding. Some students fell apart; some drew discipline and structure about themselves and accomplished the project. At least they had the choice. At the time, so did I.

At eleven I had the introduction to fiction course; at noon, the composition section; then a special session of office hours for more students who were worried about their little universe flying apart from its center. ("Listen, I don't know if I can *do* the project, and if I drop out now or if I flunk, I won't have the hours to get into nursing school, and then my parents'll kill me, but if I have to leave school they really *will* kill me, and I won't be able to get a job and then what'll I do?") Just do the project, I'd say. Develop an idea as best you can; be logically consistent; follow through; consider ramifications. Concentrate. The universe abhors chaos. If you want, I'll help you.

Today I could go home at four. Gratefully I arrived at the apartment and collapsed on the couch. As usual I turned on a *Star Trek* rerun and went to sleep for a half-hour nap. I woke up, turned off the TV, read whatever magazine had come in the day's mail. Today it was *New York*. Conscience reminded me I ought to grade last week's in-class essays. I did so for two hours until my body told me to eat. I obeyed that reassuring biological clock by fixing soup and a sandwich.

After supper I watched a made-for-television movie about a disastrous blizzard: an entire city ceased to function after a giant storm. All the inhabitants died. It was uncharacteristically pessimistic for commercial TV. Vaguely disturbed, I switched it off before the end credits. I knew I should get back to work. Again it was time. The routine must be obeyed.

I wished Elizabeth weren't visiting her parents in Michigan. I wanted to call her, see her, perhaps go out to a late film. We would return here and make love. In sleep we would touch each other all night, hip to hip, fingers on flank. But I couldn't call—it was another time zone. It was too late. I suddenly shivered. *Someone's walking across your grave,* my father would have said. I shivered again. *Someone's standing there . . . tapping a foot, tamping the fill.*

I graded essays for another three hours.

And went to bed; one more day spent.
Aberrant, logical times; I remember them.

The raucous objection of crows, as they argued with a
Manx on the fire escape over an unidentifiable bit of
carrion, echoed in my ears. The cat, ears laid back,
yowled and scimitared the air with its paw.

The cat cry merged with the rasp of the door buzzer.
Through the window, I saw the sparrow's breast explode
in a puff of gray feathers. The ragged tomcat seized the
prey between its jaws and trotted down the stairs.

Sunlight pooled around the blood on the step. It was a
beautiful day.

I left the door to my apartment open and walked down
the four flights to the side entrance; precisely thirty-one
steps. Each time I descended, I counted.

"Good morning," said Elspeth when I opened the door.
Her eyes seemed to fade to a lighter gray in the dim light
of the entryway. She carried a brown grocery sack, obviously heavy: she shifted it to the other arm and smiled.

I smiled back tentatively. "Elizabeth, I'm glad—"

"Who?"

"Elizabeth, I—"

"Nobody calls me that," she said. "Elspeth."

I realized I knew that. "Elspeth," I said. "I'm glad
you're here."

"Me too." She shook the long chestnut hair away from
her eyes. The green irises seemed to glow. "I've got plenty
of picnic things. The store had some Chenin Blanc in the
cooler. I thought we could go to the park."

"It's Febr—"

"July," she said hurriedly. "A beautiful summer day.
Can I use the john before we go?"

"Sure," I said, again defeated temporarily and tem-
porally. "I left the door open; slam it when you come
back down. I'll guard the wine."

She kissed my cheek lightly as she moved past me in
the hall. A chill breeze from the open door made me
shiver. But, for whatever reason, I felt strong this morning. For the time I was in command. From outside the
light brightened and the wind warmed as though clouds
were breaking, unmasking the sun.

I relaxed; I would get through *this* day. Considering tomorrow could wait.

Elspeth returned, breath broken. "I've got to start swimming again and get back into shape. Forty steps are killing me."

"Thirty-two," I said automatically. Thirty-two? Thirty-one? Sometimes the details were the worst part. "Close."

She ignored me. "Breath's gone—ought to stop smoking."

"You stopped smoking on your birthday."

"No," she said. "I *will*." She took a pack of Marlboros from her handbag. "On my birthday I will."

I hefted the grocery sack. "Let's go to the park." A distant siren quavered.

"What a marvelous day," said Elspeth. The remark sounded forced. "How do you feel?"

"Better. Not good."

"I didn't think so." She and I walked west along the avenue toward a crosswalk. Elspeth balked at the extra distance. "We can just jaywalk."

"I thought you wanted real exercise." The siren screamed past, the sounds scratching furrows across our ears. The tires of the ambulance shrieked nearly as loud as the vehicle rocked and skidded into the park entrance. "There's another reason why not." We waited for the light.

The edge of the park was only two blocks from the avenue. "Can we eat by the lake?" said Elspeth.

"Sure."

"I suppose I know what's wrong." Elspeth took my elbow as we left the sidewalk for the grass between the trees. "Do you want to talk about it now?"

I nodded slowly. "That's why I called you."

She glanced sidewise at me. "More attacks—" She hesitated.

"Of reality, as you called them." I nodded again.

"Disorientation?"

"Our definitions differ," I said, "but yes."

"Depression?"

"More like fear. If this is the way things really are, I'm not sure I can handle them much longer." I looked at her skeptically. "You know what I mean?"

She said, "I'm not sure I really understand, but I'm trying. I trust you."

I felt her love, and was strengthened. The center ceased its fragmentation. For a time, I would live.

We approached the south neck of the lake, the center-piece of the park. Directly ahead, a small frame building served as refreshment stand and headquarters for the rental boat concession. Segregated by a chain-link fence, brightly painted craft filled the boatyard. A crowd had gathered around the steel gate where the ambulance waited with idling engine.

Many of the spectators were children. "What's going on?" I asked an onlooker.

"Guy fell out of a boat in the middle," said the boy. "Drownded. Weeds got him right off."

"Weeds?" said Elspeth.

"There've always been two or three drownings a summer," I said. "People don't seem to be able to swim, they get careless and fall out of the boat, then they get caught in the weeds and panic."

"Hey, they found him!" someone in the crowd said. There was a surge of bodies toward the fence as people jockeyed for a good view. I saw distant wetsuited figures pulling a shapeless bundle over the side of the boat. Then, like adjusting the eyepiece of a telescope and suddenly altering scale, I saw something else.

"Let's not eat our picnic here," said Elspeth. Her voice sounded dry.

"Wait a second," I said. "Do you know what this looks like?"

She turned away from the crowd. "A circus."

"The lake," I said. "It looks like a goddamned brain."

She smiled wanly. "Or a cauliflower. So what?"

"No, it really does," I said. "Look at it. The whole thing copies the central nervous system. All the lobes are there. The medulla—that's the bulge down there." I gestured. "The brain stem . . . that spring-fed creek running past us. There's the spinal cord."

"Um," she said.

"Just *look*."

I saw the neon letters *humor him* igniting in *her* brain. "Can we walk up to the temporal lobe, okay?" she said.

I stopped, still hugging the grocery bag, staring at her. "Why did you say that?"

Elspeth said, "No reason. I just picked a lobe." She ran

her fingers through her short red hair. "Honestly." She shook her wrist. "The watch, it reminded me."

"Time sense," I said slowly. "It's partially controlled in the temporal lobe."

"Listen, I really didn't mean to say anything to upset you."

"Elspeth, I—"

"Elise," Elise said.

"Elise, let's get out of here before I—"

A police officer approached us, motioning with his nightstick. "You folks like to move back? Give the ambulance some room." The recovery boat lay alongside the small dock. Medics wheeled a litter to its side. The divers made sounds of exertion and passed them a tarpaulin-covered form, its face covered. The crowd pressed forward, unsatisfied.

Elise tugged at my fingers. "Okay, anywhere," she said. "Just not here." Her voice sounded determinedly cheerful. "We'll go to the hippocampus."

"That's worse," I said, starting to walk away from her. "The short-term memory is housed in the hippocampal region. Did you know there's a man institutionalized in the Midwest who had the wrong part of his hippocampus burned out twenty-five years ago when the doctors were trying to excise a lesion? So far as he's concerned, ever since, it's still twelve hours before the operation. It'll be that way endlessly. If he goes into a bathroom, he forgets why he's there while he's still in the doorway."

"Why are you talking about him?"

"At least he's found a kind of stability," I said. "I don't think you can understand."

Both her face and voice were frightened. "You've *never* had neurosurgery."

"Not with a knife. Not with a wire." I laughed mirthlessly. "Maybe it's the chemicals, Elise. Remember them? You lived through the sixties just as I did. Did you try everything? Did you become a mutant? Did you sample the Catastrophenol, the Entropine, the Chaozine-25? Strange conjunctions of pharmaceutical stars."

She looked at me as if I were crazy; and I suppose, briefly, I might have been. I took a few deep, shuddering breaths. "One theory," I said. "Or a joke."

Elise took my free hand tightly. "No picnic today; it's getting cold. Let's go back to the apartment."

As we started out of the park, the first powdery snow of autumn sifted down around us. Elise and Cal, changing yet unchanged. "We'll light a fire," said Elise.

"You know I don't have a fireplace."

"Then we'll turn up the radiator, mull the Burgundy, make up the bed."

I love you. More than before, the warmth flowed out. I let the grocery sack slip to the grass and hugged Elise. She framed my face with her fingers. "It will be all right," she said.

We heard the crowd shift disappointedly behind us. I turned my head back. The tarpaulin had fallen away as the man on the litter sat up. The covering over his face came free. The expression on his face transmuted from panic to bewilderment to relief. He stared at the faces looking back at him. A medic helped him to his feet.

"You're lucky, mister," said one of the police. "That was pretty close."

"Maybe . . ." I said.

"Cal?"

Can I stop the process? I thought. Even reverse it? Perhaps only for others, perhaps only temporarily, but perhaps for myself as well. I don't want only Pyrrhic victories.

But something's always lost. Already starting to blot the scene, snow clung to the lenses of my glasses. Elise's hand cooled in mine. Again I grabbed for anchored razor blades.

Life, returning; or at least in motion. "How pale your skin is," I said. "How light your eyes." She looked back at me, features expressionless. *Beth, have you changed?* The sick feeling returned.

"My eyes I was born with," said Beth. "My skin—I should have gotten out more last summer." With her fingers she urged my hands to touch her skin. "Does pallor offend your sense of aesthetics?"

I ran my fingers along the coolness of her flanks and felt no need to say anything. Now wordless as well, she offered me shelter. I shivered against her and Beth wrapped me close in her arms. I needed to touch her as I needed to be touched. I buried myself in her as though tapping submerged volcanic heat. She cried out and we rested, for the moment warm, for the second secure, cocooned in down-filled comforters.

After a time, she said, "I was reading Wilde today. I brought you something from that."

"Oscar Wilde? Doesn't seem entirely appropriate."

She didn't smile in return. "It's a paraphrase—I'm never any good with quotations. Anyway, he said that once you've loved somebody, you can do anything for them but love them that way again."

"It seems a little cynical," I said. "Do you take it literally and beyond? That the universe militates against loving anybody the same way, or to the same degree, twice?" Beth didn't answer. "Maybe it codifies some sort of second law of human dynamics?" I knew my smile had no warmth. I shivered. In the almost-darkness my fingertips proved she wasn't smiling either.

"I didn't say I understood all this. I only feel—"

"Do you want to understand?"

"I don't know that either." She paused. "Yes, no, I don't know."

Propped on an elbow, I looked down at her light champagne hair blending against the pillow, almost disappearing into its surface. Paler still were her eyes, shadowed and shading into darkness. "I'm out of phase with all this," I said. "Somehow I'm cut loose—"

"I know," said Liz, now tracing out my cheekbones with the side of her hand. I could barely feel her.

"Loving, but not enough." Had I really said that? Yes.

"No," she said. "You love me. I love you. But some processes you simply can't reverse. It has nothing to do with good or virtue or love."

I said, "It's all winding down."

"Cal." The gentle whisper faded in my ear. "I'm here."

I shook my head slowly, feeling the last resistance evaporating. It occurred to me—for perhaps an infinite time—that it's impossible to ascribe unfairness to impersonal process. It didn't help; not at all; no.

Winter, summer, autumn, spring. "Love?"

Yes.

"Liz, I can barely hear you." Light sheeted from the windows; photons flooded *away* from me, a vessel draining. Darkness overwhelmed shapes and forms with chiaroscuro.

Love? No strength, no energy, only a final railing against that which seemed inevitable; but I tried.

Starless night opened for me; a bed without heat. Emptiness champed at me; I jerked away. I reached out, grasped, groped, touching nothing, trying to secure my entropic lover.

"I'm here," she said.

And then that too changed.

Stone

Up above the burning city, a woman wails the blues. How she cries out, how she moans. Flames fed by tears rake fingers across the sky.

It is an old, old song:

> *Fill me like the mountains*
> *Fill me like the sea*

Writhing in the heat, she stands where there is no support. The fire licks her body.

> *All of me*

So finely drawn, and with the glitter of ice, the manipulating wires radiate outward. Taut bonds between her body and the flickering darkness, all wires lead to the intangible overshadowing figure behind her. Without expression, Atropos gazes down at the woman.

Face contorting, she looks into the hearts of a million fires and cries out.

> *All of me*

—As Atropos raises the terrible, cold-shining blades of the Norn-shears and with only the barest hesitation cuts the wires. Limbs spread-eagled to the compass points, the woman plunges into the flames. She is instantly and utterly consumed.

The face of Atropos remains shrouded in shadows.

II

the poster

---

alpertron presents

IN CONCERT

JAIN SNOW

with

MOOG INDIGO

sixty-track stim by RobCal

JUNE 23, 24
ONE SHOW NIGHTLY AT 2100
TICKETS $30, $26, $22

*Available at all Alpertron outlets
or at the door*

ROCKY MOUNTAIN CENTRAL ARENA — DENVER

III

My name is Robert Dennis Clary and I was born twenty-three years ago in Oil City, Pennsylvania, which is also where I was raised. I've got a degree in electrical engineering from M.I.T. and some grad credit at Cal Tech in electronics. *"Not suitable, Mr. Clary,"* said the dean. *"You lack the proper team spirit. Frankly speaking, you are selfish. And a cheat."*

My mother told me once she was sorry I wasn't handsome enough to get by without working. *Listen Ma, I'm all right. There's nothing wrong with working the concert circuit.* I'm working damned hard now. I was never genius enough that I could have got a really good job with, say, Bell Futures or one of the big space firms. But I've got one marketable talent—what the interviewer called a peculiarly coordinative affinity for multiplex circuitry. *He looked a little stunned after I finished with the stim console. "Christ, kid, you really get into it, don't you?"*

That's what got me the job with Alpertron Ltd., the big promotion and booking agency. I'm on the concert tour and work their stim board, me and my console over there on the side of the stage. It isn't that much different in principle from playing one of the instruments in the backup band, though it's a hell of a lot more complex than even Nagami's synthesizer. It all sounds simple enough: my console is the critical link between performer and audience. Just one glorified feedback transceiver: pick up the empathic load from Jain, pipe it into the audience, they react and add their own load, and I feed it all back to the star. And then around again as I use the sixty stim tracks, each with separate controls to balance and augment and intensify. It can get pretty hairy, which is why not just anyone can do the job. It helps that I seem to have a natural resistance to the sideband slopover radiation from the empathic transmissions. *"Ever think of teaching?"* said the school voc counselor. *"No,"* I said. *"I want the action."*

And that's why I'm on the concert circuit with Jain Snow; as far as I'm concerned, the only real blues singer and stim star.

Jain Snow, my intermittent unrequited love. *Her voice*

*is shagreen-rough; you hear it smooth until it tears you
to shreds.*

She's older than I am, four, maybe five years; but she
looks like she's in her middle teens. Jain's tall, with a
tumbleweed bush of red hair; her face isn't so much pretty
as it is intense. I've never known anyone who didn't want
to make love to her. *"When you're a star,"* she said once,
*half drunk, "you're not hung up about taking the last
cookie on the plate."*

That includes me; and sometimes she's let me come into
her bed. But not often. *"You like it?"* she said. *I answered
sleepily,* "You're really good." "Not me," *she said.* "I
mean being in a star's bed." *I told her she was a bitch and
she laughed.* Not often enough.

I know I don't dare force the issue; even if I did, there
would still be Stella.

Stella Vanilla—I've never learned exactly what her real
last name is—is Jain's bodyguard. Other stim stars have
whole platoons of karate-trained killers for protection. Jain
needs only Stella. *"Stella, pick me up a fifth? Yeah, Irish.
Scotch if they don't."*

She's shorter than I am, tiny and dark with curly chestnut hair. She's also proficient in any martial art I can
think of. And if all else fails, in her handbag she carries
a .357 Colt Python with a four-inch barrel. When I first
saw that bastard, I didn't believe she could even lift it.

But she can. I watched Stella outside Bradley Arena in
L.A. when some overanxious bikers wanted to get a little
too close to Jain. *"Back off, creeps." "So who's tellin' us?"*
She had to hold the Python with both hands, but the
muzzle didn't waver. Stella fired once; the slug tore the
guts out of a parked Harley-Wankel. The bikers backed
off very quickly.

Stella enfolds Jain in her protection like a raincape. It
sometimes amuses Jain; I can see that. *Stella, get Alpertron on the phone for me. Stella? Can you score a couple
grams? Stella, check out the dudes in the hall. Stella—* It
never stops.

When I first met her, I thought that Stella was the cold-
est person I'd ever encountered. *And in Des Moines I saw
her crying alone in a darkened phone booth—Jain had
awakened her and told her to take a walk for a couple
hours while she screwed some rube she'd picked up in
the hotel bar. I tapped on the glass; Stella ignored me.*

Stella, do you want her as much as I?

So there we are—a nice symbolic obtuse triangle. And yet— We're all just one happy show-biz family.

IV

This is Alpertron Ltd.'s own chartered jet, flying at twelve kilometers above western Kansas. Stella and Jain are sitting across the aisle from me. It's a long flight and there's been a lull in the usually boisterous flight conversation. Jain flips through a current Neiman-Marcus catalogue; exclusive mail-order listings are her present passion.

I look up as she bursts into raucous laughter. "I'll be goddamned. Will you look at this?" She points at the open catalogue on her lap.

Hollis. Moog Indigo's color operator, is seated behind her. She leans forward and cranes her neck over Jain's shoulder. "Which?"

"That," she says. "The VTP."

"What's VTP?" says Stella.

Hollis says, "Videotape playback."

"Hey, everybody!" Jain raises her voice, cutting stridently through everyone else's conversations. "Get this. For a small fee, these folks'll put a videotape gadget in my tombstone. It's got everything—stereo sound and color. All I've got to do is go in before I die and cut the tape."

"Terrific!" Hollis says. "You could leave an album of greatest hits. You know, for posterity. Free concerts on the grass every Sunday."

"That's really sick," Stella says.

"Free, hell," Jains grins. "Anybody who wants to catch the show can put a dollar in the slot."

Stella stares disgustedly out the window.

Hollis says, "Do you want one of those units for your birthday?"

"Nope." Jain shakes her hand. "I'm not going to need one."

"Never?"

"Well . . . not for a long time." But I think her words sound unsure.

Then I only half-listen as I look out from the plane across the scattered cloud banks and see the Rockies looming to the west of us. Tomorrow night we play Denver. *"It's about as close to home as I'm gonna get,"* Jain *had said in New Orleans when we found out Denver was booked.*

"A what?" Jain's voice is puzzled.

"A cenotaph," says Hollis.

"Shut up," Stella says. "Damn it."

V

We're in the Central Arena, the architectural pride of Denver District. This is the largest gathering place in all of Rocky Mountain, that heterogeneous, anachronistic strip city clinging to the front ranges of the continental divide all the way from Billings down to the southern suburb of El Paso.

The dome stretches up beyond the range of the house lights. If it were rigid, there could never be a Rocky Mountain Central Arena. But it's made of a flexible plastic variant and blowers funnel up heated air to keep it buoyant. We're on the inner skin of a giant balloon. When the arena's full, the body heat from the audience keeps the dome aloft and the arena crew turns off the blowers.

I killed time earlier tonight reading the promo pamphlet on this place. As the designer says, the combination of arena and spectators turns the dome into one sustaining organism. At first I misread it as "orgasm."

I monitor crossflow conversations through plugs inserted in both ears as setup people check out the lights, sound, color, and all the rest of the systems. Finally some nameless tech comes on circuit to give my stim console a run-through.

"Okay, Rob, I'm up in the booth above the east aisle. Give me just a tickle." *My nipples were sensitized to her tongue, rough as a cat's.*

I'm wired to a test set fully as powerful as the costume Jain'll wear later—just not as exotic. I slide a track control forward until it reaches the five position on a scale calibrated to one hundred.

"Five?" the tech says.

"Right."

"Reading's dead on. Give me a few more tracks."

I comply. *She kisses me with lips and tongue, working down across my belly.*

"A little higher, please."

I push the tracks to fifteen.

"You're really in a mood, Rob."

"So what do you want me to think?" I say.

"Jesus," says the tech. "You ought to be performing. The crowd would love it."

"They pay Jain. She's the star." *I tried to get on top; she wouldn't let me. A moment later it didn't matter.*

"Did you just push the board to thirty?" The tech's voice sounds strange.

"No. Did you read that?"

"Negative, but for a moment it felt like it." He pauses. "You're not allowing your emotional life to get in the way of your work, are you?"

"Screw off," I answer. "None of your business."

"No threats," says the tech. "Just a suggestion."

"Stick it."

"Okay, okay. She's a lovely girl, Rob. And like you say, she's the star."

"I know."

"Fine. Feed me another five tracks, Rob; broad spectrum this time."

I do so and the tech is satisfied with the results. "That ought to do it," he says. "I'll get back to you later." He breaks off the circuit. All checks are done; there's nothing now on the circuits but a background scratch like insects climbing over old newspapers. *She will not allow me to be exhausted for long.*

Noisily, the crowd is starting to file into the arena.

I wait for the concert.

VI

There's never before been a stim star the magnitude of Jain Snow. Yet somehow the concert tonight fails. Somewhere the chemistry goes wrong. The faces out there are as always—yet somehow they are not *involved*. They care, but not enough.

I don't think the fault's in Jain. I detect no significant difference from other concerts. Her skin still tantalizes the audience as nakedly, only occasionally obscured by the cloudy metal mesh that transforms her entire body into a single antenna. I've been there when she's performed a hell of a lot better, maybe, but I've also seen her perform worse and still come off the stage happy.

It isn't Moog Indigo; they're laying down the sound and light patterns behind Jain as expertly as always.

Maybe it's me, but I don't think I'm handling the stim console badly. If I were, the nameless tech would be on my ass over the com circuit.

Jain goes into her final number. It does not work. The audience is enthusiastic and they want an encore, but that's just it: they shouldn't want one. They shouldn't *need* one.

She comes off the stage crying. I touch her arm as she walks past my console. Jain stops and rubs her eyes and asks me if I'll go back to the hotel with her.

VII

It seems like the first time I was in Jain Snow's bed. Jain keeps the room dark and says nothing as we go through the positions. Her breathing grows a little ragged; that is all. And yet she is more demanding of me than ever before.

When it's done, she holds me close and very tightly. Her rate of breathing slows and becomes regular. I wonder if she is asleep.

"Hey," I say.

"What." She slurs the word sleepily.

"I'm sorry about tonight."

". . . Not your fault."

"I love you very much."

She rolls to face me. "Huh?"

"I love you."

"No, babe. Don't say that."

"It's true," I say.

"Won't work."

"Doesn't matter," I say.

"It can't work."

I know I don't have any right to feel this, but I'm pissed and so I move away in the bed. "I don't care." *The first time: "Such a goddamned adolescent, Rob."*

After a while, she says, "Robbie, I'm cold," and so I move back to her and hold her and say nothing. I realize, rubbing against her hip, that I'm again hard; she doesn't object as I pour back into her all the frustration she unloaded in me earlier.

Neither of us sleeps much the rest of the night. Sometime before dawn I doze briefly and awaken from a nightmare. I am disoriented and can't remember the entirety of the dream, but do remember hard wires and soft flows of electrons. My eyes suddenly focus and I see her face inches away from mine. Somehow she knows what I am thinking. "Whose turn is it?" she says. *The antenna.*

VIII

At least a thousand hired kids are there setting up chairs in the arena this morning; but it's still hard to feel I'm not alone. The dome is that big. Voices get lost here. Even thoughts echo.

"It's gonna be a hell of a concert tonight. I know it." Jain had said that and smiled at me when she came through here about ten. She'd swept down the center aisle in a flurry of feathers and shimmering red strips, leaving all the civilians stunned and quivering.

God only knows why she was up this early; over the last eight months, I've never seen her get up before noon on a concert day. That kind of sleep-in routine would kill me. I was out of bed by eight this morning, partly because I've got to get this console modified by showtime; and partly because I didn't feel like being in the star's bed when she woke up.

"The gate's going to be a lot bigger than last night," Jain had said. "Can you handle it?"

"Sure. Can you?"

Jain had flashed me another brilliant smile and left. And so I sit here substituting circuit chips.

A couple kids climb on stage and pull breakfasts out

of their backpacks. "You ever read this?" says one, pulling a tattered paperback from his hip pocket. His friend shakes her head. "You?" He turns the book in my direction; I recognize the cover.

It was two, maybe three months ago in Memphis, in a studio just before rehearsal. Jain had been sitting and reading. She reads quite a lot, though the promotional people downplay it—Alpertron Ltd. likes to suck the country-girl image for all it's worth.

"What's that?" Stella says.

"A book." Jain holds up the book so she can see.

"I know that." Stella reads the title: "*Receptacle*. Isn't that the—"

"Yeah," says Jain.

Everybody knows about *Receptacle*—the best-seller of the year. It's all fact, about the guy who went to Prague to have a dozen artificial vaginas implanted all over his body. Nerve grafts, neural rerouting, the works. I'd seen him interviewed on some talk show where he'd worn a jumpsuit zipped to the neck.

"It's grotesque," Stella says.

Jain takes back the book and shrugs.

"Would you try something like this?"

"Maybe I'm way beyond it." *A receptacle works only one-way.*

Stella goes white and bites off whatever it is she was about to say.

"Oh, baby, I'm sorry." Jain smiles and looks fourteen again. Then she stands and gives Stella a quick hug. She glances over at me and winks, and my face starts to flush. *One-way.*

Now, months later, I remember it and my skin again goes warm. "Get out of here," I say to the kids. "I'm trying to concentrate." They look irritated, but they leave.

I'm done with the circuit chips. Now the easy stuff. I wryly note the male and female plugs I'm connecting. *Jain . . .*

The com circuit buzzes peremptorily and Jain's voice says, "Robbie? Can you meet me outside?"

I hesitate, then say, "Sure, I'm almost done with the board."

"I've got a car; we're going away."

"What?"

"Just for the afternoon."

"Listen, Jain——"

She says, "Hurry," and cuts off.

It's gonna be a hell of a concert.

IX

Tonight's crowd strains even the capacity of the Rocky Mountain Central Arena. The gate people say there are more than nine hundred thousand people packed into the smoky recesses of the dome. It's not just hard to believe; it's scary. But computer ticket-totes don't lie.

I look out at the crowd and it's like staring at the Pacific after dark; the gray waves march out to the horizon until you can't tell one from the other. Here on the stage, the crowd mutter even sounds like the sea, exactly as though I were on the beach trying to hear in a six-meter surf. It all washes around me and I'm grateful for the twin earpieces, reassured to hear the usual check-down lists on the in-house com circuit.

I notice that the blowers have cut off. It's earlier than usual, but obviously there's enough body heat to keep the dome buoyed aloft. I imagine the Central Arena drifting away like that floating city they want to make out of Venice, California. There is something appealing about the thought of this dome floating away like dandelion fluff. But now the massive air-conditioning units hum on and the fantasy dies.

The house lights momentarily dim and the crowd noise raises a few decibels. I realize I can't see features or faces or even separate bodies. There are simply too many people to comprehend. The crowd has fused into one huge tectonic slab of flesh.

"Rob, are you ready?" The tech's soft voice in my earpiece.

"Ready."

"It's a big gate tonight. Can you do it?"

Sixty overlay tracks and one com board between Jain and maybe a cool million horny, sweating spectators? "Sure," I say. "Easy." But momentarily I'm not sure and I realize how tightly I'm gripping the ends of the console. I consciously will my fingers to loosen.

"Okay," the tech says. "But if anything goes wrong, cut it. Right? Damp it completely."

"Got it."

"Fine," he says. "About a minute, stand by. Ms. Snow wants to say hello."

"Hello, Robbie?"

"Yeah," I say. "Good luck."

Interference crackles and what she says is too soft to hear.

I tell her, "Repeat, please."

"Stone don't break. At least not easy." She cuts off the circuit.

I've got ten seconds to stare out at that vast crowd. Where, I wonder, did the arena logistics people scrape up almost a million in/out headbands? I know I'm hallucinating but for just a moment I see the scarlet webwork of broadcast power reaching out from my console to those million skulls. I don't know why; I find myself reaching for the shield that covers the emergency total cutoff. I stop my hand.

The house lights go all the way down; the only illumination comes from a thousand exit signs and the equipment lights. Then Moog Indigo troops onstage as the crowd begins to scream in anticipation. The group find their instruments in the familiar darkness. The crowd is already going crazy.

Hollis strokes her color board and shoots concentric spheres of hard primaries expanding through the arena: Red, yellow, blue. Start with the basics. Red.

Nagami's synthesizer spews a volcanic flow of notes like burning magma.

And then Jain is there. Center stage.

"Damn it," says the tech in my ear. "Level's too low. Bring it up in back." I must have been dreaming. I am performing stupidly, like an amateur. Gently I bring up two stim balance slides.

"—love you. Every single one of you."

The crowd roars back. The filling begins. I cut in four more low-level tracks.

"—ready. How about you?"

They're ready. I cut in another dozen tracks, then mute two. Things are building just a little too fast. The fine mesh around Jain's body seems to glitter with more than reflected light. Her skin already gleams with moisture.

"—get started easy. And then things'll get hard. Yeah?"

"YEAH!" from thousands of throats simultaneously.

I see her stagger slightly. I don't think I am feeding her too much too fast, but mute another pair of tracks anyway. Moog Indigo takes their cue and begins to play. Hollis gives the dome the smoky pallor of slow-burning leaves. Then Jain Snow sings.

And I fill her with them. And give her back to them.

> space and time
> measured in my heart

X

In the afternoon:

Jain gestures in an expansive circle. "This is where I grew up."

The mountains awe me. "Right here?"

She shakes her head. "It was a lot like this. My pa ran sheep. Maybe a hundred miles north."

"But in the mountains?"

"Yeah. Really isolated. My pa convinced himself he was one of the original settlers. He was actually a laid-off aerospace engineer out of Seattle."

The wind flays us for a moment; Jain's hair whips and she shakes it back from her eyes. I pull her into the shelter of my arms, wrapping my coat around us both. "Do you want to go back down to the car?"

"Hell, no," she says. "A mountain zephyr can't scare me off."

I'm not used to this much open space; it scares me a little, though I'm not going to admit that to Jain. We're above timberline and the mountainside is too stark for my taste. I suddenly miss the rounded, wooded hills of Pennsylvania. Jain surveys the rocky fields rubbed raw by wind and snow and I have a quick feeling she's scared too. "Something wrong?"

"Nope. Just remembering."

"What's it like on a ranch?"

"Okay, if you don't like people," she says slowly, obviously recalling details. "My pa didn't."

"No neighbors?"

"Not a one in twenty miles."

"Brothers?" I say. "Sisters?"

She shakes her head. "Just my pa." I guess I look curious, because she looks away and adds, "My mother died of tetanus right after I was born. It was a freak thing."

I try to change the subject. "Your father didn't come down to the first concert, did he? Is he coming tonight?"

"No way," she says. "He didn't and he won't. He doesn't like what I do." I can't think of anything to say now. After a while, Jain rescues me. "It isn't your hassle, and it isn't mine anymore."

Something perverse doesn't let me drop it now. "So you grew up alone."

"You noticed," she says softly. "You've got a hell of a way with understatement."

I persist. "Then I don't understand why you still come up here. You must hate this."

"Ever see a claustrophobe deliberately walk into a closet and shut the door? If I don't fight it this way—" Her fingers dig into my arms. Her face is fierce. "This has got to be better than what I do onstage." She swings away from me. "Shit!" she says. "Damn it all to hell." She stands immovable, staring down the mountain for several minutes. When she turns back toward me, her eyes are softer and there's a fey tone in her voice. "If I die—" She laughs. "When I die. I want my ashes here."

"Ashes?" I say, unsure how to respond. *Humor her.* "Sure."

"You." She points at me. "Here." She indicates the rock face. The words are simple commands given to a child.

"Me." I manage a weak smile.

Her laugh is easy and unstrained now. "Kid games. Did you do the usual things when you were a kid, babe?"

"Most of them." *I hardly ever won; but then I liked to play games with outrageous risks.*

"Paper, rock, and scissors?"

"Sure, when I was really young." I repeat by long-remembered rote: "Rock breaks scissors, scissors cut paper, paper covers rock."

"Okay," she says. "Let's play." I must look doubtful. "Rob," she says warningly.

"Okay." I hold out my right hand.

Jain says, "One, two, three." On 'three,' we each bring

up our right hand. Hers is a clenched fist: stone. My first two fingers form the snipping blades of a pair of scissors. "I win!" she crows, delighted.

"What do you win?"

"You. Just for a little while." She pulls my hands close and lays them on her body.

"Right here on the mountain?" I say.

"I'm from pioneer stock. But you—" She shrugs. "Too delicate?"

I laugh and pull her close.

"Just—" She hesitates. "Not like the other times? Don't take this seriously, okay?"

In my want I forget the other occasions. "Okay."

Each of us adds to the other's pleasure and it's better than the other times. But even when she comes, she stares through me and I wonder whose face she's seeing—no, not even that: how many faces she's seeing. *Babe, no man can fill me like* they *do.*

And then I come also and—briefly—it doesn't matter.

My long coat is wrapped around the two of us and we watch each other inches apart. "So much passion, Rob . . . It seems to build."

I remember the stricture and say, "You know why."

"You really like me so much?" *The little-girl persona.*

"I really do."

"What would you do for me, if I asked you?"

"Anything."

"Would you kill for me?"

I say, "Sure."

"Really?"

"Of course." I smile. I know how to play.

"This is no game."

My face must betray my confusion. I don't know how I should react.

Her expression mercurially alters to sadness. "You're scissors, Robbie. All shiny cold metal. How can you ever hope to cut stone?"

Would I want to?

XI

Things get worse.

Is it simply that I'm screwing up on my own hook, or is it because we're exploring a place no performance has ever been? I don't have time to worry about it; I play the console like it was the keyboard on Nagami's synthesizer.

> *Take it*
> *When you can get it*
> *Where you can get it*

Jain sways and the crowd sways; she thrusts and the crowd thrusts. It is one gigantic act. It is as though a temblor shakes the Front Range.

Insect chittering in my earpiece: "What the hell's going on, Rob? I'm monitoring the stim feed. You're oscillating from hell to fadeout."

"I'm trying to balance." I juggle slides. "Any better?"

"At least it's no worse," says the tech. He pauses. "Can you manage the payoff?"

The payoff. The precision-engineered and carefully timed upslope leading to climax. The Big Number. I've kept the stim tracks plateaued for the past three sets. "Coming," I say. "It's coming. There's time."

"You're in bad trouble with New York if there isn't," says the tech. "I want to register a jag. Now."

"Okay," I say.

> *Love me*
> *Eat me*
> *All of me*

"Better," the tech says. "But keep it rising. I'm still only registering a sixty percent."

Sure, bastard. It isn't your brain burning with the output of these million strangers. My violence surprises me. But I push the stim up to seventy. Then Nagami goes into a synthesizer riff and Jain sags back against a vertical rank of amps.

"Robbie?" It comes into my left ear, on the in-house com circuit reserved for performer and me alone.

"I'm here, Jain."

"You're not trying, babe."

I stare across the stage and she's looking back at me. Her eyes flash emerald in the wave from Hollis' color generator. She subvocalizes so her lips don't move.

"I mean it."

"This is new territory," I answer. "We never had a million before." I know she thinks it's an excuse.

"This is it, babe," she says. "It's tonight. Will you help me?"

I've known the question would come, though I hadn't known who'd articulate it—her or me. My hesitation stretches much longer in my head than it does in realtime. *So much passion, Rob . . . It seems to build. Would you kill for me?* "Yes," I say.

"Then I love you," and breaks off as the riff ends and she struts back out into the light. I reluctantly touch the console and push the stim to seventy-five. Fifty tracks are in. *Jain, will you love me if I don't?*

A bitter look

Eighty. I engage five more tracks. Five to go. The crowd's getting damn near all of her. And, of course, the opposite's true.

A flattering word

Since I first heard her in Washington, I've loved this song the best. I push more keys. Eighty-two. Eighty-five. I know the tech's happily watching the meters.

A kiss

The last tracks cut in. *Okay, you're getting everything from the decaying food in her gut to her deepest buried childhood fears of an empty echoing house.*

Ninety.

A sword

And the song ends, one last diminishing chord, but her body continues to move. For her there is still music.

On the com circuit the tech yells. "Idiot! I'm already reading ninety. Ninety, damn it. There's still one number to go."

"Yeah," I say. "Sorry. Just . . . trying to make up for previous lag-time."

He continues to shout and I don't answer. On the stage, Nagami and Hollis look at each other and at the rest of the group; and then Moog Indigo slides into the last number with scarcely a pause. Jain turns toward my side of the stage and gives me a soft smile. And then it's back to the audience and into the song she always tops her concerts with, the number that really made her.

Fill me like the mountains

Ninety-five. There's only a little travel left in the console slides.

The tech's voice is aghast. "Are you out of your mind, Rob? I've got a ninety-five here—damned needle's about to peg. Back off to ninety."

"Say again?" I say. "Interference. Repeat, please."

"I said back off! We don't want her higher than ninety."

Fill me like the sea

Jain soars to the climax. I shove the slides all the way forward. The crowd is on its feet; I have never been so frightened in my life.

"Rob! I swear to God you're canned, you—"

Somehow Stella's on the com line too: "You son of a bitch! You hurt her—"

Jain flings her arms wide. Her back arches impossibly.

All of me

One hundred.

I cannot rationalize electronically what happens. I cannot imagine the affection and hate and lust and fear cascading into her and pouring back out. But I see the antenna mesh around her naked body glowing suddenly whiter until it flares in an actinic flash and I shut my eyes.

When I open them again Jain is a blackened husk tottering toward the front of the stage. Her body falls over the edge into the first rows of spectators.

The crowd still thinks this is part of the set, and they love it.

XII

No good-byes. I know I'm canned. When I go into the Denver Alpertron office in another day and a half to pick up my final check, some subordinate I've never seen before gives me the envelope.

"Thanks," I say. He stares at me and says nothing.

I turn to leave and meet Stella in the hall. The top of her head comes only to my shoulders, so she has to tilt her face up to glare at me. She says, "You're not going to be working for any promoter in the business. New York says so."

"Fine," I say. I walk past her.

Before I reach the door, she stops me by saying, "The initial report is in already."

I turn. "And?"

"The verdict will probably end up accidental death. Everybody's bonded. Jain was insured for millions. Everything will turn out all right for everyone." She stares at me for several seconds. "Except Jain. You bastard."

We have our congruencies.

The package comes later, along with a stiff legal letter from a firm of attorneys. The substance of the message is this: "Jain Snow wished you to have possession of this. She informed you prior to her demise of her desires; please carry them out accordingly." The packet contains a chrome cylinder with a screw cap. The cylinder contains ashes; ashes and a few bone fragments. I check. Jain's ashes, unclaimed by father, friends, or employers.

I drive west, away from the soiled towers of the strip city. I drive beyond the coalstrip pits and into the mountains until the paved highway becomes narrow asphalt, and then rutted earth, and then only a trace and the car can go no farther. With the metal cylinder in one hand I flee on foot until I no longer hear sounds of city or human beings.

At last the trees end and I climb over bare mountain

grades. I rest briefly when the pain in my lungs is too
sharp to ignore. At last I reach the summit.

I scatter Jain's ashes on the wind.

Then I hurl the empty cylinder down toward the timberline; it rolls and clatters and finally is only a distant
glitter on the talus slope.

"Jain!" I scream at the sky until my voice is gone and
vertigo destroys my balance. The echoes die. *As Jain died.*

I lie down unpeacefully—exhausted—and sleep, and
my dreams are of weathered stone. And I awake empty.

Strata

Six hundred million years in thirty-two miles. Six hundred million years in fifty-one minutes. Steve Mavrakis traveled in time—courtesy of the Wyoming Highway Department. The epochs raveled between Thermopolis and Shoshoni. The Wind River rambled down its canyon with the Burlington Northern tracks cut into the west walls, and the two-lane blacktop, U.S. 20, sliced into the east. Official signs driven into the verge of the highway proclaimed the traveler's progress:

DINWOODY FORMATION
TRIASSIC
185–225 MILLION YEARS

BIG HORN FORMATION
ORDOVICIAN
440–500 MILLION YEARS

FLATHEAD FORMATION
CAMBRIAN
500–600 MILLION YEARS

The mileposts might have been staked into the canyon rock under the pressure of millennia. They were there for those who could not read the stone.

Tonight Steve ignored the signs. He had made this run many times before. Darkness hemmed him. November clawed when he cracked the window to exhaust Camel smoke from the Chevy's cab. The CB crackled occasionally and picked up exactly nothing.

The wind blew—that was nothing unusual. Steve felt himself hypnotized by the skiff of snow skating across the pavement in the glare of his brights. The snow swirled only inches above the blacktop, rushing across like surf sliding over the black packed sand of a beach.

Time's predator hunts.

Years scatter before her like a school of minnows surprised. The rush of her passage causes eons to eddy. Wind sweeps down the canyon with the roar of combers breaking on the sand. The moon, full and newly risen, exerts its tidal force.

Moonlight flashes on the slash of teeth.

And Steve snapped alert, realized he had traversed the thirty-two miles, crossed the flats leading into Shoshoni, and was approaching the junction with U.S. 26. Road hypnosis? he thought. Safe in Shoshoni, but it was scary. He didn't remember a goddamned minute of the trip through the canyon! Steve rubbed his eyes with his left hand and looked for an open cafe with coffee.

It hadn't been the first time.

All those years before, the four of them had thought they were beating the odds. On a chill night in June, high on a mountain edge in the Wind River Range, high on more than mountain air, the four of them celebrated graduation. They were young and clear-eyed: ready for the world. That night they knew there were no other people for miles. Having learned in class that there were 3.8 human beings per square mile in Wyoming, and as *four*, they thought the odds outnumbered.

Paul Onoda, eighteen. He was Sansei—third-generation Japanese-American. In 1942, before he was conceived, his parents were removed with eleven thousand other Japanese-Americans from California to the Heart Mountain Relocation Center in northern Wyoming. Twelve members and three generations of the Onodas shared one of four hundred and sixty-five crowded, tar-papered barracks for the next four years. Two died. Three more were born. With their fellows, the Onodas helped farm eighteen hundred acres of virgin agricultural land. Not all of them had been Japanese gardeners or truck farmers in California, so the pharmacists and the teachers and the carpenters learned agriculture. They used irrigation to bring in water. The crops flourished. The Nisei not directly involved with farming were dispatched from camp to be seasonal farm laborers. A historian later laconically noted that "Wyoming benefited by their presence."

Paul remembered the Heart Mountain camps only through the memories of his elders, but those recollections were vivid. After the war, most of the Onodas stayed on in Wyoming. With some difficulty, they bought farms. The family invested thrice the effort of their neighbors, and prospered.

Paul Onoda excelled in the classrooms and starred on the football field of Fremont High School. Once he overheard the president of the school board tell the coach, "By God, but that little Nip can run!" He thought about that and kept on running ever faster.

More than a few of his classmates secretly thought he had it all. When prom time came in his senior year, it did not go unnoticed that Paul had an extraordinarily handsome appearance to go with his brains and athlete's body. In and around Fremont, a great many concerned parents admonished their white daughters to find a good excuse if Paul asked them to the prom.

Carroll Dale, eighteen. It became second nature early on to explain to people first hearing her given name that it had two r's and two l's. Both sides of her family went back four generations in this part of the country and one of her bequests had been a proud mother. Cordelia Carroll had pride, one daughter, and the desire to see the Hereford Carrolls retain *some* parity with the Angus Dales. After all, the Carrolls had been ranching on Bad Water Creek before John Broderick Okie illuminated his Lost Cabin castle with carbide lights. That was when Teddy Roosevelt had been president and it was when all the rest of the cattlemen in Wyoming, including the Dales, had been doing their accounts at night by kerosene lanterns.

Carroll grew up to be a good roper and a better rider. Her apprenticeship intensified after her older brother, her only brother, fatally shot himself during deer season. She wounded her parents when she neither married a man who would take over the ranch nor decided to take over the ranch herself.

She grew up slim and tall, with ebony hair and large, dark, slightly oblique eyes. Her father's father, at family Christmas dinners, would overdo the whiskey in the eggnog and make jokes about Indians in the woodpile until her paternal grandmother would tell him to shut the hell up before she gave him a goodnight the hard way, with a rusty sickle and knitting needles. It was years before Carroll knew what her grandmother meant.

In junior high, Carroll was positive she was eight feet tall in Lilliput. The jokes hurt. But her mother told her to be patient, that the other girls would catch up. Most of the girls didn't; but in high school the boys did, though they tended to be tongue-tied in the extreme when they talked to her.

She was the first girl president of her school's National Honor Society. She was a cheerleader. She was the valedictorian of her class and earnestly quoted John F. Kennedy in her graduation address. Within weeks of graduation, she eloped with the captain of the football team.

It nearly caused a lynching.

Steve Mavrakis, eighteen. Courtesy allowed him to be called a native despite his birth eighteen hundred miles to the east. His parents, on the other hand, had settled in the state after the war when he was less than a year old. Given another decade, the younger native-born might grudgingly concede their adopted roots; the old-timers, never.

Steve's parents had read Zane Grey and *The Virginian*, and had spent many summers on dude ranches in upstate New York. So they found a perfect ranch on the Big Horn River and started a herd of registered Hereford. They went broke. They refinanced and aimed at a breed of inferior beef cattle. The snows of '49 killed those. Steve's father determined that sheep were the way to go—all those double and triple births. Very investment-effective. The sheep sickened, or stumbled and fell into creeks where they drowned, or panicked like turkeys and smothered in heaps in fenced corners. It occurred then to the Mavrakis family that wheat doesn't stampede. All the fields were promptly hailed out before what looked to be a bounty harvest. Steve's father gave up and moved into town where he put his Columbia degree to work by getting a job managing the district office for the Bureau of Land Management.

All of that taught Steve to be wary of sure things.

And occasionally he wondered at the dreams. He had been very young when the blizzards killed the cattle. But though he didn't remember the National Guard dropping hay bales from silver C-47s to cattle in twelve-foot-deep snow, he did recall, for years after, the nightmares of herds of nonplused animals futilely grazing barren ground before towering, slowly grinding bluffs of ice.

The night after the crop-duster terrified the sheep and seventeen had expired in paroxysms, Steve dreamed of brown men shrilling and shaking sticks and stampeding tusked, hairy monsters off a precipice and down hundreds of feet to a shallow stream.

Summer nights Steve woke sweating, having dreamed of reptiles slithering and warm waves beating on a ragged beach in the lower pasture. He sat straight, staring out the bedroom window, watching the giant ferns waver and solidify back into cottonwood and box elder.

The dreams came less frequently and vividly as he grew older. He willed that. They altered when the family moved into Fremont. After a while Steve still remembered he had had the dreams, but most of the details were forgotten.

At first the teachers in Fremont High School thought he was stupid. Steve was administered tests and thereafter was labeled an underachiever. He did what he had to do to get by. He barely qualified for the college-bound program, but then his normally easygoing father made threats. People asked him what he wanted to do, to be, and he answered honestly that he didn't know. Then he took a speech class. Drama fascinated him and he developed a passion for what theater the school offered. He played well in *Our Town* and *Arsenic and Old Lace* and *Harvey*. The drama coach looked at Steve's average height and average looks and average brown hair and eyes, and suggested at a hilarious cast party that he become either a character actor or an FBI agent.

By this time, the only dreams Steve remembered were sexual fantasies about girls he didn't dare ask on dates.

Ginger McClelland, seventeen. Who could blame her for feeling out of place? Having been born on the cusp of the school district's regulations, she was very nearly a year younger than her classmates. She was short. She thought of herself as a dwarf in a world of Snow Whites. It didn't help that her mother studiously offered words like "petite" and submitted that the most gorgeous clothes would fit a wearer under five feet two inches. Secretly she hoped that in one mysterious night she would bloom and grow great, long legs like Carroll Dale. That never happened.

Being an exile in an alien land didn't help either. Though Carroll had befriended her, she had listened to the president of the pep club, the queen of Job's Daughters, and half the girls in her math class refer to her as "the foreign-exchange student." Except that she would never be repatriated home; at least not until she graduated. Her parents had tired of living in Cupertino, California, and thought that running a Coast to Coast hardware franchise in Fremont would be an adventurous change of pace. They loved the open spaces, the mountains and free-flowing streams. Ginger wasn't so sure. Every day she felt she had stepped into a time machine. All the music on the radio was old. The movies that turned up at the town's one theater—forget it. The dancing at the hops was grotesque.

Ginger McClelland was the first person in Fremont— and perhaps in all of Wyoming—to use the adjective "bitchin'." It got her sent home from study hall and caused a bemused and confusing interview between her parents and the principal.

Ginger learned not to trust most of the boys who invited her out on dates. They all seemed to feel some sort of perverse mystique about California girls. But she did accept Steve Mavrakis' last-minute invitation to the prom. He seemed safe enough.

Because Carroll and Ginger were friends, the four of them ended up double-dating in Paul's father's old maroon DeSoto that was customarily used for hauling fence posts and wire out to the pastures. After the dance, when nearly everyone else was heading to one of the sanctioned after-prom parties, Steve affably obtained from an older intermediary an entire case of chilled Hamms. Ginger and Carroll had brought along jeans and Pendleton shirts in their overnight bags and changed in the restroom at the Chevron station. Paul and Steve took off their white jackets and donned windbreakers. Then they all drove up into the Wind River Range. After they ran out of road, they hiked. It was very late and very dark. But they found a high mountain place where they huddled and drank beer and talked and necked.

They heard the voice of the wind and nothing else beyond that. They saw no lights of cars or outlying cabins. The isolation exhilarated them. They *knew* there was no one else for miles.

That was correct so far as it went.

Foam hissed and sprayed as Paul applied the church key to the cans. Above and below them, the wind broke like waves on the rocks.

"Mavrakis, you're going to the university, right?" said Paul.

Steve nodded in the dim moonlight, added, "I guess so."

"What're you going to take?" said Ginger, snuggling close and burping slightly on her beer.

"I don't know; engineering, I guess. If you're a guy and in the college-bound program, you end up taking engineering. So I figure that's it."

Paul said, "What kind?"

"Don't know. Maybe aerospace. I'll move to Seattle and make spaceships."

"That's neat," said Ginger. "Like in *The Outer Limits.* I wish we could get that here."

"You ought to be getting into hydraulic engineering," said Paul. "Water's going to be really big business not too long from now."

"I don't think I want to stick around Wyoming."

Carroll had been silently staring out over the valley. She turned back toward Steve and her eyes were pools of darkness. "You really going to leave?"

"Yeah."

"And never come back?"

"Why should I?" said Steve. "I've had all the fresh air and wide-open spaces I can use for a lifetime. You know something? I've never even seen the ocean." *And yet he had* felt *the ocean.* He blinked. "I'm getting out."

"Me too," said Ginger. "I'm going to stay with my aunt and uncle in L.A. I think I can probably get into the University of Southern California journalism school."

"Got the money?" said Paul.

"I'll get a scholarship."

"Aren't you leaving?" Steve said to Carroll.

"Maybe," she said. "Sometimes I think so, and then I'm not so sure."

"You'll come back even if you do leave," said Paul. "All of you'll come back."

"Says who?" Steve and Ginger said it almost simultaneously.

"The land gets into you," said Carroll. "Paul's dad says so."

"That's what he says." They all heard anger in Paul's voice. He opened another round of cans. Ginger tossed her empty away and it clattered down the rocks, a noise jarringly out of place.

"Don't," said Carroll. "We'll take the empties down in the sack."

"What's wrong?" said Ginger. "I mean, I . . ." Her voice trailed off and everyone was silent for a minute, two minutes, three.

"What about you, Paul?" said Carroll. "Where do you want to go? What do you want to do?"

"We talked about—" His voice sounded suddenly tightly controlled. "Damn it, I don't know now. If I come back, it'll be with an atomic bomb—"

"What?" said Ginger.

Paul smiled. At least Steve could see white teeth gleaming in the night. "As for what I want to do—" He leaned forward and whispered in Carroll's ear.

She said, "Jesus, Paul! We've got witnesses."

"What?" Ginger said again.

"Don't even ask you don't want to know." She made it one continuous sentence. Her teeth also were visible in the near-darkness. "Try that and I've got a mind to goodnight you the hard way."

"What're you talking about?" said Ginger.

Paul laughed. "Her grandmother."

"Charlie Goodnight was a big rancher around the end of the century," Carroll said. "He trailed a lot of cattle up from Texas. Trouble was, a lot of his expensive bulls weren't making out so well. Their testicles—"

"Balls," said Paul.

"—kept dragging on the ground," she continued. "The bulls got torn up and infected. So Charlie Goodnight started getting his bulls ready for the overland trip with some amateur surgery. He'd cut into the scrotum and shove the balls up into the bull. Then he'd stitch up the sack and there'd be no problem with high-centering. That's called goodnighting."

"See," said Paul. "There are ways to beat the land."

Carroll said, " 'You do what you've got to.' That's a quote from my father. Good pioneer stock."

"But not to me." Paul pulled her close and kissed her.

"Maybe we ought to explore the mountain a little," said Ginger to Steve. "You want to come with me?" She stared at Steve, who was gawking at the sky as the moonlight suddenly vanished like a light switching off.

"Oh, my God."

"What's wrong?" she said to the shrouded figure.

"I don't know—I mean, nothing, I guess." The moon appeared again. "Was that a cloud?"

"I don't see a cloud," said Paul, gesturing at the broad belt of stars. "The night's clear."

"Maybe you saw a UFO," said Carroll, her voice light.

"You okay?" Ginger touched his face. "Jesus, you're shivering." She held him tightly.

Steve's words were almost too low to hear. "It swam across the moon."

"What did?"

"I'm cold too," said Carroll. "Let's go back down." Nobody argued. Ginger remembered to put the metal cans into a paper sack and tied it to her belt with a hair ribbon. Steve didn't say anything more for a while, but the others all could hear his teeth chatter. When they were halfway down, the moon finally set beyond the valley rim. Farther on, Paul stepped on a loose patch of shale, slipped, cursed, began to slide beyond the lip of the sheer rock face. Carroll grabbed his arm and pulled him back.

"Thanks, Irene." His voice shook slightly, belying the tone of the words.

"Funny," she said.

"I don't get it," said Ginger.

Paul whistled a few bars of the song.

"Good night," said Carroll. "You do what you've got to."

"And I'm grateful for that." Paul took a deep breath. "Let's get down to the car."

When they were on the winding road and driving back toward Fremont, Ginger said, "What did you see up there, Steve?"

"Nothing. I guess I just remembered a dream."

"Some dream." She touched his shoulder. "You're still cold."

Carroll said, "So am I."

Paul took his right hand off the wheel to cover her hand. "We all are."

"I feel all right." Ginger sounded puzzled.

All the way into town, Steve felt he had drowned.

The Amble Inn in Thermopolis was built in the shadow of Round Top Mountain. On the slope above the Inn, huge letters formed from whitewashed stones proclaimed: WORLD'S LARGEST MINERAL HOT SPRING. Whether at night or noon, the inscription invariably reminded Steve of the Hollywood Sign. Early in his return from California, he realized the futility of jumping off the second letter *O*. The stones were laid flush with the steep pitch of the ground. Would-be-suicides could only roll down the hill until they collided with the log side of the inn.

On Friday and Saturday nights, the parking lot of the Amble Inn was filled almost exclusively with four-wheel-drive vehicles and conventional pickups. Most of them had black-enameled gun racks up in the rear window behind the seat. Steve's Chevy had a rack, but that was because he had bought the truck used. He had considered buying a toy rifle, one that shot caps or rubber darts, at a Penney's Christmas catalogue sale. But like so many other projects, he never seemed to get around to it.

Tonight was the first Saturday night in June and Steve had money in his pocket from the paycheck he had cashed at Safeway. He had no reason to celebrate; but then he had no reason not to celebrate. So a little after nine he went to the Amble Inn to drink tequila hookers and listen to the music.

The inn was uncharacteristically crowded for so early in the evening, but Steve secured a small table close to the dance floor when a guy threw up and his girl had to take him home. Dancing couples covered the floor though the headline act, Mountain Flyer, wouldn't be on until eleven. The warmup group was a Montana band called the Great Falls Dead. They had more enthusiasm than talent, but they had the crowd dancing.

Steve threw down the shots, sucked limes, licked the

salt, intermittently tapped his hand on the table to the music, and felt vaguely melancholy. Smoke drifted around him, almost as thick as the special-effects fog in a bad horror movie. The inn's dance floor was in a dim, domed room lined with rough pine.

He suddenly stared, puzzled by a flash of near-recognition. He had been watching one dancer in particular, a tall woman with curly raven hair, who had danced with a succession of cowboys. When he looked at her face, he thought he saw someone familiar. When he looked at her body, he wondered whether she wore underwear beneath the wide-weave red knit dress.

The Great Falls Dead launched into "Good-hearted Woman" and the floor was instantly filled with dancers. Across the room, someone squealed, "Willieee!" This time the woman in red danced very close to Steve's table. Her high cheekbones looked hauntingly familiar. Her hair, he thought. If it were longer— She met his eyes and smiled at him.

The set ended, her partner drifted off toward the bar, but she remained standing beside his table. "Carroll?" he said. *"Carroll?"*

She stood there smiling, with right hand on hip. "I wondered when you'd figure it out."

Steve shoved his chair back and got up from the table. She moved very easily into his arms for a hug. "It's been a long time."

"It has."

"Fourteen years? Fifteen?"

"Something like that."

He asked her to sit at his table, and she did. She sipped a Campari-and-tonic as they talked. He switched to beer. The years unreeled. The Great Falls Dead pounded out a medley of country standards behind them.

". . . I never should have married, Steve. I was wrong for Paul. He was wrong for me."

". . . *thought* about getting married. I met a lot of women in Hollywood, but nothing ever seemed . . ."

". . . all the wrong reasons . . ."

". . . did end up in a few made-for-TV movies. Bad stuff. I was always cast as the assistant manager in a hold-up scene, or got killed by the werewolf right near the beginning. I think there's something like ninety percent of all actors who are unemployed at any given moment, so I said . . ."

."You really came back here? How long ago?"

". . . to hell with it . . ."

"How long ago?"

". . . and sort of slunk back to Wyoming. I don't know. Several years ago. How long were you married, anyway?"

". . . a year, more or less. What do you do here?"

". . . beer's getting warm. Think I'll get a pitcher . . ."

"What do you do here?"

". . . better cold. Not much. I get along. You . . ."

". . . lived in Taos for a time. Then Santa Fe. Bummed around the Southwest a lot. A friend got me into photography. Then I was sick for a while and that's when I tried painting . . ."

". . . landscapes of the Tetons to sell to tourists?"

"Hardly. A lot of landscapes, but trailer camps and oil fields and perspective vistas of I–80 across the Red Desert . . ."

"I tried taking pictures once . . . kept forgetting to load the camera."

". . . and then I ended up half-owner of a gallery called Good Stuff. My partner throws pots."

". . . must be dangerous . . ."

". . . located on Main Street in Lander . . ."

". . . going through. Think maybe I've seen it . . ."

"What do you do here?"

The comparative silence seemed to echo as the band ended its set. "Very little," said Steve. "I worked awhile as a hand on the Two Bar. Spent some time being a roughneck in the fields up around Buffalo. I've got a pick-up—do some short-hauling for local businessmen who don't want to hire a trucker. I ran a little pot. Basically I do whatever I can find. You know."

Carroll said, "Yes, I do know." The silence lengthened between them. Finally she said, "Why did you come back here? Was it because—"

"—because I'd failed?" Steve said, answering her hesitation. He looked at her steadily. "I thought about that a long time. I decided that I could fail anywhere, so I came back here." He shrugged. "I love it. I love the space."

"A lot of us have come back," Carroll said. "Ginger and Paul are here."

Steve was startled. He looked at the tables around them.

"Not tonight," said Carroll. "We'll see them tomorrow. They want to see you."

"Are you and Paul back——" he started to say.

She held up her palm. "Hardly. We're not exactly on the same wavelength. That's one thing that hasn't changed. He ended up being the sort of thing you thought you'd become."

Steve didn't remember what that was.

"Paul went to the School of Mines in Colorado. Now he's the chief exploratory geologist for Enerco."

"Not bad," said Steve.

"Not good," said Carroll. "He spent a decade in South America and the Middle East. Now he's come back home. He wants to gut the state like a fish."

"Coal?"

"And oil. And uranium. And gas. Enerco's got its thumb in a lot of holes." Her voice had lowered, sounded angry. "Anyway, we *are* having a reunion tomorrow, of sorts. And Ginger will be there."

Steve poured out the last of the beer. "I thought for sure she'd be in California."

"Never made it," said Carroll. "Scholarships fell through. Parents said they wouldn't support her if she went back to the West Coast—you know how one hundred and five percent converted immigrants are. So Ginger went to school in Laramie and ended up with a degree in elementary education. She did marry a grad student in journalism. After the divorce five or six years later, she let him keep the kid."

Steve said, "So Ginger never got to be an ace reporter."

"Oh, she did. Now she's the best writer the *Salt Creek Gazette*'s got. Ginger's the darling of the environmental groups and the bane of the energy corporations."

"I'll be damned," he said. He accidentally knocked his glass off the table with his forearm. Reaching to retrieve the glass, he knocked over the empty pitcher.

"I think you're tired," Carroll said.

"I think you're right."

"You ought to go home and sack out." He nodded. "I don't want to drive all the way back to Lander tonight," Carroll said. "Have you got room for me?"

When they reached the small house Steve rented off Highway 170, Carroll grimaced at the heaps of dirty clothes making soft moraines in the living room. "I'll clear off the couch," she said. "I've got a sleeping bag in my car."

Steve hesitated a long several seconds and lightly touched her shoulders. "You don't have to sleep on the couch unless you want to. All those years ago . . . You know, all through high school I had a crush on you? I was too shy to say anything."

She smiled and allowed his hands to remain. "I thought you were pretty nice too. A little shy, but cute. Definitely an underachiever."

They remained standing, faces a few inches apart, for a while longer. "Well?" he said.

"It's been a lot of years," Carroll said. "I'll sleep on the couch."

Steve said disappointedly, "Not even out of charity?"

"Especially not for charity." She smiled. "But don't discount the future." She kissed him gently on the lips.

Steve slept soundly that night. He dreamed of sliding endlessly through a warm, fluid current. It was not a nightmare. Not even when he realized he had fins rather than hands and feet.

Morning brought rain.

When he awoke, the first thing Steve heard was the drumming of steady drizzle on the roof. The daylight outside the window was filtered gray by the sheets of water running down the pane. Steve leaned off the bed, picked up his watch from the floor, but it had stopped. He heard the sounds of someone moving in the living room and called, "Carroll? You up?"

Her voice was a soft contralto. "I am."

"What time is it?"

"Just after eight."

Steve started to get out of bed, but groaned and clasped the crown of his head with both hands. Carroll stood framed in the doorway and looked sympathetic. "What time's the reunion?" he said.

"When we get there. I called Paul a little earlier. He's tied up with some sort of meeting in Casper until late afternoon. He wants us to meet him in Shoshoni."

"What about Ginger?"

They both heard the knock on the front door. Carroll turned her head away from the bedroom, then looked back at Steve. "Right on cue," she said. "Ginger didn't

want to wait until tonight." She started for the door, said
back over her shoulder, "You might want to put on some
clothes."

Steve pulled on his least filthy jeans and a sweatshirt
labeled AMAX TOWN-LEAGUE VOLLEYBALL across
the chest. He heard the front door open and close, and
words murmured in his living room. When he exited the
bedroom he found Carroll talking on the couch with a
short blonde stranger who only slightly resembled the
long-ago image he'd packed in his mind. Her hair was
long and tied in a braid. Her gaze was direct and more
inquisitive than he remembered.

She looked up at him and said, "I like the mustache.
You look a hell of a lot better now than you ever did
then."

"Except for the mustache," Steve said, "I could say the
same."

The two women seemed amazed when Steve negotiated
the disaster area that was the kitchen and extracted eggs
and Chinese vegetables from the refrigerator. He served
the huge omelet with toast and freshly brewed coffee in
the living room. They all balanced plates on laps.

"Do you ever read the *Gazoo?*" said Ginger.

"*Gazoo?*"

"The *Salt Creek Gazette*," said Carroll.

Steve said, "I don't read any papers."

"I just finished a piece on Paul's company," said
Ginger.

"Enerco?" Steve refilled all their cups.

Ginger shook her head. "A wholly owned subsidiary
called Native American Resources. Pretty clever, huh?"
Steve looked blank. "Not a poor damned Indian in the
whole operation. The name's strictly sham while the company's been picking up an incredible number of mineral
leases on the reservation. Paul's been concentrating on an
enormous new coal field his teams have mapped out. It
makes up a substantial proportion of the reservation's best
lands."

"Including some sacred sites," said Carroll.

"Nearly a million acres," said Ginger. "That's more
than a thousand square miles."

"The land's never the same," said Carroll, "no matter
how much goes into reclamation, no matter how tight the
EPA says they are."

Steve looked from one to the other. "I may not read the papers," he said, "but no one's holding a gun to anyone else's head."

"Might as well be," said Ginger. "If the Native American Resources deal goes through, the mineral royalty payments to the tribes'll go up precipitously."

Steve spread his palms. "Isn't that good?"

Ginger shook her head vehemently. "It's economic blackmail to keep the tribes from developing their own resources at their own pace."

"Slogans," said Steve. "The country needs the energy. If the tribes don't have the investment capital—"

"They *would* if they weren't bought off with individual royalty payments."

"The tribes have a choice—"

"—with the prospect of immediate gain dangled in front of them by NAR."

"I can tell it's Sunday," said Steve, "even if I haven't been inside a church door in fifteen years. I'm being preached at."

"If you'd get off your ass and think," said Ginger, "nobody'd have to lecture you."

Steve grinned. "I don't think with my ass."

"Look," said Carroll. "It's stopped raining."

Ginger glared at Steve. He took advantage of Carroll's diversion and said, "Anyone for a walk?"

The air outside was cool and rain-washed. It soothed tempers. The trio walked through the fresh morning along the cottonwood-lined creek. Meadowlarks sang. The rain front had moved far to the east; the rest of the sky was bright blue.

"Hell of a country, isn't it?" said Steve.

"Not for much longer if—" Ginger began.

"Gin," Carroll said warningly.

They strolled for another hour, angling south where they could see the hills as soft as blanket folds. The tree-lined draws snaked like green veins down the hillsides. The earth, Steve thought, seemed gathered, somehow expectant.

"How's Danny?" Carroll said to Ginger.

"He's terrific. Kid wants to become an astronaut." A grin split her face. "Bob's letting me have him for August."

"Look at that," said Steve, pointing.

The women looked. "I don't see anything," said Ginger.

"Southeast," Steve said. "Right above the head of the canyon."

"There—I'm not sure." Carroll shaded her eyes. "I thought I saw something, but it was just a shadow."

"Nothing there," said Ginger.

"Are you both blind?" said Steve, astonished. "There was something in the air. It was dark and cigar-shaped. It was there when I pointed."

"Sorry," said Ginger, "didn't see a thing."

"Well, it *was* there," Steve said, disgruntled.

Carroll continued to stare off toward the pass. "I saw it too, but just for a second. I didn't see where it went."

"Damnedest thing. I don't think it was a plane. It just sort of cruised along, and then it was gone."

"All I saw was something blurry," Carroll said. "Maybe it was a UFO."

"Oh, you guys," Ginger said with an air of dawning comprehension. "Just like prom night, right? Just a joke."

Steve slowly shook his head. "I really saw something then, and I saw this now. This time Carroll saw it too." She nodded in agreement. He tasted salt.

The wind started to rise from the north, kicking up early spring weeds that had already died and begun to dry.

"I'm getting cold," said Ginger. "Let's go back to the house."

"Steve," said Carroll, "you're shaking."

They hurried him back across the land.

PHOSPHORIC FORMATION
PERMIAN
225–270 MILLION YEARS

They rested for a while at the house; drank coffee and talked of the past, of what had happened and what had not. Then Carroll suggested they leave for the reunion. After a small confusion, Ginger rolled up the windows and locked her Saab and Carroll locked her Pinto.

"I hate having to do this," said Carroll.

"There's no choice anymore," Steve said. "Too many people around now who don't know the rules."

The three of them got into Steve's pickup. In fifteen minutes they had traversed the doglegs of U.S. 20 through

Thermopolis and crossed the Big Horn River. They passed the massive mobile-home park with its trailers and RVs sprawling in carapaced glitter.

The flood of hot June sunshine washed over them as they passed between the twin bluffs, red with iron, and descended into the miles and years of canyon.

TENSLEEP FORMATION
PENNSYLVANIAN
270–310 MILLION YEARS

On both sides of the canyon, the rock layers lay stacked like sections from a giant meat slicer. In the pickup cab, the passengers had been listening to the news on KTWO. As the canyon deepened, the reception faded until only a trickle of static came from the speaker. Carroll clicked the radio off.

"They're screwed," said Ginger.

"Not necessarily." Carroll, riding shotgun, stared out the window at the slopes of flowers the same color as the bluffs. "The BIA's still got hearings. There'll be another tribal vote."

Ginger said again, "They're screwed. Money doesn't just talk—it makes obscene phone calls, you know? Paul's got this one bagged. You know Paul—I know him just about as well. Son of a bitch."

"Sorry there's no music," said Steve. "Tape player busted a while back and I've never fixed it."

They ignored him. "Damn it," said Ginger. "It took almost fifteen years, but I've learned to love this country."

"I know that," said Carroll.

No one said anything for a while. Steve glanced to his right and saw tears running down Ginger's cheeks. She glared back at him defiantly. "There's Kleenexes in the glove box," he said.

MADISON FORMATION
MISSISSIPPIAN
310–350 MILLION YEARS

The slopes of the canyon became more heavily forested. The walls were all shades of green, deeper green where the runoff had found channels. Steve felt time collect in the great gash in the earth, press inward.

"I don't feel so hot," said Ginger.

"Want to stop for a minute?"

She nodded and put her hand over her mouth.

Steve pulled the pickup over across both lanes. The Chevy skidded slightly as it stopped on the graveled turnout. Steve turned off the key and in the sudden silence they heard only the light wind and the tickings as the Chevy's engine cooled.

"Excuse me," said Ginger. They all got out of the cab. Ginger quickly moved through the Canadian thistle and the currant bushes and into the trees beyond. Steve and Carroll heard her throwing up.

"She had an affair with Paul," Carroll said casually. "Not too long ago. He's an extremely attractive man." Steve said nothing. "Ginger ended it. She still feels the tension." Carroll strolled over to the side of the thistle patch and hunkered down. "Look at this."

Steve realized how complex the ground cover was. Like the rock cliffs, it was layered. At first he saw among the sunflowers and dead dandelions only the wild sweet peas with their blue blossoms like spades with the edges curled inward.

"Look closer," said Carroll.

Steve saw the hundreds of tiny purple moths swooping and swarming only inches from the earth. The creatures were the same color as the low purple blooms he couldn't identify. Intermixed were white, bell-shaped blossoms with leaves that looked like primeval ferns.

"It's like going back in time," said Carroll. "It's a whole nearly invisible world we never see."

The shadow crossed them with an almost subliminal flash, but they both looked up. Between them and the sun had been the wings of a large bird. It circled in a tight orbit, banking steeply when it approached the canyon wall. The creature's belly was dirty white, muting to an almost-black on its back. It seemed to Steve that the bird's eye was fixed on them. The eye was a dull black, like unpolished obsidian.

"That's one I've never seen," said Carroll. "What is it?"

"I don't know. The wingspread's got to be close to ten feet. The markings are strange. Maybe it's a hawk? An eagle?"

The bird's beak was heavy and blunt, curved slightly.

As it circled, wings barely flexing to ride the thermals, the bird was eerily silent, pelagic, fishlike.

"What's it doing?" said Carroll.

"Watching us?" said Steve. He jumped as a hand touched his shoulder.

"Sorry," said Ginger. "I feel better now." She tilted her head back at the great circling bird. "I have a feeling our friend wants us to leave."

They left. The highway wound around a massive curtain of stone in which red splashed down through the strata like dinosaur blood. Around the curve, Steve swerved to miss a deer dead on the pavement—half a deer, rather. The animal's body had been truncated cleanly just in front of its haunches.

"Jesus," said Ginger. "What did that?"

"Must have been a truck," said Steve. "An eighteen-wheeler can really tear things up when it's barreling."

Carroll looked back toward the carcass and the sky beyond. "Maybe that's what our friend was protecting."

GROS VENTRE FORMATION
CAMBRIAN
500–600 MILLION YEARS

"You know, this was all under water once," said Steve. He was answered only with silence. "Just about all of Wyoming was covered with an ancient sea. That accounts for a lot of the coal." No one said anything. "I think it was called the Sundance Sea. You know, like in the Sundance Kid. Some Exxon geologist told me that in a bar."

He turned and looked at the two women. And stared. And turned back to the road blindly. And then stared at them again. It seemed to Steve that he was looking at a double exposure, or a triple exposure, or—he couldn't count all the overlays. He started to say something, but could not. He existed in a silence that was also stasis, the death of all motion. He could only see.

Carroll and Ginger faced straight ahead. They looked as they had earlier in the afternoon. They also looked as they had fifteen years before. Steve saw them *in process*, lines blurred. And Steve saw skin merge with feathers, and then scales. He saw gill openings appear, vanish, reappear on textured necks.

And then both of them turned to look at him. Their

heads swiveled slowly, smoothly. Four reptilian eyes watched him, unblinking and incurious.

Steve wanted to look away.

The Chevy's tires whined on the level blacktop. The sign read:

SPEED ZONE AHEAD
35 MPH

"Are you awake?" said Ginger.

Steve shook his head to clear it. "Sure," he said. "You know that reverie you sometimes get into when you're driving? When you can drive miles without consciously thinking about it, and then suddenly you realize what's happened?"

Ginger nodded.

"That's what happened."

The highway passed between modest frame houses, gas stations, motels. They entered Shoshoni.

There was a brand-new WELCOME TO SHOSHONI sign, as yet without bullet holes. The population figure had again been revised upward. "Want to bet on when they break another thousand?" said Carroll.

Ginger shook her head silently.

Steve pulled up to the stop sign. "Which way?"

Carroll said, "Go left."

"I think I've got it." Steve saw the half-ton truck with the Enerco decal and NATIVE AMERICAN RE-SOURCES DIVISION labeled below that on the door. It was parked in front of the Yellowstone Drugstore. "Home of the world's greatest shakes and malts," said Steve. "Let's go."

The interior of the Yellowstone had always reminded him of nothing so much as an old-fashioned pharmacy blended with the interior of the cafe in *Bad Day at Black Rock*. They found Paul at a table near the fountain counter in the back. He was nursing a chocolate malted.

He looked up, smiled, said, "I've gained four pounds this afternoon. If you'd been any later, I'd probably have become diabetic."

Paul looked far older than Steve had expected. Ginger and Carroll both appeared older than they had been a decade and a half before, but Paul seemed to have aged thirty years in fifteen. The star quarterback's physique had gone a bit to pot. His face was creased with lines emphasized by the leathery curing of skin that has been exposed years to wind and hot sun. Paul's hair, black as coal, was streaked with firn lines of glacial white. His eyes, Steve thought, looked tremendously old.

He greeted Steve with a warm handclasp. Carroll received a gentle hug and a kiss on the cheek. Ginger got a warm smile and a hello. The four of them sat down and the fountain man came over. "Chocolate all around?" Paul said.

"Vanilla shake," said Ginger.

Steve sensed a tension at the table that seemed to go beyond dissolved marriages and terminated affairs. He wasn't sure what to say after all the years, but Paul saved him the trouble. Smiling and soft-spoken, Paul gently interrogated him.

So what have you been doing with yourself?

Really?

How did that work out?

That's too bad; then what?

What about afterward?

And you came back?

How about since?

What do you do now?

Paul sat back in the scrolled-wire ice-cream parlor chair, still smiling, playing with the plastic straw. He tied knots in the straw and then untied them.

"Do you know," said Paul, "that this whole complicated reunion of the four of us is not a matter of chance?"

Steve studied the other man. Paul's smile faded to impassivity. "I'm not that paranoid," Steve said. "It didn't occur to me."

"It's a setup."

Steve considered that silently.

"It didn't take place until after I had tossed the yarrow stalks a considerable number of times," said Paul. His voice was wry. "I don't know what the official company policy on such irrational behavior is, but it all seemed right under extraordinary circumstances. I told Carroll where she could likely find you and left the means of contact up to her."

The two women waited and watched silently. Carroll's

expression was, Steve thought, one of concern. Ginger looked apprehensive. "So what is it?" he said. "What kind of game am I in?"

"It's no game," said Carroll quickly. "We need you."

"You know what I thought ever since I met you in Miss Gorman's class?" said Paul. "You're not a loser. You've just needed some—direction."

Steve said impatiently, "Come on."

"It's true." Paul set down the straw. "Why we need you is because you seem to see things most others can't see."

Time's predator hunts.

Years scatter before her like a school of minnows surprised. The rush of her passage causes eons to eddy. Wind sweeps down the canyon with the roar of combers breaking on the sand. The moon, full and newly risen, exerts its tidal force.

Moonlight flashes on the slash of teeth.

She drives for the surface not out of rational decision. All blunt power embodied in smooth motion, she simply is what she is.

Steve sat without speaking. Finally he said vaguely, "Things."

"That's right. You see things. It's an ability."

"I don't know . . ."

"We think *we* do. We all remember that night after prom. And there were other times, back in school. None of us has seen you since we all played scatter-geese, but I've had the resources, through the corporation, to do some checking. The issue didn't come up until recently. In the last month, I've read your school records, Steve. I've read your psychiatric history."

"That must have taken some trouble," said Steve. "Should I feel flattered?"

"Tell him," said Ginger. "Tell him what this is all about."

"Yeah," said Steve. "Tell me."

For the first time in the conversation, Paul hesitated. "Okay," he finally said. "We're hunting a ghost in the Wind River Canyon."

"Say again?"

"That's perhaps poor terminology." Paul looked uncomfortable. "But what we're looking for is a presence, some sort of extranatural phenomenon."

" 'Ghost' is a perfectly good word," said Carroll.

"Better start from the beginning," said Steve.

When Paul didn't answer immediately, Carroll said, "I know you don't read the papers. Ever listen to the radio?"

Steve shook his head. "Not much."

"About a month ago, an Enerco mineral survey party on the Wind River got the living daylights scared out of them."

"Leave out what they saw," said Paul. "I'd like to include a control factor."

"It wasn't just the Enerco people. Others have seen it, both Indians and Anglos. The consistency of the witnesses has been remarkable. If you haven't heard about this at the bars, Steve, you must have been asleep."

"I haven't been all that social for a while," said Steve. "I did hear that someone's trying to scare the oil and coal people off the reservation."

"Not someone," said Paul. "Some *thing*. I'm convinced of that now."

"A ghost," said Steve.

"A presence."

"There're rumors," said Carroll, "that the tribes have revived the Ghost Dance—"

"Just a few extremists," said Paul.

"—to conjure back an avenger from the past who will drive every white out of the county."

Steve knew of the Ghost Dance, had read of the Paiute mystic Wovoka who, in 1888, had claimed that in a vision the spirits had promised the return of the buffalo and the restoration to the Indians of their ancestral lands. The Plains tribes had danced the Ghost Dance assiduously to insure this. Then in 1890 the U.S. government suppressed the final Sioux uprising and, except for a few scattered incidents, that was that. Discredited, Wovoka survived to die in the midst of the Great Depression.

"I have it on good authority," said Paul, "that the Ghost Dance was revived *after* the presence terrified the survey crew."

"That really doesn't matter," Carroll said. "Remember prom night? I've checked the newspaper morgues in Fremont and Lander and Riverton. There've been strange sightings for more than a century."

"That was then," said Paul. "The problem now is that the tribes are infinitely more restive, and my people are actually getting frightened to go out into the field." His voice took on a bemused tone. "Arab terrorists couldn't do it, civil wars didn't bother them, but a damned ghost is scaring the wits out of them—literally."

"Too bad," said Ginger. She did not sound regretful.

Steve looked at the three gathered around the table. He knew he did not understand all the details and nuances of the love and hate and trust and broken affections. "I can understand Paul's concern," he said. "But why the rest of you?"

The women exchanged glances. "One way or another," said Carroll, "we're all tied together. I think it includes you, Steve."

"Maybe," said Ginger soberly. "Maybe not. She's an artist. I'm a journalist. We've all got our reasons for wanting to know more about what's up there."

"In the past few years," said Carroll, "I've caught a tremendous amount of Wyoming in my paintings. Now I want to capture this too."

Conversation languished. The soda-fountain man looked as though he were unsure whether to solicit a new round of malteds.

"What now?" Steve said.

"If you'll agree," said Paul, "we're going to go back up into the Wind River Canyon to search."

"So what am I? Some sort of damned occult Geiger counter?"

Ginger said, "It's a nicer phrase than calling yourself bait."

"Jesus," Steve said. "That doesn't reassure me much." He looked from one to the next. "Control factor or not, give me some clue to what we're going to look for."

Everyone looked at Paul. Eventually he shrugged and said, "You know the Highway Department signs in the canyon? The geological time chart you travel when you're driving U.S. 20?"

Steve nodded.

"We're looking for a relic of the ancient, inland sea."

After the sun sank in blood in the west, they drove north and watched dusk unfold into the splendor of the night sky.

"I'll always marvel at that," said Paul. "Do you know, you can see three times as many stars in the sky here as you can from any city?"

"It scares the tourists sometimes," said Carroll.

Ginger said, "It won't after a few more of those coal-fired generating plants are built."

Paul chuckled humorlessly. "I thought they were preferable to your nemesis, the nukes."

Ginger was sitting with Steve in the back seat of the Enerco truck. Her words were controlled and even. "There are alternatives to both those."

"Try supplying power to the rest of the country with them before the next century," Paul said. He braked suddenly as a jackrabbit darted into the bright cones of light. The rabbit made it across the road.

"Nobody actually *needs* air conditioners," said Ginger.

"I won't argue that point," Paul said. "You'll just have to argue with the reality of all the people who think they do."

Ginger lapsed into silence. Carroll said, "I suppose you should be congratulated for the tribal council vote today. We heard about it on the news."

"It's not binding," said Paul. "When it finally goes through, we hope it will whittle the fifty percent jobless rate on the reservation."

"It sure as hell won't!" Ginger burst out. "Higher mineral royalties mean more incentive not to have a career."

Paul laughed. "Are you blaming me for being the chicken, or the egg?"

No one answered him.

"I'm not a monster," he said.

"I don't think you are," said Steve.

"I know it puts me in a logical trap, but I think I'm doing the right thing."

"All right," said Ginger. "I won't take any easy shots. At least, I'll try."

From the back seat, Steve looked around his uneasy allies and hoped to hell that someone had brought aspirin. Carroll had aspirin in her handbag and Steve washed it down with beer from Paul's cooler.

GRANITE
PRECAMBRIAN
600+ MILLION YEARS

The moon had risen by now, a full, icy disc. The highway curved around a formation that looked like a vast, layered birthday cake. Cedar provided spectral candles.

"I've never believed in ghosts," said Steve. He caught the flicker of Paul's eyes in the rearview mirror and knew the geologist was looking at him.

"There are ghosts," said Paul, "and there are ghosts. In spectroscopy, ghosts are false readings. In television, ghost images—"

"What about the kind that haunt houses?"

"In television," Paul continued, "a ghost is a reflected electronic image arriving at the antenna some interval after the desired wave."

"And are they into groans and chains?"

"Some people are better antennas than others, Steve."

Steve fell silent.

"There is a theory," said Paul, "that molecular structures, no matter how altered by process, still retain some sort of 'memory' of their original form."

"Ghosts."

"If you like." He stared ahead at the highway and said, as if musing, "When an ancient organism becomes fossilized, even the DNA patterns that determine its structure are preserved in the stone."

GALLATIN FORMATION
CAMBRIAN
500–600 MILLION YEARS

Paul shifted into a lower gear as the half-ton began to climb one of the long, gradual grades. Streaming black smoke and bellowing like a great saurian lumbering into extinction, an eighteen-wheel semi with oil-field gear on its back passed them, forcing Paul part of the way onto the right shoulder. Trailing a dopplered call from its airhorn, the rig disappeared into the first of three short highway tunnels quarried out of the rock.

"One of yours?" said Ginger.

"Nope."

"Maybe he'll crash and burn."

"I'm sure he's just trying to make a living," said Paul mildly.

"Raping the land's a living?" said Ginger. "Cannibalizing the past is a living?"

"Shut up, Gin." Quietly, Carroll said, "Wyoming didn't do anything to your family, Paul. Whatever was done, people did it."

"The land gets into the people," said Paul.

"That isn't the only thing that defines them."

"This always has been a fruitless argument," said Paul. "It's a dead past.

"If the past is dead," Steve said, "then why are we driving up this cockamamie canyon?"

AMSDEN FORMATION
PENNSYLVANIAN
270–310 MILLION YEARS

Boysen Reservoir spread to their left, rippled surface glittering in the moonlight. The road hugged the eastern edge. Once the crimson taillights of the oil-field truck had disappeared in the distance, they encountered no other vehicle.

"Are we just going to drive up and down Twenty all night?" said Steve. "Who brought the plan?" He did not feel flippant, but he had to say something. He felt the burden of time.

"We'll go where the survey crew saw the presence," Paul said. "It's just a few more miles."

"And then?"

"Then we walk. It should be at least as interesting as our hike prom night."

Steve sensed that a lot of things were almost said by each of them at that point.

I didn't know then . . .

Nor do I know for sure yet.

I'm seeking . . .

What?

Time's flowed. I want to know where now, finally, to direct it.

"Who would have thought . . ." said Ginger.

Whatever was thought, nothing more was said.

The headlights picked out the reflective green-and-white Highway Department sign. "We're there," said Paul. "Somewhere on the right there ought to be a dirt access road."

SHARKTOOTH FORMATION
CRETACEOUS
100 MILLION YEARS

"Are we going to use a net?" said Steve. "Tranquilizer darts? What?"

"I don't think we can catch a ghost in a net," said Carroll. "You catch a ghost in your soul."

A small smile curved Paul's lips. "Think of this as the Old West. We're only a scouting party. Once we observe whatever's up here, we'll figure out how to get rid of it."

"That won't be possible," said Carroll.

"Why do you say that?"

"I don't know," she said. "I just feel it."

"Women's intuition?" He said it lightly.

"*My* intuition."

"Anything's possible," said Paul.

"If we really thought you could destroy it," said Ginger, "I doubt either of us would be up here with you."

Paul had stopped the truck to lock the front hubs into four-wheel drive. Now the vehicle clanked and lurched over rocks and across potholes eroded by the spring rain. The road twisted tortuously around series of barely graded switchbacks. Already they had climbed hundreds of feet above the canyon floor. They could see no lights anywhere below.

"Very scenic," said Steve. If he had wanted to, he could have reached out the right passenger's side window and touched the porous rock. Pine branches whispered along the paint on the left side.

"Thanks to Native American Resources," said Ginger, "this is the sort of country that'll go."

"For Christ's sake," said Paul, finally sounding angry. "I'm *not* the Antichrist."

"I know that." Ginger's voice softened. "I've loved you, remember? Probably I still do. Is there no way?"

The geologist didn't answer.

"Paul?"

"We're just about there," he said. The grade moderated and he shifted to a higher gear.

"Paul—" Steve wasn't sure whether he actually said the word or not. He closed his eyes and saw glowing fires, opened them again and wasn't sure what he saw. He felt the past, vast and primeval, rush over him like a tide. It filled his nose and mouth, his lungs, his brain. It—

"Oh, my God!"

Someone screamed.

"Let go!"

The headlight beams twitched crazily as the truck skidded toward the edge of a sheer dark drop. Both Paul and Carroll wrestled for the wheel. For an instant, Steve wondered whether both of them or, indeed, either of them was trying to turn the truck back from the dark.

Then he saw the great, bulky, streamlined form coasting over the slope toward them. He had the impression of smooth power, immense and inexorable. The dead stare from flat black eyes, each one inches across, fixed them like insects in amber.

"Paul!" Steve heard his own voice. He heard the word echo and then it was swallowed up by the crashing waves. He felt unreasoning terror, but more than that, he felt— awe. What he beheld was juxtaposed on this western canyon, but yet it was not out of place. *Genius loci,* guardian, the words hissed like the surf.

It swam toward them, impossibly gliding on powerful gray-black fins.

Brakes screamed. A tire blew out like a gunshot.

Steve watched its jaws open in front of the windshield; the snout pulling up and back, the lower jaw thrusting forward. The maw could have taken in a heifer. The teeth glared white in reflected light, white with serrated razor edges. Its teeth were as large as shovel blades.

"Paul!"

The Enerco truck fishtailed a final time, then toppled sideways into the dark. It fell, caromed off something massive and unseen, and began to roll.

Steve had time for one thought. *Is it going to hurt?*

When the truck came to rest, it was upright. Steve groped toward the window and felt rough bark rather than glass. They were wedged against a pine.

The silence astonished him. That there was no fire astonished him. That he was alive— "Carroll?" he said. "Ginger? Paul?" For a moment, no one spoke.

"I'm here," said Carroll, muffled, from the front of the truck. "Paul's on top of me. Or somebody is. I can't tell."

"Oh, God, I hurt," said Ginger from beside Steve. "My shoulder hurts."

"Can you move your arm?" said Steve.

"A little, but it hurts."

"Okay." Steve leaned forward across the front seat. He didn't feel anything like grating, broken bone ends in himself. His fingers touched flesh. Some of it was sticky with fluid. Gently he pulled someone he assumed was Paul away from Carroll. She moaned and struggled upright.

"There should be a flashlight in the glove box," he said.

The darkness was almost complete. Steve could see only vague shapes inside the truck. When Carroll switched on the flashlight, they realized the truck was buried in thick, resilient brush. Carroll and Ginger stared back at him. Ginger looked as if she might be in shock. Paul slumped on the front seat. The angle of his neck was all wrong.

His eyes opened and he tried to focus. Then he said something. They couldn't understand him. Paul tried again. They made out "Good night, Irene." Then he said, "Do what you have . . ." His eyes remained open, but all the life went out of them.

Steve and the women stared at one another as though they were accomplices. The moment crystallized and shattered. He braced himself as best he could and kicked with both feet at the rear door. The brush allowed the door to swing open one foot, then another. Carroll had her door open at almost the same time. It took another few minutes to get Ginger out. They left Paul in the truck.

They huddled on a naturally terraced ledge about halfway between the summit and the canyon floor. There was a roar and bright lights for a few minutes when a Burlington Northern freight came down the tracks on the other side of the river. It would have done no good to shout and wave their arms, so they didn't.

No one seemed to have broken any bones. Ginger's shoulder was apparently separated. Carroll had a nosebleed. Steve's head felt as though he'd been walloped with a two-by-four.

"It's not cold," he said. "If we have to, we can stay in the truck. No way we're going to get down at night. In the morning we can signal people on the road."

Ginger started to cry and they both held her. "I saw something," she said. "I couldn't tell—what was it?"

Steve hesitated. He had a hard time separating his dreams from Paul's theories. The two did not now seem mutually exclusive. He still heard the echoing thunder of ancient gulfs. "I'm guessing it's something that lived here a hundred million years ago," he finally said. "It lived in the inland sea and died here. The sea left, but it never did."

"A native . . ." Ginger said and trailed off. Steve

touched her forehead; it felt feverish. "I finally saw," she said. "Now I'm a part of it." In a smaller voice, "Paul." Starting awake like a child from a nightmare, "Paul?"

"He's—all right now," said Carroll, her even tone plainly forced.

"No, he's not," said Ginger. "He's not." She was silent for a time. "He's dead." Tears streamed down her face. "It won't really stop the coal leases, will it?"

"Probably not."

"Politics," Ginger said wanly. "Politics and death. What the hell difference does any of it make now?"

No one answered her.

Steve turned toward the truck in the brush. He suddenly remembered from his childhood how he had hoped everyone he knew, everyone he loved, would live forever. He hadn't wanted change. He hadn't wanted to recognize time. He remembered the split-second image of Paul and Carroll struggling to control the wheel. "The land," he said, feeling the sorrow. "It doesn't forgive."

"That's not true." Carroll slowly shook her head. "The land just *is*. The land doesn't care."

"I care," said Steve.

Amazingly, Ginger started to go to sleep. They laid her down gently on the precipice, covered her with Steve's jacket, and cradled her head, stroking her hair. "Look," Carroll said. "Look." As the moon illuminated the glowing sea.

Far below them, a fin broke the dark surface of the forest.

The *Hibakusha* Gallery

Hibakusha: collective noun; Japanese term, the rough translation of which is "sufferers." It came into currency following the atomic bombings of Hiroshima and Nagasaki. Though one hundred thousand men, women, and children died in the initial blasts, many more survived. Their wounds were not always apparent to the eye. No one can count the burned and maimed, the genetically blasted and physically mutilated. No one can total the presumably unharmed survivors of the two target areas who were ostracized by their fellow Japanese from surrounding cities. What use assigning a number to the survivors bearing invisible scars? Sufferers. *Hibakusha* labels them all.

I have a timer for the camera and I could take a self-portrait. But at a bargain price?

Here in the Amusement Arcade, the odors remind me of a childhood further removed than I care to admit. Winter's child recalling last summer's carnival: the heavy perfume of popcorn, warm and buttery and stale; the flatulence of adults drinking too much cheap beer; the shadowed muskiness of animals pacing hidden beyond frayed canvas flaps. The arcade is less temporary than my long-ago carnival.

I suppose some people could get bored here, but I never do. It's the Chinese curse about living in interesting times all over again. These times are fascinating.

The Amusement Arcade shares a legend with Times Square and the intersection of Sunset and Vine: at one time or another, everyone in the world will travel past. I believe it. People tramp in a continual procession past the clouded panes fronting my gallery. So many humans in the world now—and they all seem to visit the arcade. Sometimes I see familiar faces. They're not just tourists examining themselves in the distorted mirrors scattered along the boardwalk. They are my past clientele, drawn back by their fascination for the gallery.

But my old customers are outnumbered by the new. Some of them are forthright; they stride directly to the door and then inside. Others hesitate, glance at my displays, and then, apparently self-conscious, walk on. Often they circle the block for another furtive peek. A few stand beyond the glass, staring hungrily in like carrion birds. These days an increasing number enter the gallery after only the most cursory examination; impulse shoppers.

I've noticed that the demographics of my customers are changing—broadening, I think. I take note, but don't speculate much. Sales increase and the management stays happy.

And I remain capable of handling the days with equanimity, save for those mornings following my nightmares.

In my dream, I dreamed that my lover had died. And then, also in my primary dream, I awoke whimpering. My lover propped herself irritatedly on one elbow and asked me what was the matter.

What could I tell her? How could I say I'd dreamed we were making love, but when I had touched her breast, the taut brown aureole around the nipple had peeled away like dead skin, leaving exposed a disc of rawness that bled a clear fluid and felt slick to the touch?

What was the *matter*?

"Nothing," I said in the primary dream. "Nothing, nothing, nothing at all," until I rolled over and my voice trailed off in the down pillow. But neither of us could go back to sleep and she finally told me she wanted to make love. We had had sex twice the previous night; yet no one I've known could excite me more. I felt my body respond. Her eyes were colorless in the half-light before morning. Her voice was husky from sleep. Drawing me down, she said, "Touch my breasts."

Her irritation rekindled when I would not. . . .

Though I had taken down the Closed sign, it was still early morning and no customers had visited the gallery. I hunched over a cup of cold coffee, waiting for a palmful of aspirin to take effect. When the door chime sounded, I didn't look up.

"Is it too early for you?"

His voice was low and husky, sounding more awake than I felt. I looked up at the man. "Too early for what? The gallery's open."

"I've known of your shop for—" The hesitation seemed deliberate. "—quite some time. I've wanted to see it."

I made a small motion with palms upward. The shop was here to see. The man looked at me uncertainly. I said, "Look around." His eyes flickered to the side as he stared past me. There was nothing in his behavior so atypical of my tourists, and yet— I felt vaguely uneasy about my first customer of the day. My clients usually come in after looking at the posters outside. Their eyes are trapped by the optical supergraphics and their minds by the subliminal voices urging them to "send home a truly 'different' souvenir." Often their spouse and kids accompany them, trailing in like a covey of quail. Generally the first question is the expense of picture postcards and I quote the rates. Then the spouse looks at husband or wife and the other says, "Oh, go ahead, dear; it'll keep the kids quiet for a while and everyone back home will just be knocked out." They both will ponder the price while they look at the photos on the wall.

This morning's first customer crossed the deep blue carpeting to my counter. "My name is Daniel," he said. I reflexively introduced myself as he extended his hand and I shook it. Daniel's skin had a light mocha richness; his palm was cool and dry and reminded me of the skin of the python I had once handled in the Arcade's reptile enclosure. Snakes were never my phobia and so the touch fascinated me. He was tall enough that he could stare down at me, though I stand a head under two meters. His dark eyes looked out of a face asymmetrically framed by a bush of curly black hair.

"I'd love some coffee," he said, though I hadn't offered any.

"The what? Coffee?" Again without thinking I picked up his cue and turned away, fumbling behind the percolator for another chipped mug. I filled it and said, "Cream? Sweetener?"

Daniel shrugged. "If you've got it. Otherwise, don't make no never mind."

"What?" The mug pivoted like a live thing in my hand and, before I caught it, spilled tepid coffee down my trouser leg.

"You okay?"

I nodded. "Percolator doesn't make it very hot." I again filled the mug to the brim and set it down on the counter. "That thing you said."

He smiled. "Just an affectation. I said all sorts of regional things after I lived in the South. A few stayed with me." He sipped the coffee and nodded appreciatively.

I was watching but not seeing, nor listening. Don't make no never mind, her self-conscious irony. Leila—it meant "dark as night" in Arabic; but she was the opposite. She loved life and brightness; I saw that while she swam and rode and flew and made love. I had picked her up on the road in an Indian summer afternoon. She was bumming her way around the world. I was hauling baled hay for a suburban farmer. She stayed—too long.

The barren glare of the corridors absorbed her brightness; the antiseptic smell smothered her clean hair. She fought, but finally nothing had made any difference. She lay there in the special bed, connected to the attending machines, progressively weaker as cells by the millions cannibalized one another and died. Each day the fingers plaited in mine were weaker. Eventually she asked me to kill her. Pull the plug. I could not.

". . . never mind, never mind," she said, finally bitter.

Again the dream died.

"Are all those authentic?" The sweep of Daniel's stare indicated the near wall of the gallery.

I motioned, paralleling the row of glossy atrocities. "Every one. If they weren't authenticated, they wouldn't be here. Look closely. They are Japanese masterworks."

"You sell these?"

"We have prints." I touched one painfully brilliant portrait with proprietary fingers. It was a twelve-by-twenty of what had been a children's playground, evidently quite close to ground zero. The three children had been vaporized by the initial blast. The heat had blackened the wall behind them, except where the children's bodies had absorbed the sear. Lighter silhouettes remained frozen. Shadow pictures. The shadow children pointed at the sky.

Daniel leaned close to the photograph. "God." I heard the pain in his voice.

"It draws a clientele."

He straightened and looked at me for a long moment. "Do you actually feel the cruelty I heard in your voice?"

For a moment I wanted to snap back the glib line: It's just a job. You get used to it. "No," I said.

Daniel turned back to the shadow portrait. "Nagasaki?"

"Hiroshima."

"I was there once," said Daniel. "I shot the complete portfolio to go with a text."

"You're a photographer?"

"What does it sound like?"

"I mean a professional," I said.

He pulled an envelope from the inside pocket of his jacket and spilled a half dozen slides out on the marble counter. He proffered me one; I held it to the light. I saw a bronze wall dwindling to a distant horizon. "The Downwind Monument," I said. I had seen it too many times before. I had read it, memorized a very small part.

Daniel said, "All thirty-seven thousand names." I must have looked at him questioningly. "Did you know they're listed alphabetically?" I said nothing. From Daniel, a mirthless smile. "The neat aesthetics are spoiled each time a new name has to be inscribed out of sequence." I still said nothing. "And when there's no more space for additional names?" His smile now was genuinely gentle.

"Shut up," I said.

"Just a simple memorial," said Daniel, "for a small nuclear accident."

I detected no maliciousness in his words. Something in my expression must have signaled him.

"I didn't mean to offend." He looked away awkwardly. "May I see the cutouts?"

"The sets," I said.

"Yes, the sets."

I touched a button behind the counter and the black

velvet curtains whispered back along the traverse. I depressed another button and the lights came up. I took a deep breath. "Aren't they fine?"

"You make them yourself?"

I'd wished I had, but I'm no artist. "They were fabricated by my predecessor."

"They are incredible." Daniel stepped close to the first and extended his hand, stopping short of actually brushing one fiberboard shoulder with his fingertips. He stared from one figure to the next. In his face I read an emulsion of horror suspended in fascination. I tried to gauge his reaction as he wandered among the faceless cutouts:

Nuclear blast victims, burn victims, figures of char and chancre. Men, children, women, flesh like seared pork, skin leprous with radiation lesions. All of them without features, ovals cut away so that other faces could be substituted. I can't say when last I had let myself look so closely at the sprawl of ravaged bodies, all linked in the anonymity of masklessness; all of them waiting for the vicarious participation of some customer.

"Is the process as simple as it appears?" said Daniel.

"Pick one." I wound my camera, counting the clicks until the first frame was set. I checked the light meter; then cocked the shutter.

"This." Daniel chose the cutout I privately called the Matisse. It was a chance parody of an odalisque, rarely picked by clients because of its inconvenient posture. Daniel took off his jacket, then lay down on his side on the carpet behind it. The set had been taken from a fire portrait, a photograph shot by rescue personnel moving back into the firestorm area:

The old man lay on his side against the juncture of sidewalk and wall, supported partially by a blistered, twisted elbow. His head was pillowed on a concrete step. What had been his garments and his skin were indistinguishable. He was still alive and not yet blessed by shock. At the end of his outstretched forearm, a hand like a charred chicken claw begged, as though for a cup of water or a sodden, cooling cloth.

"I'm ready," said Daniel.

"No," I said, "you're too tall." To smile was painful. "Your feet show."

He doubled his legs behind him. "Okay?"

"Great."

Daniel craned his neck, setting his head at the precise angle the old man's face would have occupied. "Still okay?"

"You're the perfect model." I went through the weary routine that had been taught me: "Now watch the birdie, and . . . smile."

"That I can't do," said Daniel.

"You aren't alone." The lights glared; the small muscles around his eyes twitched as he tried not to blink. "Sometimes they try, but it rarely works." I took a half dozen shots. "That should do it."

Daniel got stiffly to his feet, testing his limbs gingerly as though they were brittle. "Now what happens?"

"It takes a day to process the film and make up the cards. You want the usual package of a dozen? Fill out the slip and I'll have them mailed tomorrow morning."

"I'd rather stop back and pick them up."

"Whatever." I checked off the Will Call box.

He hesitated. "How's business?"

"Terrific."

"It's none of my affair," he said, "but as a professional I want to ask you. What did you do to get this job?"

Just lucky, I guess. "Nothing," I said. "Absolutely nothing. I just applied for the job, and I got it."

He gave me a tight bleak smile. "That's what I thought. I'll be back tomorrow."

"The pictures will be ready."

"You'll be here?"

I nodded.

"Then I'll see you in twenty-four hours. Take care, friend." As Daniel turned toward the door, something on the wall caught his eye. He gestured at the calendar pad. "When I left my hotel room an hour ago, it was still April."

I said, "Here in the gallery, it's always the sixth of August."

I awoke disoriented and staring at streaked windowpanes, gray dawn beyond. My lover's face, drawn tight like a silk stocking across a skull, faded. The daylight had a texture and taste: cold copper metal clenched between my jaws. My tongue was dry and cracked; sore where I'd bitten it. My head throbbed.

When I could no longer stand the feeling of damp sheets entangling my body, I got up and dressed in yesterday's clothes. Still not fully oriented, I stumbled and nearly fell on the stairs down from my apartment above the gallery. I entered a new morning, the sun not fully risen above the horizon. I walked along the boardwalk toward the beach and listened to the hollow cadence of my heels upon the wood.

This dawn the sea was quiet, the waves restrained. I slipped off my shoes and walked in the cold sand. The sky brightened above the ocean, but my mind was still night, pondering the eerie aesthetic of bombed and burning cities. I walked blindly, but saw an alien beauty: Guernica, Shanghai, Dresden, Hiroshima, Nagasaki, Quang Tri City, Haifa, Denver. The bombers fell from the sky like burning angels; the sea accepted them all.

Children's voices pulled me back. They were the only other human beings on this gray beach. Two boys and a girl, they played with their toy soldiers in the sand. One boy yelped and pointed to the sky: a white gull. I followed its flight with my eyes until it soared up into the east and full into the sun.

I don't remember returning to the gallery. I only remember sitting in my chair behind the counter and looking up as the door chime pealed and Daniel walked into the gallery.

"You look terrible," he said.

"I feel lousy."

"Do you want me to leave you alone?"

I shook my head. Without a word, Daniel made coffee for me. And then somehow, without deliberation or prompting, I started talking about my nightmares. After a while I stopped speaking because it had all been said. I checked beneath the counter and scavenged a half-full liter of brandy for the coffee. We silently sat and drank and I contemplated him looking back pensively at me.

Then we both jumped as the door chimed. They trooped in single file—an early-venturing tourist family out looking for unusual souvenirs. All five were clad in bright beachwear.

"Good morning," I said, faking professional courtesy. "May I help you?"

The male met my eyes. He was a florid, hearty man who

looked to be in his fifties. His sports shirt seemed to burn with flame-wreathed orchids. "Those cards," he said. "How much?"

The family proceeded with uncanny exactness to play out the scenario I'd described to myself the previous day. The five of them—the three children ranged from about five to fifteen—decided jointly on a family grouping. I shot an extra roll as a precaution against poses ruined by the squirming of their youngest. It must have been close to the end of their vacation: the father scowled, the mother displayed her own irritation, and none of the kids smiled. Part was my fault; there was little heart in my clown act this morning.

The father gave me a traveler's check and an address while I wrote out a receipt. His mood apparently buoyed up, he gestured expansively around the gallery. "I was a military adviser once." He grinned. "This is tame stuff."

I gave him the receipt and thanked them all for their patronage. "Nice place," said the man. "Really educational." He tried to give me a dollar back from his change as a tip; I put the wadded bill into his shirt pocket; he seemed affronted.

At the door, the middle child turned and looked back at the *hibakusha* sets with wide eyes. She said, "Are they really people?"

Her father answered: "No, they're dead."

"Unassailable logic," said Daniel after the door had swung shut. " 'Forget the dead you've left. . . .' "

More than once Leila had said, "I don't understand it."

"What don't you understand?"

"You were downwind too." She looked up from the sterile slate of the hospital bed, her blue eyes briefly accusing. "Why not you too?"

"I don't know," I said. "I wish it were me."

"No," she said. "Never wish that."

"I can't help it."

"No," she repeated. "It wouldn't help." But she rang for the nurse and told me to leave.

"What?" I said.

"Just a poet."

"I've had poets come into the gallery," I said. "I've had nearly everybody." I suddenly remembered the packet that lay at one end of the counter. "Here, the cards are ready." I slipped one off the top and handed it to him.

Daniel turned it over and over, examining first the side that showed the dying old man with his face, and then the opposite side with space for the address and message. "It's very professional."

"I'll take that as a compliment."

Daniel riffled the pictures as though they were a deck of playing cards. "Have you ever refused a customer?"

"Once. A man wanted to deface a set."

"How do you mean?"

"He wanted to cut an additional hole so he could expose his genitals."

"Was that so bad?"

I drew a breath. "The sets were mutilated sufficiently in life. In death . . ." My palms spread. "I drew an arbitrary limit."

"You do recognize the *hibakusha?*" said Daniel. "The sufferers?"

"Each day and night."

"And you don't recognize me?"

I stared. "What—"

"I thought it was very plain." Daniel shrugged. "Maybe not." He examined the backs of his hands. "There are no sores, no scar tissue."

I started to say a word but it stuck in my throat. "You?"

"I was visiting a city at the far edge of the downwind zone that day. I didn't *have* to be there—just a weekend trip to see friends. The doctors tell me I breathed at least eighty micrograms of plutonium oxide dust . . . not even enough to see with the naked eye." He looked at me calmly. "In the hospital they gave me a lung lavage to try to remove most of the particles; they pumped my lungs full of saline solution and then drew it off. Three times I was drowned, and thrice revived."

I said, "Then perhaps it was—"

"It wasn't. Some òf the dust was encapsulated in the lung tissue. It's still there."

"Years have passed," I said.

He shook his head. "Even thanks to the accident, there are no actuarial tables for dust victims. The half-life of plutonium is longer than I care to consider. I don't expect I'll be waiting to see."

I said awkwardly, "I'm sorry."

He again showed me his humorless smile. "I didn't travel this far for your stumbling sympathy."

"Then why?"

Again the click and chime of the opening door; more customers. These were both young and beautiful; I guessed that they were still in their teens. Each was a creation of the summer: skin tanned to a rich shade of cocoa, hair bleached to drawn gold. They dressed expensively, were well fed and healthy. The two shared a youthful arrogance. The boy smelled of lime and oranges. I distractedly asked them if I could help.

"We're just looking," said the girl.

I directed them to the wall of photographs. Fingers entwined, the pair roamed along the lines of portraits. The examination was cursory. They returned to the counter where I stood rigid and Daniel was pouring more bitter black coffee.

I said, "Find anything interesting?"

"No," said the girl.

"What we were looking for," said the boy, "was something special."

"What's more special that you could wish?"

"Don't you have a scene with people making love?"

"The victims?" They nodded. "No."

As if suspicious that I might be holding out and concealing other pictures beneath the counter, the girl said, "Are you sure?"

"Perhaps you ought to try a straight porn shop."

"No," the girl said. "This is the shop we want."

"Then I'm sorry. I don't have what you wish."

The pair exchanged glances. The boy said, "Is there another gallery like this one?"

"None."

"Do you think maybe you'll be getting some more pictures?"

I said, "I wouldn't know."

The girl shrugged and took the boy's hand. She said to him, "Come on. We'll try somewhere else."

"Sorry," I said. "Maybe another time."

They left without answering, taking with them their fresh citrus scent. I slowly turned back toward Daniel, who was again shuffling through his deck of photo cards. He laid them out on the counter facedown in a Tarot configuration.

"But they're identical," I said.

"How astute."

"I don't need sarcasm."

"You need honesty." He shook his head. "I don't know what you need." As he had the previous day, Daniel pulled out the envelope of slides. "Let me show you something."

They stood framed against evergreens and snow; her eyes flashed blue like the clear winter morning.

I stared unbelieving at the transparency. "Leila and you?"

"I was her lover long before you."

"Daniel?" I said. "Daniel." I shook my head. "She never mentioned you."

"She was too private a person."

I continued drinking Leila's beauty from the slide; my thirst had never abated. Daniel gently plucked her from my hand. Reflexively I reached for her. Daniel recoiled, his fist closing upon the transparency; when he opened his hand, the film was creased and split, the frame crushed. Blood gathered on his palm like a jewel.

"She's dead." I looked away from the ruin in his hand. "Why did she leave you?"

"She would have left you eventually. She wasn't a woman to be held." As I watched, he set the crumpled slide in an ashtray and lighted it from a pack of matches.

"You bastard," I said. "You didn't come here for the postcards." The question was implicit.

Smoke curled briefly upward from the ashtray. Daniel took a handkerchief from a coat pocket and blotted the dot of blood on his palm. The sadness in his face was overpowering. "I shouldn't have come—not now."

"So why *did* you?"

"I took it upon myself to judge."

"Judge?" I said. He didn't respond. "Me?" Finally he nodded. "What for?"

Gesturing around the gallery, he said, "How you, a survivor, one of the few fortunate ones, can do *this*. I'd hoped to make you feel guilty that you survived. I was stupid. I failed to realize there was no need."

I recognized what was filtering into his words. "Don't pity me," I said. "Don't pity *me*."

"All right," Daniel said. But his eyes contradicted his voice. And with the pity was a sick understanding. "I'd wanted to see what sort of man had loved her, and then survived her so badly."

I didn't reply.

"Such a luxury, self-pity. You don't use it well."

"At least," I said, "I'm alive."

He inclined his head as though to indicate I'd scored a minor point in a meaningless game. Then Daniel turned and walked out, leaving behind his pack of picture postcards. They remained on the marble slab of the counter.

"Hey," I called. "Don't forget your cards."

"I didn't." He paused at the door without turning. "Nor will you." And was gone.

I slowly sat down at my desk in front of the windows overlooking the ocean. I sat listening to the faint carnival sounds of the Amusement Arcade. I heard the tread of my potential customers outside on the boardwalk. Their footsteps echoed and deepened to a roar like the long march of waves tramping up the beach and then back into the sea.

I counted the waves and multiplied them into the days and weeks and years to come. Within each day is buried another night; and within that, the certain knowledge that I will live through it.

giANTS

Paul Chavez looked from the card on the silver plate to O'Hanlon's face and back to the card. "I couldn't find the tray," she said. "Put the thing away maybe twelve years ago and didn't have time to look. Never expected to need it." Her smile folded like parchment and Chavez thought he heard her lips crackle.

He reached out and took the card. Neat black-on-white printing asserted that one Laynie Bridgewell was a bona fide correspondent for the UBC News Billings bureau. He turned the card over. Sloppy cursive script deciphered as: *Imperitive I talk to you about New Mexico Project.* "Children of electronic journalism," Chavez said amusedly. He set the card back on the plate. "I suppose I ought to see her in the drawing room—if I were going to see her, which I'm not."

"She's a rather insistent young woman," said O'Hanlon.

Chavez sat stiffly down on the couch. He plaited his fingers and rested the palms on the crown of his head. "It's surely time for my nap. Do be polite."

"Of course, Dr. Chavez," said O'Hanlon, sweeping silently out of the room, gracefully turning as she exited to close the doors of the library.

Pain simmered in the joints of his long bones. Chavez shook two capsules from his omnipresent pill case and poured a glass of water from the carafe on the walnut desk. Dr. Hansen had said it would only get worse. Chavez lay on his side on the couch and felt weary—seventy-two years' weary. He supposed he should have walked down the hall to his bedroom, but there was no need. He slept better here in the library. The hardwood panels and the subdued Mondrian originals soothed him. Endless ranks of books stood vigil. He loved to watch the windblown patterns of the pine boughs beyond the French windows that opened onto the balcony. He loved to study the colors as sunlight spilled through the leaded DNA double-helix pane Annie had given him three decades before.

Chavez felt the capsules working faster than he had expected. He thought he heard the tap of something hard against glass. But then he was asleep.

In its basics, the dream never changed.

They were there in the desert somewhere between Albuquerque and Alamogordo, all of them: Ben Peterson, the tough cop; the FBI man Robert Graham; Chavez himself; and Patricia Chavez, his beautiful, brainy daughter.

The wind, gusting all afternoon, had picked up; it whistled steadily, atonally, obscuring conversation. Sand sprayed abrasively against their faces. Even the gaunt stands of spiny cholla bowed with the wind.

Patricia had struck off on her own tangent. She struggled up the base of a twenty-foot dune. She began to slip back almost as far as each step advanced her.

They all heard it above the wind—the shrill, ululating chitter.

"What the hell is that?" Graham yelled.

Chavez shook his head. He began to run toward Patricia. The sand, the wind, securing the brim of his hat with one hand—all conspired to make his gait clumsy.

The immense antennae rose first above the crest of the dune. For a second, Chavez thought they surely must be branches of windblown cholla. Then the head itself heaved into view, faceted eyes coruscating with changing hues of red and blue. Mandibles larger than a farmer's scythe clicked and clashed. The ant paused, apparently surveying the creatures downslope.

"Look at the size of it," said Chavez, more to himself than to the others.

He heard Peterson's shout. "It's as big as a horse!" He glanced back and saw the policeman running for the car.

Graham's reflexes were almost as prompt. He had pulled his .38 Special from the shoulder holster and swung his arm, motioning Patricia to safety, yelling, "Back, get back!" Patricia began to run from the dune all too slowly, feet slipping on the sand, legs constricted by the ankle-length khaki skirt. Graham fired again and again, the gun popping dully in the wind.

The ant hesitated only a few seconds longer. The wind sleeked the tufted hair on its purplish green thorax. Then it launched itself down the slope, all six articulated legs churning with awful precision.

Chavez stood momentarily frozen. He heard a coughing stutter from beside his shoulder. Ben Peterson had retrieved a Thompson submachine gun from the auto. Gouts of sand erupted around the advancing ant. The creature never hesitated.

Patricia lost her race in a dozen steps. She screamed once as the crushing mandibles closed around her waist. She looked despairingly at her father. Blood ran from both corners of her mouth.

There was an instant eerie tableau. The tommy gun fell silent as Peterson let the muzzle fall in disbelief. The hammer of Graham's pistol clicked on a spent cylinder. Chavez cried out.

Uncannily, brutally graceful, the ant wheeled and, still carrying Patricia's body, climbed the slope. It crested the dune and vanished. Its chittering cry remained a moment more before raveling in the wind.

Sand flayed his face as Chavez called out his daughter's name over and over. Someone took his shoulder and shook him, telling him to stop it, to wake up. It wasn't Peterson or Graham.

It was his daughter.

She was his might-have-been daughter.

A concerned expression on her sharp-featured face, she was shaking him by the shoulder. Her eyes were dark brown and enormous. Her hair, straight and cut short, was a lighter brown.

She backed away from him and sat in his worn, leather-covered chair. He saw she was tall and very thin. For a moment he oscillated between dream-orientation and wake-fulness. "Patricia?" Chavez said.

She did not answer.

Chavez let his legs slide off the couch and shakily sat up. "Who in the world are you?"

"My name's Laynie Bridgewell," said the young woman.

Chavez's mind focused. "Ah, the reporter."

"Correspondent."

"A semantic distinction. No essential difference." One level of his mind noted with amusement that he was articulating well through the confusion. He still didn't know what the hell was going on. He yawned deeply, stretched until a dart of pain cut the movement short, said, "Did you talk Ms. O'Hanlon into letting you up here?"

"Are you kidding?" Bridgewell smiled. "She must be a great watchdog."

"She's known me a long while. How *did* you get up here?"

Bridgewell looked mildly uncomfortable. "I, uh, climbed up."

"Climbed?"

"Up one of the pines. I shinnied up a tree to the balcony. The French doors were unlocked. I saw you inside sleeping, so I came in and waited."

"A criminal offense," said Chavez.

"They were unlocked," she said defensively.

"I meant sitting and watching me sleep. Terrible invasion of privacy. A person could get awfully upset, not knowing if another human being, a strange one at that, is secretly watching him snore or drool or whatever."

"You slept very quietly," said Bridgewell. "Very still. Until the nightmare."

"Ah," said Chavez. "It was that apparent?"

She nodded. "You seemed really upset. I thought maybe I ought to wake you."

Chavez said, "Did I say anything."

She paused and thought. "Only two words I could make out. A name—Patricia. And you kept saying 'them.' "

"That figures." He smiled. He felt orientation settling around him like familiar wallpaper in a bedroom, or old friends clustering at a departmental cocktail party. "You're from the UBC bureau in Billings?"

"I drove down this morning."

"Work for them long?"

"Almost a year."

"First job?"

She nodded. "First real job."

"You're what—twenty-one?" said Chavez.

"Twenty-two."

"Native?"

"Of Montana?" She shook her head. "Kansas."

"University of Southern California?"

Another shake. "Missouri."

"Ah," he said. "Good school." Chavez paused. "You're here on assignment?"

A third shake. "My own time."

"Ah," said Chavez again. "Ambitious. And you want to talk to me about the New Mexico Project?"

Face professionally sober, voice eager, she said, "Very much. I didn't have any idea you lived so close until I read the alumni bulletin from the University of Wyoming."

"I wondered how you found me out." Chavez sighed. "Betrayed by my alma mater . . ." He looked at her sharply. "I don't grant interviews, even if I occasionally conduct them." He stood and smiled. "Will you be wanting to use the stairs, or would you rather shinny back down the tree?"

"Who is Patricia?" said Bridgewell.

My daughter, Chavez started to say. "Someone from my past," he said.

"I lost people to the bugs," said Bridgewell quietly. "My parents were in Biloxi at the wrong time. Bees never touched them. The insecticide offensive got them both."

The pain in Chavez's joints became ice needles. He stood—and stared.

Even more quietly, Bridgewell said, "You don't have a daughter. Never had. I did my homework." Her dark eyes seemed even larger. "I don't know everything about the New Mexico Project—that's why I'm here. But I can stitch the rumors together." She paused. "I even had the bureau rent an old print of the movie. I watched it four times yesterday."

Chavez felt the disorientation return, felt exhausted, felt —damn it!—old. He fumbled the container of pain pills out of his trouser pocket, then returned it unopened. "Hungry?" he said.

"You better believe it. I had to leave before breakfast."

"I think we'll get some lunch," said Chavez. "Let's go downtown. Try not to startle Ms. O'Hanlon as we leave."

O'Hanlon had encountered them in the downstairs hall, but reacted only with a poker face. "Would you and the young lady like some lunch, Dr. Chavez?"

"Not today," said Chavez, "but thank you. Ms. Bridgewell and I are going to eat in town."

O'Hanlon regarded him. "Have you got your medicine?"

Chavez patted his trouser leg and nodded.

"And you'll be back before dark?"

"Yes," he said. "Yes. And if I'm not, I'll phone. You're not my mother. I'm older than you."

"Don't be cranky," she said. "Have a pleasant time."

Bridgewell and Chavez paused in front of the old stone house. "Why don't we take my car?" said Bridgewell. "I'll run you back after lunch." She glanced at him. "You're not upset about being driven around by a kid, are you?" He smiled and shook his head. "Okay."

They walked a hundred meters to where her car was pulled off the blacktop and hidden in a stand of spruce. It was a Volkswagen beetle of a vintage Chavez estimated to be a little older than its driver.

As if reading his thoughts, Bridgewell said, "Runs like a watch—the old kind, with hands. Got a hundred and ten thousand on her third engine. I call her Scarlett." The car's color was a dim red like dried clay.

"Do you really miss watches with hands?" said Chavez, opening the passenger-side door.

"I don't know—I guess I hadn't really thought about it. I know I don't miss slide rules."

"*I* miss hands on timepieces." Chavez noticed there were no seat belts. "A long time ago, I stockpiled all the Timexes I'd need for my lifetime."

"Does it really make any difference?"

"I suppose not." Chavez considered that as Bridgewell drove onto the highway and turned downhill.

"You love the past a lot, don't you?"

"I'm nostalgic," said Chavez.

"I think it goes a lot deeper than that." Bridgewell handled the VW like a racing Porsche. Chavez held on to the bar screwed onto the glove-box door with both hands. Balding radial tires shrieked as she shot the last curve and they began to descend the slope into Casper. To the east, across the city, they could see a ponderous dirigible-freighter settling gracefully toward a complex of blocks and domes.

"Why," she said, "are they putting a pilot fusion plant squarely in the middle of the biggest coal deposits in the country?"

Chavez shrugged. "When man entered the atomic age he opened a door into a new world. What he may eventually find in that new world no one can predict."

"Huh?" Bridgewell said. Then: "Oh, the movie. Doesn't it ever worry you—having that obsession?"

"No," said Chavez. Bridgewell slowed slightly as the road became city street angling past blocks of crumbling budget housing. "Turn left on Rosa. Head downtown."

"Where are we eating? I'm hungry enough to eat coal by-products."

"Close. We're going to the oil can."

"Huh?" Bridgewell said again.

"The Petroleum Tower. Over there." Chavez pointed at a forty-story cylindrical pile. It was windowed completely with bronze reflective panes. "The rooftop restaurant's rather good."

They left Scarlett in an underground lot and took the high-speed exterior elevator to the top of the Petroleum Tower. Bridgewell closed her eyes as the ground level rushed away from them. At the fortieth floor she opened her eyes to stare at the glassed-in restaurant, the lush hanging plants, the noontime crowd. "Who *are* these people? They all look so, uh, professional."

"They are that," said Chavez, leading the way to the maître d'. "Oil people. Uranium people. Coal people. Slurry people. Shale people. Coal gasification—"

"I've got the point," Bridgewell said. "I feel a little underdressed."

"They know me."

And so, apparently, they did. The maître d' issued orders and Bridgewell and Chavez were instantly ushered to a table beside a floor-to-ceiling window.

"Is this a perk of being maybe the world's greatest molecular biologist?"

Chavez shook his head. "More a condition of originally being a local boy. Even with the energy companies, this is still a small town at heart." He fell silent and looked out the window. The horizon was much closer than he remembered from his childhood. A skiff of brown haze lay over the city. There was little open land to be seen.

They ordered drinks.

They made small talk.

They ordered food.

"This is very pleasant," said Bridgewell, "but I'm still a correspondent. I think you're sitting on the biggest story of the decade."

"That extraterrestrial ambassadors are shortly to land near Albuquerque? That they have picked America as a way station to repair their ship?"

Bridgewell looked bemused. "I'm realizing I don't know when you're kidding."

"Am I now?"

"Yes."

"So why do you persist in questioning me?"

She hesitated. "Because I suspect you want to tell someone. It might as well be me."

He thought about that awhile. The waiter brought the garnish tray and Chavez chewed on a stick of carrot. "Why don't you tell me the pieces you've picked up?"

"And then?"

"We'll see," he said. "I can't promise anything."

Bridgewell said, "You're a lot like my father. I never knew when he was kidding either."

"Your turn," said Chavez.

The soup arrived. Bridgewell sipped a spoonful of French onion and set the utensil down. "The New Mexico Project. It doesn't seem to have anything to do with New Mexico. You wouldn't believe the time I've spent on the phone. All my vacation I ran around that state in Scarlett."

Chavez smiled a long time, finally said, "Think metaphorically. The Manhattan Project was conducted under Stagg Field in Chicago."

"I don't think the New Mexico Project has anything to do with nuclear energy," she said. "But I have heard a lot of mumbling about DNA chimeras."

"So far as I know, no genetic engineer is using recombinant DNA to hybridize creatures with all the more loathsome aspects of snakes, goats, and lions. The state of the art improves, but we're not that good yet."

"But I shouldn't rule out DNA engineering?" she said.

"Keep going."

"Portuguese is the official language of Brazil."

Chavez nodded.

"UBC's stringer in Recife has it that, for quite a while now, nothing's been coming out of the Brazilian nuclear-power complex at Xique-Xique. I mean there's *news,* but it's all through official release. Nobody's going in or out."

Chavez said, "You would expect a station that new and large to be a concern of national security. Shaking down's a long and complex process."

"Maybe." She picked the ripe olives out of the newly arrived salad and carefully placed them in a line on the plate. "I've got a cousin in movie distribution. Just real scutwork so far, but she knows what's going on in the industry. She told me that the U.S. Department of Agriculture ordered a print from Warner Brothers dubbed in Portuguese and had it shipped to Brasília. The print was that movie you're apparently so concerned with—*Them!* The one about the ants mutating from radioactivity in the New Mexico desert. The one about giant ants on the rampage."

"Only a paranoid could love this chain of logic," said Chavez.

Her face looked very serious. "If it takes a paranoid to come up with this story and verify it," she said, "then that's what I am. Maybe nobody else is willing to make the jumps. I am. I know nobody else has the facts. I'm going to get them."

To Chavez, it seemed that the table had widened. He looked across the linen wasteland at her. "The formidable Formicidae family . . ." he said. "So have you got a conclusion to state?" He felt the touch of tiny legs on his leg. He felt feathery antennae tickle the hairs on his thigh. He jerked back from the table and his water goblet overturned, the water stain spreading smoothly toward the woman.

"What's wrong?" said Bridgewell. He heard concern in her voice. He slapped at his leg, stopped the motion, drew a deep breath.

"Nothing." Chavez hitched his chair closer to the table again. A waiter hovered at his shoulder, mopping the water with a towel and refilling the goblet. "Your conclusion." His voice strengthened. "I asked about your theory."

"I know this sounds crazy," said Bridgewell. "I've read about how the Argentine fire ants got to Mobile, Alabama. And I damned well know about the bees—I told you that."

Chavez felt the touch again, this time on his ankle. He tried unobtrusively to scratch and felt nothing. Just the touch. Just the tickling, chitinous touch.

"Okay," Bridgewell continued. "All I can conclude is that somebody in South America's created some giant mutant ants, and now they're marching north. Like the fire ants. Like the bees."

"Excuse me a moment," said Chavez, standing.

"Your face is white," said Bridgewell. "Can I help you?"

"No." Chavez turned and, forcing himself not to run, walked to the restroom. In a stall, he lowered his trousers. As he had suspected, there was no creature on his leg. He sat on the toilet and scratched his skinny legs until the skin reddened and he felt the pain. "Damn it," he said to himself. "Stop." He took a pill from the case and downed it with water from the row of faucets. Then he stared at himself in the mirror and returned to the table.

"You okay?" Bridgewell had not touched her food.

He nodded. "I'm prey to any number of ailments; goes with the territory. I'm sorry to disturb your lunch."

"I'm apparently disturbing yours more."

"I offered." He picked up knife and fork and began cutting a slice of cold roast beef. "I offered—so follow this through. Please."

Her voice softened. "I have the feeling this all ties together somehow with your wife."

Chavez chewed the beef, swallowed without tasting it. "Did you look at the window?" Bridgewell looked blank. "The stained glass in the library."

Her expression became mobile. "The spiral design? The double helix? I loved it. The colors are incredible."

"It's exquisite; and it's my past." He took a long breath. "Annie gave it to me for my forty-first birthday. As well, it was our first anniversary. Additionally it was on the occasion of the award. It meant more to me than the trip to Stockholm." He looked at her sharply. "You said you did your homework. How much *do* you know?"

"I know that you married late," said Bridgewell, "for your times."

"Forty."

"I know that your wife died of a freak accident two years later. I didn't follow up."

"You should have," said Chavez. "Annie and I had gone on a picnic in the Florida panhandle. We were driving from Memphis to Tampa. I was cleaning some catfish. Annie wandered off, cataloguing insects and plants. She was an amateur taxonomist. For whatever reason—God only knows; I don't—she disturbed a mound of fire ants. They swarmed over her. I heard her screaming. I ran to her and dragged her away and brushed off the ants. Neither of us had known about her protein allergy—she'd just been lucky enough never to have been bitten or stung." He hesitated and shook his head. "I got her to Pensacola. Annie died in anaphylactic shock. The passages swelled, closed off. She suffocated in the car."

Bridgewell looked stricken. She started to say, "I'm sorry, Dr. Chavez. I had no—"

He held up his hand gently. "Annie was eight months pregnant. In the hospital they tried to save our daughter. It didn't work." He shook his head again, as if clearing it. "You and Annie look a bit alike—coltish, I think is the word. I expect Patricia would have looked the same."

The table narrowed. Bridgewell put her hand across the distance and touched his fingers. "You never remarried."

"I disengaged myself from most sectors of life." His voice was dispassionate.

"Why didn't you reengage?"

He realized he had turned his hand over, was allowing his fingers to curl gently around hers. The sensation was warmth. "I spent the first half of my life single-mindedly pursuing certain goals. It took an enormous investment of myself to open my life to Annie." As he had earlier in the morning when he'd first met Bridgewell, he felt profoundly weary. "I suppose I decided to take the easier course: to hold on to the past and call it good."

She squeezed his hand. "I won't ask if it's been worth it."

"What about you?" he said. "You seem to be in ferocious pursuit of your goals. Do you have a rest of your life hidden off to the side?"

Bridgewell hesitated. "No. Not yet. I've kept my life directed, very concentrated, since—since everyone died. But someday . . ." Her voice trailed off. "I still have time."

"Time," Chavez said, recognizing the sardonicism. "Don't count on it."

Her voice very serious, she said, "Whatever happens, I won't let the past dictate to me."

He felt her fingers tighten. "Never lecture someone three times your age," he said. "It's tough to be convincing." He laughed and banished the tension.

"This *is* supposed to be an interview," she said, but didn't take her hand away.

"Did you ever have an ant farm as a child?" Chavez said. She shook her head. "Then we're going to go see one this afternoon." He glanced at the food still in front of her. "Done?" She nodded. "Then let's go out to the university field station."

They stood close together in the elevator. Bridgewell kept her back to the panoramic view. Chavez said, "I've given you no unequivocal statements about the New Mexico Project."

"I know."

"And if I should tell you now that there are indeed monstrous ant mutations—creatures as large as horses—tramping toward us from the Mato Grosso?"

This time she grinned and shook her head silently.

"You think me mad, don't you?"

"I still don't know when you're kidding," she said.

"There are no giant ants," said Chavez. "Yet." And he refused to elaborate.

The field station of the Wyoming State University at Casper was thirty kilometers south, toward the industrial complex at Douglas-River Bend. Two kilometers off the freeway, Scarlett clattered and protested across the pot-holed access road, but delivered them safely. They crossed the final rise and descended toward the white dome and the cluster of outbuildings.

"That's huge," said Bridgewell. "Freestanding?"

"Supported by internal pressure," said Chavez. "We needed something that could be erected quickly. It was necessary that we have a thoroughly controllable internal environment. It'll be hell to protect from the snow and wind come winter, but we shouldn't need it by then."

There were two security checkpoints with uniformed guards. Armed men and women dubiously inspected the battered VW and its passengers, but waved them through when Chavez produced his identification.

"This is incredible," said Bridgewell.

"It wasn't my idea," said Chavez. "Rules."

She parked Scarlett beside a slab-sided building that

adjoined the dome. Chavez guided her inside, past another checkpoint in the lobby, past obsequious underlings in lab garb who said, "Good afternoon, Dr. Chavez," and into a sterile-appearing room lined with electronic gear.

Chavez gestured at the rows of monitor screens. "We can't go into the dome today, but the entire installation is under surveillance through remotely controlled cameras." He began flipping switches. A dozen screens jumped to life in living color.

"It's all jungle," Bridgewell said.

"Rain forest." The cameras panned past vividly green trees, creepers, seemingly impenetrable undergrowth. "It's a reasonable duplication of the Brazilian interior. Now, listen." He touched other switches.

At first the speakers seemed to be crackling with electronic noise. "What am I hearing?" she finally said.

"What does it sound like?"

She listened longer. "Eating?" She shivered. "It's like a thousand mouths eating."

"Many more," Chavez said. "But you have the idea. Now, watch."

The camera eye of the set directly in front of her dollied in toward a wall of greenery wound round a tree. Chavez saw the leaves ripple, undulating smoothly as though they were the surface of an uneasy sea. He glanced at Bridgewell; she saw it too. "Is there wind in the dome?"

"No," he said.

The view moved in for a close-up. "Jesus!" said Bridgewell.

Ants. Ants covered the tree, the undergrowth, the festooned vines.

"You may have trouble with the scale," Chavez said. "They're about as big as your thumb."

The ants swarmed in efficient concert, mandibles snipping like garden shears, stripping everything green, everything alive. Chavez stared at them and felt only a little hate. Most of the emotion had long since been burned from him.

"Behold *Eciton*," said Chavez. "Driver ants, army ants, the *maripunta*, whatever label you'd like to assign."

"I've read about them," said Bridgewell. "I've seen documentaries and movies at one time or another. I never thought they'd be this frightening when they were next door."

"There is fauna in the environment too. Would you like to see a more elaborate meal?"

"I'll pass."

Chavez watched the leaves ripple and vanish, bit by bit. Then he felt the tentative touch, the scurrying of segmented legs along his limbs. He reached out and tripped a single switch; all the pictures flickered and vanished. The two of them sat staring at the opaque gray monitors.

"Those are the giant ants?" she finally said.

"I told you the truth." He shook his head. "Not yet."

"No kidding now," she said.

"The following is a deliberate breach of national security," he said, "so they tell me." He raised his hands. "So what?" Chavez motioned toward the screens. "The *maripunta* apparently are mutating into a radically different form. It's not an obvious physical change, not like in *Them!* It's not by deliberate human agency, as with the bees. It may be through accidental human action—the Brazilian double-X nuclear station is suspected. We just don't know. What we do understand is that certain internal regulators in the *maripunta* have gone crazy."

"And they're getting bigger?" She looked bewildered.

He shook his head violently. "Do you know the square-cube law? No? It's a simple rule of nature. If an insect's dimensions are doubled, its strength and the area of its breathing passages are increased by a factor of four. But the mass is multiplied by eight. After a certain point, and that point isn't very high, the insect can't move or breathe. It collapses under its own mass."

"No giant ants?" she said.

"Not yet. Not exactly. The defective mechanism in the *maripunta* is one which controls the feeding and foraging phases. Ordinarily the ants—all the millions of them in a group—spend about two weeks in a nomadic phase. Then they alternate three weeks in place in a statary phase. That's how it used to be. Now only the nomadic phase remains."

"So they're moving," said Bridgewell. "North?" She sat with hands on knees. Her fingers moved as though with independent life.

"The *maripunta* are ravenous, breeding insanely, and headed our way. The fear is that, like the bees, the ants won't proceed linearly. Maybe they'll leapfrog aboard a charter aircraft. Maybe on a Honduran freighter. It's inevitable."

Bridgewell clasped her hands; forced them to remain still in her lap.

Chavez continued, "Thanks to slipshod internal Brazilian practices over the last few decades, the *maripunta* are resistant to every insecticide we've tried."

"They're unstoppable?" Bridgewell said.

"That's about it," said Chavez.

"And that's why the public's been kept in the dark?"

"Only partially. The other part is that we've found an answer." Chavez toyed with the monitor switches but stopped short of activating them. "The government agencies with this project fear that the public will misunderstand our solution to the problem. Next year's an election year." Chavez smiled ruefully. "There's a precedence to politics."

Bridgewell glanced from the controls to his face. "You're part of the solution. How?"

Chavez decisively flipped a switch and they again saw the ant-ravaged trees. The limbs were perceptibly barer. He left the sound down. "You know my background. You were correct in suspecting the New Mexico Project had something to do with recombinant DNA and genetic engineering. You're a good journalist. You were essentially right all down the line." He looked away from her toward the screen. "I and my people here are creating giant ants."

Bridgewell's mouth dropped open slightly. "I—but you—"

"Let me continue. The purpose of the New Mexico Project has been to tinker with the genetic makeup of the *maripunta*—to create a virus-borne mutagen that will single out the queens. We've got that agent now."

All correspondent again, Bridgewell said, "What will it do?"

"At first we were attempting to readjust the ants' biological clocks and alter the nomadic phase. Didn't work; too sophisticated for what we can accomplish. So we settled for something more basic, more physical. We've altered the ants to make them huge."

"Like in *Them!*"

"Except that *Them!* was a metaphor. It stated a physical impossibility. Remember the square-cube law?" She nodded. "Sometime in the near future, bombers will be dropping payloads all across Brazil, Venezuela, the Guianas . . . anywhere we suspect the ants are. The weapon is dispersal bombs, aerosol canisters containing the viral mutagen to trigger uncontrolled growth in each new generation of ants."

"The square-cube law . . ." said Bridgewell softly.

"Exactly. We've created monsters—and gravity will kill them."

"It'll work?"

"It should." Then Chavez said very quietly, "I hope I live long enough to see the repercussions."

Bridgewell said equally quietly, "I *will* file this story."

"I know that."

"Will it get you into trouble?"

"Probably nothing I can't handle." Chavez shrugged. "Look around you at this multimillion-dollar installation. There were many more convenient places to erect it. I demanded it be built here." His smile was only a flicker. "When you're a giant in your field—and needed—the people in power tend to indulge you."

"Thank you, Dr. Chavez," she said.

"Dr. Chavez? After all this, it's still not Paul?"

"Thanks, Paul."

They drove north, back toward Casper, and watched the western photochemical sunset. The sun sank through the clouds in a splendor of reds. They talked very little. Chavez found the silence comfortable.

Why didn't you reengage?

The question no longer disturbed him. He hadn't truly addressed it. Yet it was no longer swept under the carpet. That made all the difference.

I'll get to it, he thought. Chavez stared into the windshield sun-glare and saw his life bound up in a leaded pane like an ambered insect.

Bridgewell kept glancing at him silently as she drove up the long mountain road to Chavez's house. She passed the stand of pine where she had hidden Scarlett earlier in the day and braked to a stop in front of the stone house. They each sat still for the moment.

"You'll want to be filing your story," said Chavez.

She nodded.

"Now that you know the way up my tree, perhaps you'll return to visit in a more conventional way?"

Bridgewell smiled. She leaned across the seat and kissed him on the lips. It was, Chavez thought, a more than filial kiss. "Now *I'm* not kidding," she said.

Chavez got out of the Volkswagen and stood on the flagstone walk while Bridgewell backed Scarlett into the drive and turned around. As she started down the mountain, she turned and waved. Chavez waved. He stood there and watched until the car vanished around the first turn.

He walked back to the house and found O'Hanlon waiting, arms folded against the twilight chill, on the stone step. Chavez hesitated beside her and they both looked down the drive and beyond. Casper's lights began to blossom into a growing constellation.

"Does she remind you considerably of what Patricia might have been like?" said O'Hanlon.

Chavez nodded, and then said quickly, "Don't go for easy Freud. There's more to it than that—or there may be."

A slight smile tugged at O'Hanlon's lips. "Did I say anything?"

"Well, no." Chavez stared down at the city. He said, with an attempt at great dignity. "We simply found, in a short time, that we liked each other very much."

"I thought that might be it." O'Hanlon smiled a genuine smile. "Shall we go inside? Much longer out here and we'll be ice. I'll fix some chocolate."

He reached for the door. "With brandy?"

"All right."

"And you'll join me?"

"You know I ordinarily abstain, Dr. Chavez, but—" Her smile impossibly continued. "It is rather a special day, isn't it?" She preceded him through the warm doorway.

Chavez followed with a final look at the city. Below the mountain, Casper's constellation winked and bloomed into the zodiac.

Twelve hours later, the copyrighted story by Laynie Bridgewell made the national news and the wire services.

Eigheen hours later, her story was denied by at least five governmental agencies of two sovereign nations.

Twelve days later, Paul Chavez died quietly in his sleep, napping in the library.

Twenty-two days later, squadrons of jet bombers dropped cargoes of hissing aerosol bombs over a third of the South American continent. The world was saved. For a while, anyway. The grotesquely enlarged bodies of *Eciton burchelli* would shortly litter the laterite tropical soil.

Twenty-seven days later, at night, an intruder climbed up to the balcony of Paul Chavez's house on Casper Mountain and smashed the stained-glass picture in the French doors leading into the library. No item was stolen. Only the window was destroyed.

Afterword: To See

through eyes . . .

Eyes of crystal, mirror

Eyes: reflecting, refracting. Eyes lit bright with fires from infinity.

Infinitely subtle eyes registering the invisible.

She sees through eyes of quasars . . .

—blazing in night's countenance.

"God is gracious," says the voice.

"What *are* you speaking of?"

"A loose translation from the Hebrew."

"Don't try to be subtle." Amusement—a shade of impatience? "Who are you?"

"You could call me Charon."

"Then I'm dead."

"Charon's ferry voyages each way."

"I still don't like it," she says.

"Then call me Guardian."

"Where are we?"

"Our feet are on Terra." A gust of hard radiation blurs the final word.

"Tara?"

"Close enough."

"I'm not sure I know what I'm seeing," she says.
—but she looks away and sees

—behind her, the ranch, the house on the mountain.
Diminishing. The hills rush in; it is like leaning over a
topographical map.

Distance.^{2}

The continent below, cloud-crossed.

Distance.^{2}

The disc of the planet, shadow crescent eaten away by
the sun.

Distance.^{2}

The star system. See the dot of light in the center called
the sun; around it circle the almost infinitesimal planetary
motes. Count them.

She gauges the orbit of the outermost world; the entire
star system is held like a tiny cat's cradle between the
taut tips of her thumb and index finger. It takes light
eleven hours to travel across this pool of planets.

Distance.^{2}

In a sphere fifty light-years across, the sun has thirty-
six neighboring stars: gasballs such as Capella and Procy-
on, Sirius and Pollux. Alpha Centauri, the closest, is little
more than four years away as the photon flies.

"My love, she speaks like silence—"

At the speed of light, it's said, radio signals just keep
on traveling to infinity. Perhaps the songs play now on the
planets of Arcturus or Beta Hydri under alien skies. Un-
human audiences listen bemusedly.

"—without ideals or violence."

Distance.^{2}

The sun's neighborhood of stars dwindles. Massed thousands of millions of other suns glow.

Distance.[2]

Comprehend the radiance of the Milky Way, our galaxy;
a great turning pinwheel of stars. In 200,000,000 years it
ponderously revolves only once. In a ragged spiral arm,
perhaps two-thirds the distance out from the hub, somewhere there is the sun. Our sun.

Distance.[2]

Eleven galaxies congregate in our local group. No one's
counted exactly, but those who have tried estimate there
are perhaps 3,000,000,000 galaxies in the observable universe. If each galaxy contains an average 100,000,000,000
stars, and if maybe each hundredth star has a solar system
with an inhabited planet, then there could be 3,000,000,-
000,000,000,000 populated worlds.

"Are you paying attention?"

"How am I supposed to comprehend all the zeroes?"
she says. "I want to be able to see it."

"Start out small," says Guardian. "Envision the number
of atoms that make up the Earth; or try counting the seconds since the solar system was formed."

"I'm not amused."

Distance.[2]

●

A stellar shark charting the deeps between galaxies . . .

inviolate in the void

She swims space, dives toward time.

●

She sees through eyes of supernovae . . .
—burning in the mind.

"Those dots," says Guardian, "are *groups* of galaxies."

She stares into the spangled blackness. Synesthetized,
the dark touches velvet to her eyelids. The bonfires prickle,
but do not hurt. She starts to count. And stops.

Distance.

She could span the glittering cloud with one step.

Distance.

The vista actually appears to remain unchanged. Guardian says, "The farthest of the galaxies we can see from Earth with telescopes lie two thousand million light-years distant."

"Numbers," she says disgustedly. "Figures. I want to see—"

Distance.

The perspective still seems unaltered. "Why doesn't the universe of galaxies diminish?" she says.

Guardian's voice sounds uncomfortable for the first time. "We're up against the curvature of the universe now. There is no further point from which to observe."

"So find one."

"I cannot."

"Show me."

"I cannot."

"Then I'm disappointed," she says.

"Wait. What I can show you is

●

the other entrance to the star-tunnels. You can view through a singular eye." Guardian chuckles. She is puzzled. Guardian explains the joke. "Cosmologists call the black holes 'singularities' . . ."

Her impatience vaults the explication. "Where do they go? When?"

"All places. All times."

"And to get there—?"

"Just go. It

●

—works *thus*."

She is delighted. "Anywhere?"

"And anytime."

"I've seen all of space now—"

"You're so thirsty in this mode," says Guardian. "This mood."

"—so show me time. Show me the end."

"What about the beginning?"

Eagerly: "That too."

Guardian says dryly, "They are the same."

"*All* of it." Her voice trembles slightly with excitement, as though from the exhilaration of riding or swimming, or about to make love.

"I'm not sure you are ready."

She badgers him.

At length he agrees. With resignation Guardian says, "*All* of it."

⬤

"Aren't you tired yet?"

"No," she says. "Why should I be?"

"In the nineteenth century," Guardian says, "Clausius killed the age of the perpetual-motion machine. His theory of entropy asserted that all energy systems must finally run down."

"Heat death—"

And then again they sail beyond the black event horizon.

⬤

She sees through eyes of final darkness . . .

—through the hearts of guttering suns.

In the beginning there was life. And a microtomed section of a second later, there was death. The universe was birthed, and then began to die. Call it the big bang, the primal egg, the crack of bloom. Energy flowed, flooded, filled the cosmic circuits. Matter shotgunned into the immensity.

So it all began. For some 41 billion years the forces of countergravity overcame the tendency of gravity to pull everything back together. Indeed, the center could not hold; not for more than forty eons. The *stuff* of the universe pushed ever outward. All that we know formed, cycled, died; and lived again, but diminished. With every exchange, something was lost. Available energy.

Some points are not negotiable. You are either on a diving board or off it. You are either pregnant or not. Even on a scale of 41 billion years there comes a knife-edge time. No tangible intelligence was there to mark it.

But we are.

It is a time of final balance when gravity and counter-gravity have canceled each other. The universe expands no longer; no energy persists to push the limits further. Stasis. Equality of time and energy and matter pushed to its logical extreme.

Even time has slowed and stopped. A function of speed, time depends for definition upon differences of potential. All potentials have been satisfied. No peak remains unsmoothed, no valley still unfilled.

All spectra are silent.

Yet final peace can never—cannot—exist.

On the knife edge of forty-one eons nothing balances. Almost . . . but not quite. From our vantage we sense one final unit of gravity slide back from the brink and affect a final amenable particle. It takes no more. Raveled spacetime reverses, begins again to weave.

Tilt. Backward from the brink. Slowly at first. But surely. Collapse. All falls toward the center. It takes another 41 billion years. Time runs backward. The universe reverses history. And who is to say which is the positive and which the negative process? It's all relativity.

Finally—and after how many times before?—it all comes together. The gravity tide pulls all the universe into the focal point, down to the critical mass of the primal egg, the *ylem*, the incompressible point at which the universe-seed explodes and the cycle begins again.

At the end there is life.

Or to put it another way . . .

●

She woke to night-darkness and the sound of crickets. The glowing dial of the alarm on the bed table told her it was just past midnight. The moon had not yet set; furniture surfaces appeared softly phosphorescent. The drapes shivered as air moved through the half-open window. Something—a moth, probably—batted against the screen.

A night-bird cried to its hunting mate. A confused day-bird twittered softly. The woman spread arms and legs to the sides of the bed that had seemed to grow smaller with the passing years.

Someone called her name. "Are you all right?" Shape

was indistinguishable from shadows in the doorway. Her mother.

"Yes. I'm fine."

"I heard you cry out," said her mother. "I didn't know whether you were afraid, or were having a nightmare, or were hurt—"

"It was a dream. I don't think it was a nightmare. It woke me, but I'm all right." It had not been a nightmare, but still she wanted to reach out, hold, be held.

Hair silver and luminous in the moonlight, her mother moved across the bedroom and carefully sat on the edge of the bed. As though by touch, or perhaps from long custom, she reached through the night and picked up the hairbrush from beside the alarm. "Here," she said. "Sit up against the pillow." With slow, gentle, steady strokes, she brushed her daughter's hair. And again broke the silence: "If you'd rather not, you needn't tell me."

"I don't know." She considered it, let her taut neck relax against the seductive hiss of the strokes, decided. "All right. I grew old."

Her mother's hand never faltered.

"I never expect to be old, but there I was. It was a process and not sudden. I started by remembering my birth."

"Do you really?" said her mother.

"I did in the dream. More than that, I remembered my conception." She sensed her mother smiling. "All of it—I followed everything through: birth, infancy, childhood, youth, adulthood, maturity. I grew and gained and changed until—" She hesitated.

Her mother set down the brush and gently but firmly drew her daughter against her bosom.

"I was old. Everything turned gray and unchanging. I hated it."

"It happens," her mother said.

The daughter shook her head. "It was like climbing a long, steady slope, with not so much a peak ahead as a plateau. I almost made it. Not quite. An inch short, a millimeter, whatever, I started to fall back. I couldn't help myself. It felt right, so right. My entire fragmented life and youth and childhood and infancy; back through birth cohered again as I plunged backward through adulthood to the beginning." She smiled and felt her lips curve against her mother's neck. "It was an inconceivable conception."

Her mother kissed her gently.

There is no one more beautiful, she thought. No one I would rather be.

And realized that they both—mother and daugher—were points on the same continuum.

●

Cycles. She is silent for a long while. Then: "All of it? All over again, repeated?"

"Yes," says Guardian.

"The specifics too? Even—me?"

"Context and content obviously aren't the same. The particulars may change."

"But you aren't sure?"

"I am not certain."

Wonder steeps her voice. "But haven't you looked?"

"Not yet."

"Then let me."

"You're sure you want to—"

"Didn't I say so?"

Guardian is silent for a time and a space. "Are you to be denied nothing?"

There is certainty in her voice. "Nothing."

The final free warmth in the universe flows between them then and Guardian says

●

"Look."

She sees

[for Jo]

Fantasy Novels
from
POCKET BOOKS